The
Coach
TRIP

IZZY BROMLEY

PUBLISHING

Published by Lake Union Publishing, Seattle

www.apub.com

Amazon, the Amazon logo, and Lake Union Publishing are trademarks of Amazon.com, Inc., or its affiliates.

ISBN-13: 9781662511462
eISBN: 9781662511479

Cover design by Emma Rogers
Cover image: ©aliaksei kruhlenia / Shutterstock; ©Greens87 / Shutterstock; ©Little Hand Creations / Shutterstock; ©Wise ant / Shutterstock

Printed in the United States of America

The
Coach
TRIP

1

I'm SO sorry

'Mel, what can I say? I'm SO sorry.'

I press my hands together in a prayer of sorts as I try to get across to my best friend just how very, very sorry I am.

Mel stands, arms folded and her head tipped to one side, and stares at me. In the twenty-odd years that we've been friends and over the very, very many cock-ups I've made in that time, I've rarely seen her look as cross as this. Even her hair looks cross.

'You had one thing to do, Emma,' she says. 'One thing!'

I wish our grotty carpet would split and swallow me up so that I wouldn't have to look at her any more. It's not so much her anger. I know that'll pass. Mel's temper is like a firework – all bangs and sparks and then lost to the night sky as quickly as it arrived. But it's the disappointment that lies beneath that's harder to deal with. I've let her down.

Again.

I hang my head.

'If I could turn back time . . .' I try, which sounds pathetic even to me.

Mel is having none of it.

'And it's not only me that you wrecked things for. There's poor Jonathan too. All that effort he made. Ruined.'

This isn't entirely true. I didn't ruin the entire evening. And actually, I bet this was the most interesting thing to happen to Mel's new boyfriend in years. But of course, this isn't the moment to point that out.

'Well, at least you managed to salvage the end of the night,' I say, and then, when I see Mel's raised eyebrows, instantly wish that I hadn't. I shake my head and look down at the swirls on the carpet again. 'I know, I know,' I say. 'That's not the point.'

'What I don't get,' continues Mel, 'is how you could have forgotten. It's not like we didn't talk about Valentine's night. We've talked about virtually nothing else for days.'

This isn't strictly accurate either. Mel talked about Valentine's for days. I, having no one in my life to surprise me with a huge romantic gesture, just listened to her endless speculations about what Jonathan might have planned.

She's right, though. I'm not sure how could I have forgotten. He'd sneakily passed me the card, all cloak and dagger, with instructions to hand it to Mel before she left for work on Valentine's Day.

And somehow the blessed thing slipped my mind.

How was I supposed to know that it contained all the instructions for the romantic night that he'd arranged? He should have mentioned that it was more than just your common-or-garden card when he gave it to me and then I might have taken more notice.

But no.

There is no excuse.

Whichever way you cut it, I am a rubbish friend.

'I don't know what to say,' I try again. 'I really am sorry. But I'll make it up to you. I promise.'

This is a rash statement as I doubt there is anything I can do to fix her ruined night. It was a once-in-a-lifetime experience, the kind of story you'd be telling your grandchildren decades later, and I'd blown it for her.

'I keep picturing Jonathan waiting on that train platform,' Mel says, her eyes straying to the stained ceiling as she imagines the scene. 'He must have thought I'd stood him up. And he had that massive bunch of red roses. It was all so romantic.' And then she tightens her lips into a thin line. 'Or it would have been. If you'd just given me the card.'

Suddenly, and I'm really not proud of this, I want to laugh. The desire to giggle is almost overwhelming, even though giggling now would be about the most inappropriate thing I could do. This is the time to be contrite, remorseful, repentant. I need Mel to understand that even though I am a crap friend and I let her down more often than Northern Rail, I am very, very sorry.

But my mouth doesn't seem to understand the importance of this moment and my lips start to twitch. I bite them together, but I fear it's too late. The giggle is building from my stomach. I can feel it making its bubbling way up my spine.

I tense my shoulders to try and stop it escaping, but it's a determined little blighter and before I can say 'sackcloth and ashes' it's out of my mouth. A full-blown guffaw made all the worse by my trying to contain it.

Mel looks at me as if I've just produced a steak at a vegan barbecue. Her jaw drops and she begins to shake her head slowly in disbelief.

'God, I'm sorry,' I say, trying to stifle my laughter with a futile hand. 'But it is kind of funny.'

'What is? You single-handedly wrecking my extraordinarily romantic Valentine's night out? Oh yes, Emma,' she says coldly. 'It's absolutely hilarious. Pardon me while I pee my pants.'

'But Jonathan standing there at the station waiting for you,' I splutter, 'with all those roses and the table booked and everything, and you waiting here for him to turn up, getting crosser and crosser. You've got to see the funny side.'

And then Mel's mouth creases a little at the edges. It's not much, but it's enough, and I know that it's going to be all right. She rolls her eyes and lets out a sigh.

'I suppose it is a bit funny,' she concedes. 'If you ignore the fact that you wilfully forgot . . .'

'It wasn't wilful,' I interrupt. 'A genuine accident.'

She looks at me down her nose like our headmistress used to do.

'. . . that you wilfully forgot to give me a Valentine's card that my boyfriend had entrusted to you. And on Valentine's Day, which should have been a pretty big memory jogger.'

'But you did get to the club,' I say. 'After he texted to find out where you were. I mean, I know you missed the candlelit dinner, but the evening wasn't a complete disaster.'

Mel holds up a warning finger.

'Don't push it, Em,' she says, and I know that if I'm not entirely forgiven already, it won't be far away.

'Listen,' I say. 'What if I pay for you and Jonathan to go for a romantic dinner somewhere to make up for it?'

As I say this, I'm thinking of my meagre bank balance and the overdraft that I absolutely promised myself I wouldn't dip into again this month. But needs must.

Mel considers my offer and nods slowly, as if it's a good start. My mind is running into overdrive now as I scrabble for other ways to make it up to her, because I really am sorry, and I can't bear the idea that I might have wobbled our friendship. Mel has a lot to put up with, living with me and my chaos. I want her to know that I really appreciate her.

'And how about we go away for a girly weekend?' I add. 'Just the two of us.'

Mel is smiling at me now in the way you might smile at a puppy that's just walked dirty paw prints all over a clean floor but is just so cute that you can't get annoyed.

Encouraged, I press on.

'How about the weekend of your birthday?' I suggest, ignoring the fact that she'll probably want to spend her birthday with boring Jonathan. 'We could go to Edinburgh. We've always wanted to go there together. What do you say? Shall we do it? I can find us a nice Airbnb.'

It's on the tip of my tongue to offer to pay for that too, but luckily I manage to restrain myself. I haven't been that bad a friend.

I can tell from her face that she's considering saying no because I'm not quite forgiven. But then she can't resist, and she grins.

'Okay,' she says. 'You're on. Let's do it! But if you let me down like that one more time, Emma Lewis, then I swear we are over. *Finito.*'

I nod vigorously. Mel's birthday is a few weeks away. Plenty of time to clear my diary and get something booked in Edinburgh. It'll be fabulous, just like the weekends we used to go on before grown-up life started to get in the way. I can feel excitement fizzing in my stomach already. This is the perfect way to make it up to Mel and show her how much she means to me.

And I'll make sure that everything runs like clockwork.

2

You've gotta kiss a lot of frogs.

After that initial contretemps, I seem to get away with my Valentine's Day cock-up without too much fallout. Mel continues to make spiky comments about how I ruined the most romantic night of her life for a few days, which is fair enough, but then the incident joins the rich folklore of stories that runs through our twenty-year friendship like a ribbon.

The first time Jonathan comes round to the flat afterwards is a tad awkward. When the doorbell rings I stop still in my tracks, frozen to the spot. I can't answer it. What will I say to him? I'm really sorry that I totally screwed your hugely romantic evening with my friend, but don't worry, I won't do it again!

'You go,' I hiss at Mel, but she stands, arms folded, and shakes her head slowly at me, a grin on her lips.

'Oh no,' she says. 'I'm not digging you out of this one. You owe it to him to face up to him. And you need to apologise.'

The doorbell goes again and even though it's only one chime, somehow it sounds annoyed. I imagine Jonathan standing on the other side tapping his foot in irritation.

I throw a desperate look at the door and then back at Mel, who is smirking at me unhelpfully, one eyebrow raised. There is no escape. I am going to have to face the wrath of Jonathan.

Running a hand through my hair, I make for the door. I'm tempted to put my hands over my eyes like I did when I was little and pretend I'm not there, but instead I plaster a huge, idiotic smile across my face and open up.

'Jonathan!' I bellow at him, as if volume might help make the moment less awkward. 'How lovely to see you. Come in, come in.'

Jonathan looks a little taken aback by my hail-fellow-well-met greeting, but he steps into the flat, conscientiously wiping his feet on the mat, even though our carpets aren't much up from the pavement outside in the cleanliness stakes.

'Emma,' he says, nodding at me tightly.

I scan the greeting for ill will and think I detect an air of frostiness, so I continue with my over-the-top enthusiasm.

'Let me take your coat,' I say, like I'm the maid. 'Is it still cold out there? Would you like some coffee? Or tea? And can I just say how sorry I was about the little thing with the card. Just a silly misunderstanding . . .'

I'm virtually bolting from him as I speak, and disappear straight into my bedroom, shutting the door firmly behind me. I have escaped. I know it's cowardly, but I'm just not up for yet another post-mortem of my incompetencies.

I stay incarcerated until I hear them retire to Mel's bedroom, when I risk sneaking out for a crisp and salad cream sandwich. Don't judge me. Sometimes only crisps and salad cream will do.

❖ ❖ ❖

Since then, no one has mentioned the V Day incident again, which suits me just fine. I don't need any more reminders of my inadequacies. They're nothing new, though. I've always been a little bit crap at stuff. I remember when I was little my dad used to tease me for not being able to tie my shoelaces properly. My brother's bows were always even and tidy whereas I couldn't get my loops the same length and they sat kind of wonkily on my shoes.

'I don't know how you do it, Emma, my little angel,' Dad used to say, 'but if there's a way of making a dog's dinner of something you'll find it.' Then he'd ruffle my hair and they'd all laugh and I'd stand there looking at my shoes and wishing they looked like James's. My bows are still a bit wayward to this day.

Anyway, I really want to make things up to Mel so I start trying to plan the best weekend ever for her birthday. Resources are a little limited, but I'm determined to find something perfect for our jaunt to Edinburgh. After several false starts I come across a tiny but super-quirky flat in the old town not far from the castle. From the pictures, it looks like you could stand in the centre of the rooms and touch all four walls. Plus we'll have to share the one double bed, but as we'll be out sampling the delights of Edinburgh most of the time, the cosiness of the place will be a boon, not a disadvantage.

After a few emails backwards and forwards with Marcus the owner, the place is ours – for the weekend at least.

In my ideal world, the one where I live in my head, I'd keep the details secret and then do a big reveal when we're on the train. I can see Mel squealing and me popping the first prosecco of the weekend and everyone else in the carriage looking up smiling and wishing they were us.

But I'm just too excited to keep the secret, so it all comes blurting out almost as soon as I've booked it, and moments later Mel and I are poring over the pictures on my laptop. Mel is suitably excited and I'm relieved that I've finally managed to get something right.

'I love that dark blue,' she says, peering at the photo of the kitchen. 'It's so classy. Do you think we could paint ours that colour?'

Our kitchen units are orange, some kind of hideous eighties throwback that the landlord calls vintage so that he doesn't have to modernise. I'm pretty certain that slopping blue paint on top would be a mistake.

'We can certainly ask,' I say, not wanting to dampen Mel's enthusiasm when it feels like I might be back in her good books. 'Are you sure you like this place, though?' I add anxiously. 'It's not too small? I can find one with two bedrooms instead if you like, but it might be a bit further out.' And more expensive, I think but don't say.

Mel leans across, throws her arms around me and pulls me in for a big squeeze.

'It's perfect,' she says into my hair. 'It's going to be the best birthday weekend ever.'

A glow starts up in my heart and spreads to all my extremities.

'Oh, and I've kicked Jonathan into touch,' she adds, like she's telling me that she's bought more loo roll. 'He kept going on about Valentine's, like he wanted a medal or something for organising it. Turns out I'm not that keen on grand romantic gestures after all.'

'Okay,' I say slowly. So much fuss over one forgotten card and now he's gone anyway. I push this thought away, though, because the weekend is going to be amazing, even if it might be less necessary than it was. I also judge that this isn't the moment to say that I never liked him anyway, so I add, 'And you're all right with that?'

'Yeah,' replies Mel. 'You've gotta kiss a lot of frogs, right?'

'And a fair few toads as well,' I agree, thinking about my most recent boyfriend, but that's a whole different story.

'I think I'm off men for a bit,' says Mel. 'I'm just going to concentrate on me for change, and on having the best birthday instead.'

I nod and grin at her, basking in the fact that for once I've hit the jackpot with my plan.

'Edinburgh, here we come!' I say raising my mug in a toast, although it's empty.

Does that still count?

3

She takes up less space on the planet.

This morning I decide to go and see my grandma. She's always lived nearby so I used to call in on her and Grandad on my way home from school for pink wafer biscuits and kind words. That's what grandparents are there for, after all.

Whenever life didn't go quite my way, Dad would explain how it was probably something that I'd got wrong and Mum would give me clear, practical advice on how to improve matters. And that was all very helpful. But sometimes all I *really* wanted to hear was how everyone else was being mean to me and that I was very badly done by.

So that was Grandma's job. She never doled out chunks of unwelcome advice or suggested solutions to my problems. She just listened, told me everyone else was a rotter, and made me big mugs of creamy hot chocolate. And then Grandad would give me a massive squeeze and make me laugh with one of his truly terrible jokes, and suddenly all the horrible stuff wouldn't be important any more.

But a couple of months back my grandad died. It was totally unexpected and incredibly sad. He and my grandma had been married for ever and they were the strongest couple I've ever known.

I almost never saw a cross word pass between them. Occasionally they would disagree about something, but when that happened Grandma used to wink at me behind his back, tell him what he wanted to hear to stop the argument, and then do the complete opposite anyway. Grandad knew what she was up to, of course, but it always took the heat out of any row. They made such an amazing team.

Since Grandad died, Grandma isn't the same. She's smaller somehow. It's like she takes up less space on the planet. She hasn't fallen apart or anything dramatic like that, although you could totally understand if she did – I'd be in bits if I lost my partner of fifty years. She's just getting on with things, like there's nothing else to be done. Her sparkle has gone, though, and she suddenly seems every one of her seventy years, although she could have passed for ten years younger before Grandad died.

You wouldn't know any of this from looking at the front of her house, mind you. She hasn't let anything slip, and the flowerbeds and lawn are still neat as ninepence, as she'd say. The front path is always swept and her windows gleam. I hate to think what she'd say if she ever saw how me and Mel live, but as I always visit her that's unlikely to come up.

When I arrive, next door's cat is sitting on the front step looking for all the world as if he owns the place. I bend to stroke him and he purrs loudly and rubs his black and white head into my open hand. Then I knock on the door and go straight in. The cat sneaks in with me.

'Grandma,' I call as I make my way to the kitchen at the back of the house. 'It's me. Emma.'

The kitchen is tiny, and if anyone were to get their hands on the house now they'd no doubt knock a wall or two down to make it bigger and stick a glass extension on the back. There's room for a tiny wooden table, though, and that's where I find Grandma, sitting with a pot of tea and a teetering pile of photo albums in front of her.

'Oh Emma, love,' she says as I approach. 'What a lovely surprise.' But there's a false brightness to her tone, and I wonder whether I should have given her a ring rather than turning up unannounced.

'Hi, Grandma,' I say. 'I was just passing and I thought I'd pop in. I'm afraid the cat came in with me.' I pull a face, but she doesn't seem to notice. 'What have you got there?' I try instead.

It's obvious that she's been looking at photos of her and Grandad, but she scoops up the albums as if she's going to put them away.

'Oh, nothing,' she says. 'Just being a sentimental old fool.'

She tries to keep her face turned away from me but I can see that her eyes are red-rimmed.

'Don't put them away,' I say quickly. 'Show me some of your favourites. You know how I love those old ones.'

She gives me a grateful smile and puts the albums back down on the table.

'Tea first,' she says, reaching me a mug from the cupboard and handing it over.

I pour myself a cup from the pot and sit down, pulling the chair round so that we're shoulder to shoulder.

'I was just looking at our wedding album,' she says.

She reaches for a brown linen-backed album and it falls open on a page of pictures of her and Grandad in front of a church. Grandma's dress is long, cream satin with a boat neckline and three-quarter-length sleeves. Her dark hair is piled on top of her head in a complicated chignon and she's holding a bouquet of red roses. Grandad, dressed in a brown suit and tie, is grinning like the cat that got the cream. They both look so young, which they were at the time; much younger than I am, anyway.

13

'How old were you?' I ask, even though I know the answer.

'I was twenty and your grandad was twenty-two,' she says.

'You look radiant, Grandma,' I say, and she does. Everything about her glows.

'It was a lovely day,' she says. Her voice cracks at the end of her sentence and she covers her eyes with her hand. 'I'm sorry, Emma.'

'You have nothing to be sorry for,' I reply. 'You must miss him so much.'

She drops her hand and tears start trickling freely down her cheeks. I don't think I've ever seen her cry before. Even at the funeral she was composed, carrying herself with so much dignity. But seeing the photos of them together looking so young and happy seems to be more than she can bear.

'It'll be fifty years soon,' she says, speaking more to herself than me.

Mum's mentioned that the golden wedding anniversary is coming up, but to be honest I hadn't really taken that much notice now that Grandad isn't here to share it.

'We'd booked a holiday to celebrate,' Grandma continues. 'A trip up north.'

I nod and smile at her, encouraging her to go on.

'A coach trip,' she continues. 'From Leeds to Edinburgh. It stops at lots of lovely places on the way. Your grandad said it would be a wander down memory lane for us, but with someone else doing all the hard work. We made almost the same trip for our honeymoon, you know, but we did it on the back of his Harley. He said the coach might be more comfy.'

She gives me a weak smile and I overcompensate by giving her a huge one back.

'I'd forgotten you went on honeymoon on his motorbike,' I say, which is true.

'It was all we could afford. Cheap B&Bs and the bike. But it was so romantic. That's why when I saw this trip I thought it would be perf—'

She can't finish her sentence. I watch as she pulls a cotton hanky from her sleeve and uses it to cover her eyes.

'Oh, I am sorry, Emma,' she says. 'I don't know what's got into me this morning.'

I put my arm around her shoulder and give her a squeeze. Her body feels tiny underneath her clothes. Has she always been this thin? I daren't squeeze too hard in case I break a bone.

'You just let it all out,' I say, conscious of how many times she must have said those exact same words to me, but where I would have wailed and gnashed teeth, Grandma just trembles slightly beneath my arm.

Eventually, she recovers herself. She wipes her eyes dry and sits up straight.

'Would you help me cancel the trip, please, Emma?' she says. 'Your grandad used to do all that kind of thing. I wouldn't know where to start.'

'I can,' I say, 'but when is it? You could go anyway. It could be a way of saying goodbye to Grandad. You could take his ashes and scatter a few in each place.'

I flinch as I say this, thinking that I've gone too far, but Grandma is nodding like she thinks it's a good idea. I can almost see her thoughts cross her face as she considers it. But then she slumps back a little.

'But who would I go with?' she says. 'I can't go on my own. Not with a coach full of strangers.'

The idea comes to me straight away.

'I'll go with you,' I say, without even thinking about it. 'I've got some holiday to take. We can do the trip together as a tribute to Grandad.'

Grandma looks so grateful that I think it might set me off crying too.

'Oh, would you really? Are you sure, Emma? That would be wonderful. But it'll be a bus of old folks. I can't imagine there'll be anyone under sixty-five.'

'I don't care,' I say. 'It would be a privilege to come with you. When is it?'

Grandma smiles and her whole face lights up like it used to before Grandad died.

'We leave Leeds on the 25th and then it calls at York, and Durham and Berwick, I think, maybe some other places too. I can't remember exactly. And then we get into Edinburgh on the 30th.'

'Great!' I say, already starting to wonder what I've agreed to. 'Which month?'

'Well, this month of course. March.'

I feel every part of me go cold. March 30th. Mel's birthday. That must be a Saturday then. The Saturday right in the middle of the 'I'm so sorry I screwed up your Valentine's, but I'll make it up to you' weekend.

Shit.

4

A BUNCH OF HANDSOME BACKPACKERS?

So, before we get much further into this story, I should probably tell you a bit more about me, although there's not that much to tell. I'm one of your truly average people. Sounds harsh, but I'm self-aware enough to know that it's true. Just about clever enough, attractive enough, funny enough, I am what my grandad would have called 'fair to middling'. Of course, he wouldn't have described me in those terms, but I'd say it's pretty accurate.

I'm twenty-eight and I live with my best friend, Mel, as you'll have gathered, in a slightly damp flat in the small northern town where I was born. I haven't always lived here – I managed to escape to uni for three years – but somehow I got pulled back into the orbit of the place after my course finished, and I've been here ever since.

My parents have moved away, though. My big brother, James, did all the right things in the right order: got an important job in London, found a competent, independently minded woman to marry him and had two lovely children shortly thereafter. And when it became apparent that none of that was going to happen to me any time soon, my parents hedged their bets and upped sticks to be nearer to him and their grandchildren, leaving me here with Grandma and Grandad to underachieve in accordance with expectations.

Contrary to the impression I might have made so far, I'm not completely hopeless. Apart from being a bit chaotic and held together with duct tape in places, my life is going reasonably well just now. I work as a visual merchandiser, which is a posh way of saying that I arrange displays in shops to try to tempt you to buy things you didn't know you needed. I think I'm not too bad at it – I haven't been sacked yet, at any rate – but it doesn't set my heart alight. It's just a job that I fell into because I couldn't think of anything else. No boyfriend currently, or for a while if truth be told, but I keep frantically telling myself that Mr Right will come along soon. In the meantime, my circle of single friends dwindles year on year and I continue to ignore how desperate my internal monologue is becoming.

Mel and I have been living together since we left uni and things generally run quite smoothly. We know each other inside out and can usually swerve to avoid incoming meteors if need be. I mess up on a fairly regular basis, and I can live with the fact that she never seems to.

Mel works in the office of a company that sells double glazing. She hates it, but they get an annual bonus that acts like a gigantic magnet, keeping her stuck there with little hope of escape. She hates her boss too, and so do I out of loyalty to her. He's old, in his late fifties or something, and he thinks all the orders should be written in triplicate on a pad in biro because that's how he's always done it, which means that Mel has to do all her work and then his on top so the orders can be inputted on to the system. He won't even try to learn how to use the computer. He drives her potty and the first fifteen minutes or so of every evening are spent with her ranting about what he's done that day to annoy her.

I wait until she's got the Colin the Luddite boss stories out of her system before I summon up the courage to tell her about the clash of dates between her birthday and Grandma's coach trip. She takes the news surprisingly calmly, I think because she knows how upset I've been about Grandad dying, and that makes me feel even more guilty.

'Listen, there'll be other birthdays,' she says, her expression resigned to disappointment but her voice gentle. 'It's not like being twenty-nine is anything special. And it sounds like your grandma would really appreciate you going with her, what with her golden wedding anniversary and everything. I can see how hard it must be for her now your grandad's gone.'

I nod weakly. Guilt is eating away at my insides. It doesn't matter what I choose to do. I'm going to let one of them down. And the fact that Mel is being so reasonable about it just makes it worse, especially when I was trying desperately to make things up to her after the last time. And then I think about Grandma and how upset she was when she was looking at the photos. And I think about Grandad and how much I miss him, and suddenly it's all a bit much.

'I'm so sorry,' I say, my eyes stinging with the tears that I'm fighting to hold back. 'I didn't mean for this to happen. If I'd known it was going to be that weekend I'd never have offered to go with her. I feel so crap for letting you down again.'

Mel sweeps me up in her arms and gives me a huge hug.

'Hey. Don't get upset. It's okay. I do have other friends, you know. I'll sort something out with them for my actual birthday and we can do something when you get back. Okay?'

I nod into her collarbone.

'Thanks, Mel,' I whisper.

She holds me for a few moments more, and then releases me in a 'Right, that's sorted' kind of way. I wipe my eyes on my sleeve.

'What's for tea?' she asks.

It's my turn to cook. I've forgotten.

'I'm on it,' I lie, despite the fact that there are no tempting smells floating in from the kitchen, or indeed any evidence of meal preparation whatsoever.

Mel sighs and heads to her room.

I'm just shrugging on my coat to go to the tiny Co-op on the corner and forage for something we can eat when she emerges from her room dressed in loungewear and ready to snuggle down for an evening in front of the telly.

'What if I came with you?' she asks.

I'm thrown.

'To the Co-op? No. You've only just got in. I can go. I should have gone to the supermarket before it closed but . . .'

'No. On the coach trip. If I don't use my holiday up by the end of the month, then I'm going to lose it anyway, so why not do this?'

I stand still, one coat sleeve dangling.

'What?' I ask, my brain not quite computing because the idea seems so outlandish.

'Come on, Emma. Keep up! The coach trip with you and your grandma.'

I'm still a bit baffled. She must see it in my face because her expression is so gentle and caring and it makes me want to cry all over again.

'I know how hard it's been for you with your grandad dying and everything,' she continues. 'And now this on top. I'm not going to ask you to choose between me and your grandma. That would be awful. But we really could do both. I come with you on the trip and then we have our Edinburgh night out at the end.'

She stares at me, waiting for me to say something, but I'm still trying to process what she's saying so she carries on.

'I've been thinking about it, and I bet it won't all be old people on board. There's bound to be some our age too. Stands to reason.'

'What? Like a bunch of handsome backpackers doing Europe by coach, all tall and blond and muscly from carrying their rucksacks everywhere?' I joke.

'Yes! Exactly like that,' she replies, and I can't tell if she thinks I'm serious. 'If we play our cards right we could both have dates for the Saturday night in Edinburgh. Let's cancel the Airbnb and do this instead. It might actually be a laugh.'

'Okay . . .' I say slowly as I think it all through.

She grins at me, her eyes shining, and I start to see that this could work out quite well. She seems genuinely excited, which gets me off the hook, and this way I will get to be there for both her and my grandma.

'I'll need to check that Grandma doesn't mind,' I say cautiously, buying more thinking time, but I'm pretty certain she'll be fine with it. She's always up for some fun, or she was until Grandad died. Having Mel and me to lighten up the mood of the coach couldn't be a bad thing.

'She won't mind,' replies Mel confidently. 'She likes me.'

Well, that's true enough. Grandma has had a soft spot for Mel ever since we were girls and Mel used to offer to pick Grandad's raspberries for him when all I wanted to do was eat them.

My brain is slowly pulling all the threads together.

'We could take the room she booked for her and Grandad. It'll have twin beds, I assume, which is fine. And then we can just book a single for her and it should all work out perfectly.'

Mel is nodding enthusiastically.

'Maybe it'll turn out to be a bit of a party bus with wall-to-wall cocktails and a banging playlist,' she says, her enthusiasm running amok now. 'And moving on to a new place every day sounds cool.

We should call it "Em and Mel on Tour". We can get some t-shirts printed. We could get one for your grandma.'

I can't help but laugh as I picture the three of us in cowboy hats and feather boas, but then I rein myself back in.

'But we mustn't forget that the whole idea is to say goodbye to my grandad,' I say.

Mel's face falls to solemn immediately and she nods soberly.

'Yes, of course,' she says. 'I'm only messing, Em. I know that's what it's about really.'

I give her a sad smile because, despite all the fun that we might have, the most important thing is to make sure that Grandma feels loved and supported.

'I'll ring Grandma later,' I say, finally wriggling my second arm into my coat. 'Check that she's okay with it all.'

Mel nods. 'Okay, but now can you go forth and buy us food, please,' she says. 'Or we'll have to eat that tin of macaroni cheese!'

The macaroni cheese, best before July 1994, was at the back of the cupboard under the sink when we moved in and we didn't throw it out because it seemed like an antiquity. It now sits in pride of place on a shelf in the kitchen as a testament to what life can become if you don't grab it by both horns.

5

I'm busy being awesome.

I speak to Grandma about Mel tagging along on the trip. I build myself up to the conversation because I don't want her to think that I'm not keen on it being just me and her, but Grandma sees the sense of it straight away.

'Well, I think that's a lovely idea, Emma,' she says. 'It'll give you someone else to talk to, and I've always liked Mel, ever since . . .'

'She picked the raspberries,' I finish.

'And it's nice to be high-spirited,' she adds, with such a tiny raise of her eyebrow that I almost think I imagined it.

I feel like I should defend my friend. Yes, she can be a bit fiery, and I've caught myself making excuses for her to strangers more than once, but I think that feisty side of her personality is all part of her charm, and as long as you don't press her buttons too hard, she's lovely. Grandma knows that too so I just smile and agree with her.

I ring the holiday company, rejig all the sleeping arrangements, and a few days later it's all booked. Now we just have to wait for the time to pass.

I wander into work on Monday. I say 'wander', but that implies a leisurely stroll through the streets of Leeds, carefully taking in the work of other visual merchandisers as I pass the shop fronts.

This is inaccurate. What actually happens is that I hurtle to the station at a pace rarely seen since Donald Campbell broke the land speed record, pelt to work from the station, leaving old ladies spinning in my wake, and skid horizontally into the staff room with one eye on its occupants and the other on the big, judgey clock that hangs on the wall above the kettle.

My colleague Gavin is already there, sipping his cup of peppermint tea with little finger and eyebrow cocked in harmony. He nods at the clock and then raises his mug (pale blue and sporting a picture of a French pug in a beret) at me in salute.

'And here she is,' he says. 'A mere two minutes late. Not bad for a Monday. I've made you a cuppa, so whip your coat off and you can swig it fast.'

I smile at him gratefully. Gavin is my guardian angel, in a professional capacity at least. He has my back so often that I swear we must be surgically attached. Over the years he has dug me out of more holes than a dachshund on heat, and I have rarely ever had cause to repay his kindness, but he doesn't seem to mind.

I tear my coat off and throw it at the pegs in the corner of the room. There is nothing more likely to signal lateness than an inappropriately timed outer garment. Then I grab the mug (white with 'I'm busy being awesome' and a picture of a unicorn in a Superman cloak on it), hurl myself at the easy chairs and try to look as if I've been there for a good twenty minutes.

Rarely for me, my timing is impeccable. The boss bustles into the room mere seconds later. This is Suki, merchandising director. She's barely older than I am, which always seeks to remind me just how well I have underachieved in my life thus far, but she dresses as if she stepped out of the nineties, in tight pencil skirts, silk blouses and court shoes. This makes me feel like all is not quite lost. At least I have style.

Suki's skirts limit the length of step that she can take, a form of human hobbling, and she compensates by taking lots of tiny steps very quickly. Gavin does a fearsome impression of her, and we spend a fair amount of time with our fists in our mouths trying to stifle laughter.

She looks up from her iPad and I swear she seems disappointed to see me sitting there and not missing in action. Still, from her expression, she clearly thinks I should be somewhere else by now and I leap to my feet, slop most of my tea into the sink and give my awesome mug a cursory rinse under the tap.

'I want you two in the Kitchen department this morning,' she says. 'Those new mixers aren't selling. Go and sort it out.'

Gavin is up too now and on the move. He at least squirts some washing-up liquid into his cup, but he leaves it to soak. Gavin has a theory that most people are too lazy to wash a cup and so if he leaves his half-done they will choose someone else's to use. I know that only half-completing the task of washing-up pains him sorely, but it is better than having to share his precious mug with all and sundry.

'On it, boss,' he says, and heads for the door.

'Can I have a quick word?' I ask Suki. 'Is now a good time?'

I know it isn't. There is never a good time for a quick word with Suki, but needs must. I sense rather than see Gavin slowing down to earwig.

'Is it all right if I book some time off at the end of the month? I have plenty of holiday to use up, and I need to take my grandma away. My grandad died, you see, and . . .'

Suki's nose crinkles and she sucks her lip. I am clearly giving her too much detail, but I can't seem to stop.

'And she was going on a coach trip for her golden wedding, but . . .'

She puts her hand up, the flat of her palm almost touching my nose.

'Fine,' she says. 'Fill the form in and get it up to HR.'

And then she's gone, taking her ludicrously small strides to go and torment some other poor soul.

Gavin, who had loitered to see what was happening, grins at me as soon as Suki is out of earshot.

'That is the best excuse for booking holiday late that I've ever heard,' he says. 'No wonder you were tardy this morning. I bet you were awake all night coming up with that one.'

I drop my jaw in indignation.

'It happens to be true,' I say. 'I'm taking Grandma on a coach trip to Edinburgh because she can't go with Grandad.'

Gavin's expression slips from a smirk to a genuine smile.

'Oh, that is the sweetest thing,' he says. 'Well done you.'

I nod, forgiving him immediately.

'Thank you,' I say.

We head off in the direction of the escalators. The shop isn't yet open, so there's no one to get in our way. Gavin stops to give himself a little foof of his favourite scent as we pass the stand. It's strictly against the rules, but everybody loves Gavin so he gets away with murder.

'You do know that those coach trips are where the world's most miserable pensioners congregate in numbers?' he says. 'It's like a breeding ground for them.'

'How would you know?' I ask. 'When was the last time you went on a coach holiday?' Gavin holidays in the bougiest places.

He taps the side of his nose with his finger.

'Trust me,' he says. 'It's common knowledge. Only the most crabby, waspish, grumpy and cantankerous need apply for trips like that.' Then he seems to realise that this may be insulting and quickly adds, 'Except for your grandma, of course.'

'Oh shut up, Gavin,' I say, punching him on his shoulder. 'Don't say that. It wouldn't be my holiday of choice and it clashes with Mel's birthday, but I couldn't just abandon Grandma.'

Gavin's eyes open wide.

'So, have you ditched Mel? She's not going to be best pleased about that,' he says with a knowing dip of his chin.

'It's okay. Mel's coming with me.'

'Oh sweet Jesu,' he says. 'And she's okay with that?'

I bite my lip and screw my nose up. 'I might have accidentally given her the impression that the coach is going to be full of hot backpackers.'

'Ah,' replies Gavin. 'She's going to kill you when she finds out who really takes a coach trip.'

'There might be a few travellers under seventy,' I say.

He's shaking his head slowly.

'Just one or two?' I add weakly.

'Well, yes. There'll be you and Mel,' he laughs.

'Oh God. You're probably right. Should I tell her?'

'That's up to you, lovely. Tell her now so she cancels, or let her find out when she gets on board and deal with her being pretty peevish until she sees the funny side. If I were you I'd keep schtum and then just pretend to be as disappointed as she is.'

I'm not sure it's the right thing to do, but I suspect it's what I'll end up doing anyway.

Gavin wafts off in the direction of the food mixers and I trail in his wake, wondering if I might have made a colossal error of judgement.

6

THERE WON'T BE MUCH CALL FOR MY BACKLESS BLUE DRESS.

Mel and I are having a pamper night, mainly because what with having to fork out for the forthcoming trip, we don't really have enough money left to go out.

I'm lying on the sofa in my dressing gown with a face pack on. It's one of those sheet things with holes cut out for your eyes and mouth. It's making me feel quite claustrophobic, but the packet promises that my skin will be rehydrated and rejuvenated by the end, so I'm pushing any feelings of mild panic to the back of my mind.

Mel has gone for one of the more traditional masks that you slather on and leave to dry. Both of us have cucumber on our eyes but mine keeps sliding off on to the sofa cushions because I have to sit up quite often to get a mouthful of wine. We do have a couple of scented candles burning, but I'm not sure we've managed to re-create the expensive spa vibe entirely successfully.

As we luxuriate, Mel is entertaining me with stories about the worst customers of the week at the double-glazing company.

'There was this one woman this week,' she says, 'who spent half an hour telling me that uPVC windows are common and she wouldn't dream of having them fitted at her house, and then accused me of wasting her time when I finally got a word in edgeways and informed her that those are the only kind we do.'

'Oh dear,' I say, knowing how this story is likely to end.

'So I told her that in fact she'd been wasting my time because it quite clearly says that we only do uPVC windows on the website, and she said she'd never been spoken to so rudely, which I found very hard to believe, and then she asked to speak to my manager.'

'Did you put her through?' I ask, thinking that a complaint to Mel's boss, Colin, wouldn't have been good.

'Colin was on the phone,' Mel said, 'so I put her on hold.'

'How long for?' I ask, fearing the worst.

'I'm not sure. When I checked on her an hour or so later she'd rung off.'

'Oh Mel! You'll get sacked,' I say, although the thought of the woman being on hold is quite funny.

'Well, it's old people,' she says. 'They get on my nerves. They complain about everything. And this one was old and a snob on top!'

'How do you know she was old?' I ask.

'I just did from the stuff she said. She'd clearly not been anywhere near the website or she'd have known. Who rings a company up without checking out the website? Old people, that's who.'

My stomach lurches and Gavin's warning looms into my mind.

'And Colin was a nightmare today too,' Mel continues, as her head of steam builds. 'If I've shown him how to use the online ordering system once I must have shown him a million times, but he still can't work it. Or won't, more likely. And why should he when he can carry on just as he always has done, knowing that I'm there to input all his orders on to the system for him?'

'I'm sure it's hard for him,' I say. 'It's not always easy to learn something new.'

'Well, it wouldn't hurt him to try,' Mel snaps back. 'I caught him trying to use the fax machine the other day. No one uses that any more. I don't know why we still have it. It wasn't even plugged in.'

I snigger because I know that's what is expected of me.

'And then he had a right go at me because I told him to email the bloke instead. Called me a nasty little know-it-all. I was tempted to say that I'd rather be that than a dinosaur like him, but Hannah stopped me by dropping her bin and causing a distraction.' She reaches for her wine and takes a long slug. 'Anyway, this time next week we'll be on the way to Scotland with a bunch of hunky backpackers and Colin will have to work out how to sort his orders on his own.'

This is the perfect moment to mention my fears about the average age of our fellow travellers, but given how wound up she is it feels like a foolhardy venture. I promise myself I'll manage her expectations tomorrow.

'Anyway,' she says, sitting up and refilling our glasses. 'More important than my miserable Luddite boss is what we are going to pack for our forthcoming adventure. I'm assuming there won't be much call for my backless blue dress, and my silk negligée is at the dry cleaners, so that can't come with us.'

I grin at her.

'It's not like packing for Ibiza,' I say. 'But we will need nice things for the evening and a going-out outfit for Edinburgh on Saturday.'

'Oh yes,' she says, nodding sagely. 'That better be a humdinger of a night, what with all this build-up.'

This makes my stomach clench as I pray I can deliver something that matches her expectations.

'During the day, though, it'll be mainly woollies,' I say. 'The north-east of England in March isn't known for its tropical weather patterns.'

Plucking the cucumber slices from my eyes and dropping them on the already dirty carpet, I reach for my phone and open the weather app, typing in Newcastle as a kind of benchmark for our entire trip. The page looks very busy, with most weather conditions catered for.

'Well, it looks like it could do pretty much anything,' I say. 'In general, though . . .' I let my eyes trail across the temperatures for the week ahead, 'I'd go with layers.'

Mel nods and settles back down into her spa pose.

'Next time we go on a coach trip,' she says, 'can we go to Bora Bora?'

7

MONDAY: THE DAY OF THE TRIP

A BRIGHT RED SUIT IN SCRATCHY POLYESTER.

The taxi drops us off at the coach park ludicrously early. What is it about old people and time-keeping? I tried to suggest to Grandma that we really didn't need to allow two hours for a ten-mile journey, but my words fell on stony ground. That said, we're not the first to arrive by a long chalk. The place is teeming with activity, with passengers, coach drivers dressed in smart navy jackets and a woman bustling about efficiently with iPad in hand who looks as if she's in charge.

I cast an eye around and my heart sinks. Mel and I seem to be bringing the average age of passengers down by quite some margin, and there's no sign of any backpackers, handsome or otherwise.

Mel is helping Grandma with her case, and I hope she can't sense my mood as I feel a knot tighten in my stomach. I still haven't quite got round to levelling with her about the chances of any young people being on the bus, and it appears I'm too late. She's going to work it out for herself any minute now. Flak helmets at the ready.

The buses are all lined up in a neat row like as many kids' toys and our first job is to locate ours. I spot one with a big sign saying 'Odyssey of the North' in the window and point it out to Mel with a sly nod of my head. We both smirk. It's just a coach trip, but it clearly has ideas of grandeur.

The driver is standing by the open luggage hold, the gaping hole in the side of the coach already half-filled with suitcases. He seems cheerful enough, a far cry from the bus drivers I generally encounter, and he gives us a Cheshire Cat smile when he sees us hovering.

'Now then, now then,' he says, with echoes of a long-dead celebrity that no one wants to remember, and I wonder if he uses the expression on purpose or if it's just an unfortunate verbal tic. 'I'm Dave the Driver . . .' He points enthusiastically to a plastic name badge on his jacket lapel. 'And are you three lovely ladies coming my way?'

'If you're going to Edinburgh, then yes, we are,' Mel replies coolly. No smile.

Dave's smile slips just a notch and I want to nudge her and tell her to play nice, but instead I decide to ignore it. Mel has never been much good at dealing with what she calls the inherent condescension of men towards women. I'm more likely to cut them a bit of slack, particularly men like Dave, whose heart appears to be in the right place, even if his vocabulary is stuck somewhere back in the seventies. Mel, however, takes no prisoners.

'Righty ho. Let's get those cases on board,' Dave says, with slightly less warmth than before. He grabs the handle of mine and swings it into the luggage hold with practised ease. 'Robin will be over in a minute to tick you off his list.'

Then he turns his attention to the elderly couple waiting behind us.

'Now then, my love,' he says to the woman, who has tight hold of the handle of her case, as if she fears someone might steal it from her at any second. 'Let me take that for you.'

He means no harm. In fact, I quite like him.

We move away from the coach, not quite sure what we're supposed to do next. Grandma suddenly looks smaller than ever, her shoulders hunched inside her woollen coat and her eyes fearful. This must be hard for her, I realise, harder than I'd thought. I tuck my arm through hers and give her a reassuring squeeze. She offers me a brave smile, and I know that she must be thinking about Grandad and wishing that it was him escorting her to her seat and not me.

Mel has slipped into taking charge mode and she strides over to the person we assume is Robin. He's around our age and is wearing a bright red suit in a scratchy-looking polyester. The jacket alone would have been statement enough but teaming it with the red trousers, a white shirt and a red tie makes him look like he should be hosting proceedings at a holiday camp.

The couple he's been dealing with, also elderly, move towards the coach. The woman stops at the front steps, stares up at them as if they are the north face of the Eiger, casts a sorrowful glance at her husband, and then purposefully lifts one shaking leg towards the first tread. Two things cross my mind. Firstly, this really is a trip for old people. I mean, I knew that already, but I hadn't really thought about the implications. And secondly, if I were running a coach trip for pensioners I would provide a ramp.

Robin turns his attention to us. He has the air of someone who is perpetually bewildered but is trying hard to look in control.

'Good morning,' he says eagerly. 'And you are . . .' He speaks with the kind of Midlands accent that makes you want to mimic him.

'Phyllis Potter,' says Grandma. 'And this is my granddaughter, Emma, and her friend Mel.'

Robin looks at us, and I swear he does a double take. I assume this is to do with our age and the consequential rarity of our type of client on his coach. Then he consults his clipboard. The pink tip of his tongue protrudes from his lips as he traces a finger down the list of names.

'Potter, Potter, Potter . . . ah yes. Here you are,' he says. 'Potter times three. So, welcome to the Odyssey of the North. Climb aboard and find yourselves a seat. You can sit wherever you like. We'll be underway in . . .' He consults his watch and I notice that it's got Tintin on its face. 'In forty-five minutes.'

I'm pleased to see that Grandma makes a much better stab at the stairs than the woman before, not struggling at all, and soon the three of us are standing in the aisle surveying the seating arrangements. It's certainly a very plush coach, the poshest I've ever been on. It's got leather seats – or they might be pleather, I can't really tell from the touch and I don't want to get my nose down to seat level to smell it. There are tables between some of the seats, a bit like on a train, and a set of steps that I assume descend to the onboard facilities. I shudder at the thought of trying to do a wee at sixty miles an hour on the motorway with a bunch of strangers only the width of a door away, but I suppose it might be handy for some of the older passengers and it'll mean that we don't need to stop every ten miles for comfort breaks.

The coach is about a third full with a mixture of people sitting in couples and on their own. Every single pair of eyes is on us and I see one woman nudge her husband as she stares at Mel and me. We are the youngest by at least forty years.

Mel widens her eyes at me and I know she's saying, 'Are we on the right coach?' I give her what I hope is a reassuring nod. Then, anxious to stop being the coach entertainment, I turn to Grandma.

'Where would you like to sit?' I ask her. 'Front or back?'

'Somewhere in the middle,' she says in a small voice. 'But not over a wheel. Stan always said it makes you travel-sick if you sit over the wheel.'

I have no idea where the wheels might be, so I guess and point to a table seat in what I hope is a wheel-free place. There are four seats arranged around the table and Grandma chooses the one by the window facing the front. I'm going to slip in next to her but Mel tugs at my arm.

'I can't go backwards,' she says. 'I need to be able to see where we're going.'

She has a point. Mel could sit next to Grandma, but then I'll be facing the wrong way, and now I think about it, I realise that I'm not that keen on going backwards either.

'Erm . . .' I mutter as I struggle to find a solution. Maybe Mel could sit on her own behind us. But then I'd have to talk to Grandma all the time and while I love her to pieces, I'd much rather chat to Mel.

But I don't want to hurt Grandma's feelings. I dither, and then another man gets on the coach and, obviously, we are blocking the aisle. I can feel irritation radiating off him as I try to decide what to do. He tuts, then coughs, then says, 'Could you say your goodbyes and get off the coach now, please? You're blocking the way for the passengers.'

'Actually,' replies Mel, 'we're passengers too and we're just choosing our seats, so please can you just be patient for a moment?'

She's polite, but barely. Because I know her so well, I recognise the barbs in her tone, but I hope they aren't obvious to the man, who seems to have plenty of barbs of his own. We don't want to be starting a fight before we've even left the coach park.

Grandma, who had been searching for something in the depths of her handbag, now looks up and works out what the delay-causing issue is at once.

'Oh, silly me, sitting here and taking up all this space,' she says. 'I didn't think. But I'm here now. Why don't you two find a double and sit together?'

'Will you be okay?' I ask.

'Of course,' she says. 'I'm fine. It's a lovely seat and I have the table to put my book on.'

The man behind us tuts again and I can feel Mel building up to an inappropriate comment, so I say, 'If you're sure,' and slide myself into the pair of seats behind her. I do it so quickly that I clatter my knee on the seat in front and have to press my lips together hard to stop me swearing. Something tells me that these old people wouldn't appreciate an expletive.

It's clear, however, that Mel has no intention of doing anything quickly. She lifts her bag up into the overhead rack with all the speed of a sloth, turns to look up and down the coach as if she's familiarising herself with her surroundings then finally sits down, at which point the irritated man makes a kind of grunt and mutters 'Thank you' under his breath.

'Behave,' I whisper to Mel with a grin.

'Well,' she tuts. 'That kind of rudeness really gets on my nerves. It's not like we're about to set off. It wouldn't have killed him to wait for a second or two.' She drops her voice lower still and adds, 'They're all quite old so far, aren't they?'

I nod and give her a sidelong glance.

'But I bet the younger passengers will rock up just before we're due to leave,' she says. 'You know, like we would have done if we hadn't been bringing Phyllis.'

'Mel,' I begin. 'You do know . . .'

But I'm interrupted by the arrival of the next passenger.

8

I'm quite partial to a bit of tea loaf.

'Well, what do we have here? This all looks very jolly,' trills a woman's voice with a clear overtone of amusement, and Mel and I look up to see who is speaking. Another single old lady, with a navy silk scarf knotted jauntily at her neck and a pink trilby stops next to Grandma's table.

'Are these seats free?' she asks in the cut-glass tone of someone you wouldn't generally expect to find on a coach. 'Would you mind awfully if I joined you? Just until York, of course. I'm not trying to foist myself on you for the entire week. My name is Gloria. Gloria Finchley-Browne.'

She holds out a leather-gloved hand for Grandma to shake. I can't see how Grandma reacts because the seat is in the way, but the woman sits down next to her and I hear Grandma introduce herself.

'I'm not travelling alone,' she adds as Gloria settles herself down. 'My granddaughter and her friend are with me.'

Gloria's face immediately appears above the seat in front. She is what they used to call 'a handsome woman', with high cheekbones and fine features. Her skin, though lined, is still like porcelain. She smiles broadly at us and there's a twinkle in her eyes. I like her at once.

'Hello, granddaughter and granddaughter's friend,' she says in her clipped voice.

'I'm Emma,' I reply. 'And this is Mel.'

'Short for Melanie, I assume,' says Gloria. 'Or Melissa perhaps?'

I can feel Mel tense.

'Carmel, actually,' she says. 'After a singer that my mum liked in the eighties.'

It's not often that Mel lets this little nugget out and I'm quite surprised that she's confessed it now to a total stranger, but Gloria has the air of someone you want to be your friend as soon as you meet them.

'Oh, how totally delicious,' Gloria says.

As she speaks her eyes widen and her head gives a little shiver, like it really is the most exciting thing she's heard all day. Then she drops back behind the seat to talk to Grandma.

Mel and I indicate our approval with mutual raised eyebrows.

'Well, she might be a breath of fresh air,' I say, thinking of the other passengers we've encountered so far.

'Time will tell,' replies Mel with a hint of dark foreboding. 'She's certainly more promising than the rest of them.'

I gird my loins.

'I think it is just going to be old people,' I whisper, cocking my head backwards. 'On the coach, I mean.'

The knot in my stomach tightens just a little more as I watch Mel's expression settle into something closer to irritated than I'd like it to be right now. She lets out a sharp sigh.

'So it appears,' she says crisply.

'You didn't really think . . .' I begin, but then there's a sharp little bark in the air as the onboard PA system comes to life. Robin is standing at the front of the coach, his red suit glowing. He has a clump of unruly brown curls falling almost to his shoulders and patchy stubble that might be an attempt at a beard but which isn't quite working for him. He also wears little round glasses that do nothing to improve the look of bewilderment that I noticed before.

He starts speaking into the microphone.

'Can everyone hear me?' he asks.

It doesn't sound as if the system is amplifying his voice at all.

'We can't hear you,' comes an indignant voice from behind us.

'Is that thing working?' comes another that I suspect belongs to Grumpy Aisle Man.

'Could you speak up?' asks a third.

'I'm not sure they're getting it,' chips in Gloria, and even though I can't see her face, I sense a wink.

The tip of Robin's nose blushes and he fiddles with the microphone.

'Is that better?' he asks, his voice now louder. It's possibly too loud for those of us with normal hearing but it appears that we are in the minority.

There is a general affirmative chorus from further down the coach and he continues.

'Now, as you all know, my name is Robin, and I'm going to be your tour guide for the trip.'

There is what I can only describe as an expectant hush as we all hang on his every word.

'So, our first stop is York!'

He says this as if it will come as a surprise to us, like it's a mystery tour, and then looks disappointed when no one reacts. He looks down at his clipboard to cover his embarrassment and I feel for him. He's one of those men who make you want to say 'Bless' every time they speak.

'It's only a short hop,' he continues, 'so we'll be there in plenty of time to get settled into the hotel before lunch. Then this afternoon, those of you that would like to can accompany me on a tour of the world-acclaimed York Minster, followed by a wander down the Shambles and finishing up with a lovely cream tea back at the hotel. You then have time to yourself before we meet for dinner at seven in the hotel dining room.'

There is a general murmuring of approval down the coach.

'Of course, the joy of these trips is that you can join in with as much or as little as you like . . .' At this point he looks directly at me and Mel.

'Do you think he doesn't want us?' whispers Mel. 'I could be quite hurt.'

I stifle a giggle.

'. . . but if you choose to eat somewhere else could you please let me know by midday each day so that I can tell the hotels. I'm afraid that if you do eat elsewhere that will be entirely at your own expense . . .'

A male voice pipes up behind us. 'We mentioned when we booked that we'd like our rooms to be upgraded wherever possible.'

'Yes, we're used to staying in very nice places,' says a female voice, his wife I assume, whose suspiciously peculiar accent sounds like she's trying to make herself appear posher than she actually is. She emphasises 'very' and I'm desperate to turn around and get a proper look at her, but I manage to resist.

'And so it begins,' whispers Mel, and I snigger.

Robin is on it and replies with an air of well-practised tact.

'Here at Odyssey Luxury Coach Holidays we pride ourselves on selecting the best hotel rooms for all our guests, but if upgrades have been requested then the office will have passed that on as required, er, Mr . . . ?'

'Mr Anderson. Frank. And this is my wife, Vivienne,' supplies the man. He places an unnatural stress on the final syllable, which seems to sit well with her fake accent.

'I'm sure, Frank, that you and Vivienne . . .' – Robin parrots the unusual pronunciation of the name, and I feel Mel shaking in the seat next to me – '. . . will be delighted with the standard of the rooms.'

There is a kind of grunt from Frank that says, 'We better had be' quite loud and clear.

'I'm not fussed about a cream tea,' says another voice, a woman this time. 'Cream doesn't sit easy with me, especially not after a journey. Will there be other cakes? I'm quite partial to bit of tea loaf. Or maybe a crumpet.'

Mel snorts and I nudge her hard with my elbow.

'It's generally just scones with cream,' says Robin.

'And jam, I assume.' This time it's Gloria who speaks, but I get the impression that she's doing it out of naughtiness. I decide I definitely like Gloria.

'Yes. And jam,' confirms Robin patiently.

'But if you don't like cream, can you have the scones plain?' asks the woman.

The temptation to turn round and take a look is almost overwhelming.

'I can't eat cream, you see,' she repeats in a quieter voice, pre-sumably to whoever has the misfortune to be sitting near her.

'The cream is entirely optional,' says Robin, and Mel gives him a cheerful thumbs-up behind the seat in front.

'So,' Robin continues, 'I'll leave you now to enjoy the journey. When we get near to York I'll tell you about the arrangements for the hotel.'

He turns off the microphone, blows his wayward fringe from his forehead and takes his seat at the front.

'Poor old Robin seems to have his hands full,' I whisper to Mel.

'Looks like he's used to it,' she says. 'Do you think they're going to be this miserable all the way to Edinburgh? I've come on holiday to get away from Colin the Luddite and his moaning, and now it appears that I'm trapped with a whole coachload of miseries.'

'Except us,' I say. 'And Grandma, and that Gloria. And not all the others have said anything yet so maybe some of them are okay too.'

Mel sniffs.

'And Robin seems quite sweet,' I add. 'In a slightly space-cadet kind of way.'

'No gorgeous Kiwis, though,' she says with a resigned air, and I can't tell if she's joking or cross.

9

River view. Prosecco on tap.

We are less than fifteen minutes out of Leeds when we make our first unscheduled stop. It's the woman who can't eat cream. It appears she can't eat much at all because she leaves most of it on the edge of the A64.

Mel and I avert our eyes. I've never been much good with vomit, not since I went on a school residential and had to share a room with a girl with gastroenteritis. Mel just isn't interested and spends the time on her phone.

All around us the reactions range from sympathy to irritation, with irritation prevailing. They don't seem to be a very patient bunch and I distinctly hear Grumpy Aisle Man complaining that we'll have lost fifteen minutes from our schedule. Like that's going to matter. None of this is life and death stuff.

I take the opportunity to stand up and check in on Grandma, but she is merrily chatting away with Gloria and barely seems to have noticed that we've stopped. I should be pleased that she's found a friend. It takes the pressure off me. But I find that my nose is ever so slightly out of joint.

When the woman has finished being sick, she clambers back aboard, wiping at her mouth with a tissue and apologising on repeat. She stops to inform Robin that we may continue and then makes her way down to her seat. Gloria passes her a tube of extra strong mints as she passes. She tries to take just one, her swollen fingers fumbling with the packet, but Gloria waves her away.

'Keep them,' she says. 'Keep them.'

The coach sets off again and we manage to reach York without further incident. As the traffic on the outskirts of York begins to build and our pace slows, Robin gets to his feet again and switches on the microphone. Silence descends on the coach like snowfall.

'So,' he says, 'we'll be arriving at the hotel shortly. Our driver, Dave, will help you with your bags and then please make your way into reception, where they will be waiting to allocate your rooms in accordance with the preferences you stated at the time of booking.'

Yet again there is a general twittering as passengers either confirm their preferences to their partner or wonder whether they've missed a trick by not putting any down.

Mel looks at me. She's smiling and I'm relieved. Maybe she's over the lack of younger travellers.

'Twin beds,' she says. 'River view. Prosecco on tap. Gorgeous men ready and waiting to tend to our every whim. Have I forgotten anything?'

'Chocolate,' I say. 'You didn't mention the unlimited supplies of chocolate.'

Someone near us shushes us loudly. I want to turn round, hoping that it's Grumpy Aisle Man, but I think the voice was too close by to be him. My heart sinks. Can there be two such miserable so and sos among our number?

Robin continues.

'There will then be a quick buffet lunch' – he drops his gaze at this point so that he doesn't have to make eye contact and prompt any queries about what the buffet will entail – 'and then those who wish to join us on the city tour should congregate in the hotel reception at one o'clock. Now, are there any questions?'

'Will there be many steps, Robin? On the tour, I mean. I'm fine on the flat, but steps play havoc with my knees.' This seems to be from the woman who struggled to get on the bus in the first place.

Mel rolls her eyes. 'For God's sake,' she mutters under her breath. 'It's a bloody tour. There are likely to be some steps involved. Or did she think we were going to see all the places from inside the bus?'

'Shhh,' I say. 'She'll hear you.'

Mel tuts loudly. 'I doubt it. They'll all be deaf as posts. But I really don't care either way,' she says. 'It's ridiculous to want to avoid steps.'

This change of tone is making me slightly nervous. We haven't even reached the first stop yet and it seems like Mel's old-lady tolerance is failing already.

'Just ignore them,' I whisper. 'Let them twitter about whatever worries them. In the meantime, we can focus on having the best time.'

I give her my brightest smile, but the one I get back is a bit half-hearted. I can't have Mel taking against the trip so early. This is supposed to be fun and something special to make up for, etc., etc., but she has a tendency to come to snap judgements that are hard to reverse out of. We definitely can't run the risk of that happening here.

'I'm looking forward to seeing York Minster,' she says, and I relax a little. 'I've never been in. Mum says that God tried to burn it down in the eighties because someone high up in the Church was sceptical about His existence. Nearly succeeded as well, by all accounts.'

'Is that true?' I ask.

'Apparently.'

She picks up her phone and does a quick Google search and then turns the screen round so I can see the results. The page is full of articles about the fire.

'Well, that's interesting,' I say. 'I love a good conspiracy theory. Let's see if Robin brings it up on his tour.'

'If not, maybe we could mention it,' says Mel with a mischievous grin. 'Or do you think God will smite us down?'

Now we seem to be back in dangerous territory. It's a fair assumption, given their age, that a number of the other passengers won't take kindly to casual God jokes. Then again, if I keep second-guessing what might offend them, then Mel and I are going to have absolutely no fun at all, so I choose to ignore it.

'If He does, let's make sure He does it right in the middle of the cathedral so that we go out in a blaze of Twitter feeds!'

We snigger to ourselves and then realise we've missed whatever Robin said about steps and tune back in.

'One final point,' he says. 'We haven't introduced ourselves as yet. You all know who I am, of course, but you need to meet each other. I won't do that now because it's hard to see and hear one another on the coach. We'll have a proper introduction session at the cream tea. And I'd like you all to tell us one surprising thing about yourself, so that should give you plenty of time to think of something.'

I groan inwardly. I hate being forced to do things like this, not least because there is absolutely nothing surprising about me at all. But I suppose none of them know anything about me, so I can probably dredge something up and put some tinsel on it so it's more interesting.

The coach rolls into York and I see first the ancient city walls and then Clifford's Tower basking in the clear morning light. I let myself sink back into the seat.

'I've had an idea,' says Mel, her voice suitably low this time. 'Let's have a bet. Make this trip a bit more interesting.'

I glance at her through narrowed eyes.

'What on?' I ask her suspiciously. I've been part of her bets before and they aren't always as much fun as she supposes.

'The first one to ask Robin out for a drink,' she says.

I look over towards Robin. He's staring out of the window as the coach negotiates the one-way system. He's not good-looking, but he's not ugly either. And he seems quite sweet. Nice enough to have a drink with at least.

'Okay,' I say. 'But it can't be as simple as that. You'll just ask him out now, and I'll lose before I've even started.' I think for a moment. 'How about he has to say yes? That means there'll need to be a bit of a build-up to asking.'

Mel pulls a face, considering my terms, and then nods.

'Okay.'

'And what are we playing for?' I ask.

'Loser washes up for a month,' she says.

We have no dishwasher in our flat so this is quite a big deal.

'High stakes indeed,' I say. I consider her proposal for a minute and then I say, 'Okay. You're on!'

We shake on it and I can feel the tension starting to ebb out of Mel. I have to say, I'm quite relieved.

10

HIDING WHAT THEY DON'T EAT IN THEIR HANDBAGS.

The coach pulls up outside the hotel in York and there's a new air of expectation as everyone waits to see what it's like. It looks quite smart. It's got one of those huge revolving doors that I always want to spin round and round in, like I did when I was little. I look to see if there's a doorman or a bellboy too, but there's no sign of either. There are none of those tall brass luggage racks they're always pushing about either, although maybe they're only in American films. I haven't stayed in enough hotels to know. Mel and I usually choose apartments. It's cheaper for one thing, and we like having the freedom and flexibility of our own front door key.

But nothing about this week is to do with freedom and flexibility. If we hadn't realised that already then we certainly understand it now as we watch Robin tick everyone off his list and usher them first to their cases and then into the reception area. It reminds me a lot of a school outing. In fact, so far the old people remind me quite a lot of children, with all their questions and fussing.

When Robin gets to me and Mel he peers at this clipboard even harder, as if he's checking that our names are still there. He really doesn't know what to make of us. Even though we've explained that we're here to chaperone Grandma, he doesn't seem to have got his head round the idea and he still looks thoroughly confused. That bewildered look he has is quite cute, though, in a lost puppy kind of way.

Mel seems to be making a start on our bet already. She gives Robin one of her best megawatt smiles, all teeth and eye contact.

'That's great. Thanks, Robin,' she simpers.

I elbow her in the ribs as we go to join the queue at reception.

'What??' she asks indignantly, and I just shake my head at her, but I can see I'm going to have to raise my game if I don't want to be doing the washing-up for a month.

We retrieve our cases and follow the others into the foyer. It's nice enough. A bit old-fashioned, with lots of dark wood and red and gold, but smarter than anywhere I've stayed for a while and definitely quite a few steps up from our flat.

Whilst we wait, I take the chance to have a proper look at our fellow passengers. They are all old, I'd guess in their seventies, although I'm not great at judging the ages of old people. They look about the same age as Grandma, anyway. It's a mixture of couples and singletons.

One of the pairs, who are dressed in matching khaki cagoules and walking trousers, cling to each other as if they are about to be wrenched apart. It would be romantic at their age if they didn't look so terrified. There's a man who seems to be on his own and who looks quite sweet, sort of soft around the edges. He's got that air of confusion that Robin also radiates, and I wonder for a moment if they might be related, like me and Grandma, but then dismiss the thought when I realise that this is the only thing they seem to share. Robin is tall and a bit lanky and the sweet-looking man is as round as a ball.

Apart from him, the only other passenger who seems at all interesting is Gloria. There's a confidence about her, and she gives off that air of being completely in control. Where the others look thrown by not quite knowing what's going on, Gloria seems to be taking it all in her stride. She chats to Grandma, but her eyes never stop darting about as she gets the measure of everything. And everyone.

The woman who had to get off the coach on the way here still looks a little green around the gills and I hope that she's not ill every time we move on. I do feel sorry for her, though. She's still blushing and she doesn't meet anyone's eyes. I wonder about going to say hello, just to put her at her ease, but then I look at Mel standing next to me and change my mind.

Mel sighs loudly.

'If I get to be as dithery as this lot when I'm old then please shoot me,' she says, and mimes putting a revolver to her temple and pulling the trigger. I laugh, despite myself. It's not funny – but then again, it really is. I scan the old people. They are fizzing either with anxiety or irritation. There doesn't seem to be much in between. I decide Mel has got a point.

'Deal,' I say.

Oh so very slowly, everyone is allocated their room for the night and we are finally released to go and drop off our cases.

'Lunch in the restaurant in twenty minutes, and then the city walking tour will leave from here at one,' calls Robin to his guests as they wander off in search of the lifts.

Our room is on the first floor and, seeing the length of the queue for the lift, we decide to take the stairs.

Once we are out of earshot of our fellow travellers we drop our guard. Mel blows her lips out as she heaves her case up to the first landing.

'Oh my God,' she says. 'Aren't they hilarious? Your grandma seems like the only normal one of the lot. And that Gloria. She seems okay. I thought old Grumpy-drawers would lose his schnit in the queue to check in. Anyone would think he had never queued before.'

'Maybe he hasn't,' I say. 'Maybe he's actually a secret royal, or the boss of the whole company and is only here to get the guest experience.'

Mel's eyes open wide.

'Do you think so?' she asks, quite excited by the idea.

'Er, no,' I reply. 'He's just a grumpy old man who has an over-inflated sense of his own importance and doesn't like to wait his turn.'

She laughs. 'Yeah, I suppose so. That would have been cool, though. I wonder what his surprising fact will be. What are you going to say for yours?'

I have no idea what she's talking about, but then I remember that we're supposed to be telling each other something surprising at the introductions later that day.

'God, I don't know,' I say. 'I'll have to think. What about you?'

Mel sets off again, grabbing her case with two hands as she lugs it up the next return of stairs.

'No idea,' she says. 'I'll probably make something up.'

'You can't do that!' I say, some deep part of me feeling outraged by the idea of lying, as if I'm still eight years old.

'Why not? It's not like anyone is going to be checking up on us. It might be fun to pretend to be something different for a while, like giving a fake name for your coffee in Starbucks.'

'I don't do that. Do you do that?' I ask, pulling the fire door open and holding it for Mel to pass through.

'Always,' she says.

'It never even occurred to me,' I reply, but as I speak I wonder why not.

'Oh, it's great fun,' says Mel. 'I tend to go for something that's hard to spell, like Anastasia.'

'You're so mean!' I laugh, and she shrugs.

We find the door with our room number on and use the key card to open it. The room is predominantly lilac, and is bright and airy with a feature wallpapered wall in an abstract design. There are twin beds dressed with sumptuous silver cushions and throws, a desk, a wardrobe and a door that I assume must lead to the en suite.

'Well, this is very nice,' I say, swinging my case so that it has enough momentum to land on the nearest bed. 'It's almost like being on holiday! Shall I sleep here?'

'Fine by me.'

Mel struts over to the window and pulls back the net curtain.

'Great view,' she says, letting it fall again.

We appear to be overlooking a service shaft and a brick wall.

'Oh well,' I say brightly. 'It's not like we're going to be in here much.'

I open my case to unpack, but then stop.

'I suppose there's not much point unpacking,' I say. 'We'll only have to pack it all back up again in the morning.'

'Living out of a suitcase,' says Mel, flopping on to the bed and staring up at the ceiling. 'How very rock and roll.'

And then we laugh because if there's one thing this trip is not, it's rock and roll.

'Shall we go downstairs and find this buffet before the old people scoff it all?' I ask.

Mel grins at me. 'They'll be hiding what they don't eat in their handbags for later,' she says. 'You know what old people are like!'

We're still laughing as our room locks silently behind us.

11

You should have a system.

We don't notice that we've locked ourselves out until we head back to get our bags after lunch.

'Damn,' says Mel as we round the corner into our part of the corridor. She pats at her jeans pockets.

'I think I left my key card in the thing that makes the lights come on,' she says. 'Have you got yours?'

I realise with a sinking feeling that I put mine in my purse for safekeeping and that it is now in my bag, which is safely locked in our room. I shake my head.

'I'll go down and get another one from reception,' Mel says, turning on her heel to head back the way we just came. Not wanting to loiter in the corridor on my own and being just as responsible as she is for the cock-up, I follow her.

We have to walk right past the rest of the group, who are just finishing their coffee, clearly determined to get every last penny's worth out of the included food and drink.

'You were very quick,' says Cream Tea Woman, who we learned over lunch is called Cynthia.

'We've locked ourselves out,' I reply with a smile and a little self-deprecating shrug.

'Well, that was stupid,' says Grumpy Aisle Man, now known as Keith. 'You should have a system. Always check you have your keys before you leave the room and always put them in the same place so you know where they are.'

He speaks to us as if we are children, not independent women with brains and a flat of our own. It's not like we've never been responsible for a key before. Although, given that we have just locked ourselves out, I decide that perhaps this isn't the moment to set him straight.

Cynthia is more sympathetic.

'Such an easy mistake to make,' she says, and gives us a simpering smile. 'I'm sure they will have a spare one at the desk.'

'They can just program a new card,' replies Mel dismissively, and moves off to speak to the woman on reception, leaving me to face more life lessons from Keith.

'That's the trouble with this new-fangled technology,' he says to no one in particular. 'When we had a proper key, you had to turn it in the lock to secure the room, so this couldn't happen.'

'Unless it was a Yale lock,' Cynthia adds helpfully.

The look Keith gives her would turn milk sour. I smile broadly at Cynthia, partly because she's right but mainly because I approve of her little act of rebellion and I want her to know.

'You won't lock yourself out if you just follow a system,' repeats Keith, sticking firmly on message. 'I'm constantly aware of the stiffness in my pocket so I always know I haven't lost the card.'

It's a good job that Mel is at the desk because she wouldn't have been able to ignore his unintentional innuendo, but as I'm on my own I can disregard it, and Cynthia, who doesn't look as if stiff things have ever featured in her life, doesn't even notice.

'I write the room number down too,' he continues. 'In code.'

He reaches into his pocket, takes out a wallet and removes a tiny piece of paper, which he shows to us.

'See. I write the numbers down, but I reverse them. So, three is the floor number and . . .' Then he seems to think better of breaching his own security system. He slips the paper back into his wallet and gives me a smug look. It makes me want to punch him.

Mel returns a moment later brandishing a new key card.

'All sorted,' she says, and keeps walking towards the stairs without even stopping. I give Cynthia a little smile and follow after her. As I walk away, Keith is sallying forth about the inadequacies of today's young people. Whilst I'm delighted to be referred to as 'young', I am mildly insulted by his comments on behalf of my generation and the one that comes behind. It wasn't us, after all, who climbed up to the treehouse and then pulled the trap door up after ourselves.

We get back into our room, gather what we need for the afternoon's tour, including the key cards, and head back down to meet Robin.

When we get to reception there is a little gaggle of our fellow passengers already waiting. They are wrapped up as if we are venturing forth into Siberia in January when in fact it's a relatively mild March afternoon. I'm glad to see that Grandma is there, standing next to her new bestie, Gloria. A teeny-tiny prick of jealousy stabs at my heart, but I ignore it. It's great that she has found someone of her own age to talk to. I realise, as I have this thought, that I sound like a helicopter parent in a playground. Grandma is a grown woman and I am not responsible for her, nor she me, for that matter. And this trip will be a whole lot easier if she has something or someone to take her mind off Grandad.

When she sees us, Grandma waves and calls out.

'Yoo-hoo, Emma.'

We make our way across to her.

'Ooh, are you going to be warm enough in that thin jacket?' she asks. 'The wind can be bitter at this time of year.'

'I'll be fine,' I tell her. 'We're looking forward to this, aren't we, Mel?'

'Definitely,' replies Mel, giving Grandma one of her prize-winning smiles.

Grandma beams back at her, reminded no doubt of how much she has always liked Mel. I'm hoping she hasn't noticed how close to the edge of politeness Mel has been sailing this morning.

'I've been to the minster before, of course,' says Grandma, 'but it's always nice to go with a proper guide. You learn so much more that way.'

'I've never been in a cathedral,' says Gloria breezily, and we all stare at her, aghast. Gloria definitely looks the cathedral type.

'Really?' I say before I can stop myself.

Gloria's lip twitches for a moment and then she says, 'My mother was such a staunch atheist. Would never let us set foot in the places, growing up. After she died, it felt disrespectful to go against her wishes, and then it just never occurred to me to visit one.'

Concern washes over Grandma's face.

'Well, are you sure you want to go inside?' she asks. 'If it's a matter of respect. We can always stay behind.'

I'm about to wade in to tell Grandma that she can come with us, but Gloria waves a hand airily.

'Oh no. Let's all go. My mother has been dead a long time. I don't suppose she'll care now, and I've always felt as if I was missing out.'

Keith, who has clearly been earwigging on our conversation, steps over.

'Very short-sighted not to visit our magnificent cathedrals,' he says huffily. 'You don't need to have a faith to appreciate their majesty.'

'Indeed,' says Grandma, and I do a double take. What is she doing agreeing with this abominable man?

'As a matter of fact, the cathedrals are the main reason I'm on the trip,' Keith continues.

He speaks with the kind of self-assured pomposity that I associate with white, middle-class men of his age, as if he assumes that everyone will be interested in what he has to say. It grates on my nerves, but I listen all the same.

'I'm working my way around all forty-two of them,' he continues. 'This week is an easy way of ticking a few off. It's a shame we don't stop at Newcastle, but I might have a word with Robin, see if we can't squeeze in a detour.'

I want to point out that that would be extraordinarily selfish of him, but at that moment Robin, as if summoned by mention of his name, appears. He is wearing a bright red overcoat to match his bright red suit. The poor man.

'Robin redbreast!' Mel whispers into my ear, and I stifle a giggle. I suspect there's going to be a fair amount of giggle-stifling this week.

'Everybody ready?' he asks.

There is a general murmuring of assent and then we shuffle as one towards the revolving doors. The Northern Odyssey is about to meet York.

12

And so, shall we go round the table?

York is as glorious as ever. We perhaps don't see quite as much of it as we would have done had we been progressing at a reasonable speed, but as I've been so many times before I don't mind.

Robin leads us round, not, as I had feared, by brandishing a red umbrella for us to follow, but with a far more modern approach. As we leave the hotel, he distributes headsets to everyone. There is a degree of confusion from those among our group who have never moved into the twenty-first century in terms of technology, and of course Keith has a thing or two to say. But they all change their tune when they put the headphones on and realise how well the system works. It's like having your own private tour with Robin talking directly into your ear. The microphone only works one way, though, and a couple of times I reply to him and then feel foolish when I realise that he can't hear me.

Overall, however, the outing is declared a success and there is a buzz around the group as we re-enter the hotel and make our way to the dining room for our cream tea. A large table has been set for us. It's dotted with cake stands ladened with dainty sandwiches and plates piled high with scones.

'This'll be interesting,' whispers Mel into my ear.

I don't understand what she's getting at and give her a quizzical look.

'Isn't this when we're doing the "get to know each other" introductions?' she says with an eye roll.

She's right. I had completely forgotten again. A little flurry of anxiety rushes through me as I realise that I still haven't thought of anything surprising about myself to tell the group. Maybe I should make something up, like Mel suggested. Then again, I'm a terrible liar and I'm bound to pick something and then find that the world's expert on the subject is among us. I'd better just come up with something true.

There is the expected amount of fuss made as we all decide where to sit. Obviously, couples want to sit as couples. Even though most of them must have been married longer than I've been alive, they don't show any desire to branch out and connect with a stranger. Then the woman with the matching husband doesn't want to sit in a draught so that requires more seat shuffling, even though her moving means that someone else has to sit in the probably imagined chilly spot.

Cynthia is left with a chair at the head of the table. She looks about her, clearly uncomfortable with the arrangement, although I can't understand why she would be.

'I can't sit here,' she tells the air space in her vicinity. 'Not at the head of the table.'

She looks positively horrified at the idea, and I wonder briefly what has happened to Cynthia to make her so unsure of herself and her place in the world.

But there are no other seats left. She seems to decide that sitting at the head of the table rather than making everyone else move round one is the lesser of two evils and finally lowers herself into the chair. She perches on the edge, though, as if ready to leap up should someone more worthy of the position come along.

Everyone sits and eyes the food politely. Then Vivienne, whose hair, I notice, is an unlikely shade of chestnut brown, makes a grab for a smoked salmon sandwich and suddenly they're off. It's like feeding time at the zoo, with hands shooting out left and right. There appears to be a tussle over a ham and mustard on white opposite me but luckily no one is hurt. I notice that Keith has put both sandwiches and scones on his plate at the same time, as if claiming his fair share. I'm tempted to spit on a scone like we did when we were kids but I resist.

'For God's sake,' mutters Mel to my left. 'It's as if they've never been fed.'

The mutter is quite loud. I think she assumes that our fellow tourists are all deaf, but I see the gentle-looking man's head rise at her words so I'm pretty sure he heard her.

Nobody else speaks as they consume their food. A waiter arrives with pots of tea and little silver jugs of milk. I thought a cream tea came with a glass of fizz and I'm disappointed when none materialises. Keith asks for coffee. I mean, of course he does.

After a remarkably short amount of time, the plates are clear. It looks as if the table has been visited by a swarm of locusts. Even Cynthia, she of the professed concern about cream and misadventure on the A64, seems to have done herself proud. The waiter buzzes around freshening tea pots, and Robin, with the air of a man who knows exactly when to begin these things, taps his spoon against his cup and brings us to order.

'I trust you all enjoyed your tea,' he begins, and there is a general hum of approval from the others. 'So now, as we will be spending the next week in each other's company, I think it would be nice if we introduced ourselves. Nothing formal. Just a couple of sentences to tell the group a little bit about yourself so that we're not all strangers. And it always adds a little bit of fun if you add something that we probably couldn't guess about you just from looking.'

My stomach flips over again. I really do need to think of something. I hope that Robin asks the people to his left first, which will give me a few more precious moments to come up with an idea.

'I'll start with myself,' continues Robin. 'My name is Robin, as you know. I'm originally from Solihull in the East Midlands and I've been working as a rep for Odyssey Travel for three years. Before that I sold drugs . . .'

There is an audible gasp around the table. Robin waits for a beat, lets an impish smile creep on to his lips. It's quite sweet, in a playful kind of way. When he judges that his words have had long enough to sink in, he continues, 'By which I mean I was a sales rep for a large pharmaceutical company.'

He looks triumphant at his little gag. He must use that line on every tour, I think, and I imagine it has a similar impact each time he delivers it. It takes some of the group longer than others to catch up, but after a moment or two there is a general relaxation as everyone realises that it was a joke, and all is well.

'And a surprising thing about me,' Robin continues, 'is that I keep bees.'

Am I imagining it, or does he look at me when he says this? It's hard to tell because his curls keep falling over his face and obscuring his eyes. Just when I think he might be talking to me, he whips his gaze away to the others around the table, but then I feel his attention creeping back to me again.

Bee-keeping is actually quite interesting as it goes. I once thought about doing a course. I didn't get any further than just thinking about it, but I would like to talk to him about it if we get a moment. I give him a broad smile and cock my head slightly to show him that I'm intrigued. Then I make a mental note to ask him about it later. I may be wrong, but I think the tip of his nose goes a bit pink. I throw a sidelong glance at Mel to see if she's either noticed or is getting the same attention, but she's picking at her fingers and is oblivious to what just seemed to happen. Is that a point to me, maybe?

The other passengers nod their approval of Robin's surprising fact. A couple of them nudge each other as if it is significant in some way, although I can't see how Robin's bee-keeping skills are relevant to his duties as our tour guide.

'And so, shall we go round the table?' he asks.

He turns to his left.

13

Eleven hours, forty-eight minutes and twenty seconds, give or take.

Sitting to Robin's left is Arthur, the soft-edged man.

'So, Arthur,' says Robin. 'Would you like to tell us something about yourself?'

Arthur looks a little flustered, as if this has come as a surprise.

'Oh, goodness,' he says, his eyes shooting to the ceiling as he tries to gather his thoughts. 'My name is Arthur. I'm from a little village near Doncaster. I'm a widower. Er . . .' He looks to Robin, a mild panic in his eyes.

'And something that we couldn't guess about you?' prompts Robin.

'Oh well, let me see,' says Arthur. 'Erm.'

'He's only had all day to think of something,' whispers Mel.

I shush her. I'm more sympathetic because I haven't come up with anything to say yet either.

'I grow award-winning roses,' Arthur says, relief washing over his face as he speaks. 'Is that enough?'

'Oh, that's definitely enough,' pipes up Gloria. 'How fabulous. What kind of roses?'

Arthur sits up a little and looks less at sea.

'Hybrid tea,' he replies. 'Usually cream ones, although I do stray into peach from time to time.'

'And what did you win?' Gloria presses.

Arthur drops his head bashfully. 'Silver gilt at Chelsea. And a gold at Tatton Park one year too.'

'Wow!' says Gloria appreciatively. 'That's impressive. We have a champion in our midst.'

There is a little ripple of applause and Arthur blushes. It's not often you see a man blush. It's endearing and makes me warm to him even more than I did before. He seems so genuine and guile-less: a proper gent.

'Actually, you're not the only champion amongst our number,' says Frank, who is sitting next to Mel. He reminds me of one of those kids from school, the ones who want to answer every ques-tion, and bounce up and down with their hands thrust skywards to get attention. Also, there's a kind of smugness about him that I'm not keen on.

'All in good time,' says Robin, cutting him off, and I feel a new kind of respect for our tour guide that wasn't entirely there before. He's more in control than I'd given him credit for.

Next up it's the matching couple, who it turns out are called Rita and Derek. They're the sort who finish each other's sentences, and they seem to lead very quiet lives. Derek's surprising thing about himself is that he once ate two burgers on the trot, and Rita says she just can't think of anything to say, which is definitely cheat-ing, and, annoyingly, now that she's done this in all earnestness I can't say the same as a joke.

Gloria is more interesting, although given how flamboyant she is, I was expecting something a bit more exotic from her. She tells us she once put her arm inside a cow to help it give birth, so that was better than Derek's rather feeble two burgers story at least.

Cynthia goes a bit pale when Gloria describes her arm when it came out of the cow. That makes me feel a bit sick, too, on the back of the afternoon tea we've just wolfed down, but we get past it without mishap.

Cynthia's thing is that she makes tiny quilts for premature babies in hospital. She barely makes eye contact with anyone when she tells us, as if she's sorry that it isn't something more exciting, but I'm really touched. I get the impression that she's never married or had children, so that makes what she does even more poignant. All that love and care for people who are in a situation that she has never experienced herself. It's so very kind.

It feels like a bit of a roller-coaster ride, getting all these pieces of information thrown at me so quickly without time to process any of them. And the next one really knocks me for six. It comes from a couple who I haven't heard speak yet. They haven't even smiled as far as I know. They introduce themselves as Angela and Ian. He is very tall and rangy, looks like he keeps himself fit. She's tall too and has lovely curly hair, but it's pulled into a ponytail at the nape of her neck like she doesn't care what it looks like. She isn't wearing any make-up either. Not anything at all.

Angela speaks first. Her voice is low with the hint of an accent I can't quite place.

'I'm Angela, and I grew up on a sheep farm in Australia,' she says, and I immediately recognise the twang.

'How fascinating,' says Robin with an expression that I assume is there to invite elaboration, but Angela drops her eyes to the table and doesn't say anything else, so Robin has to move us along rather awkwardly.

'And you?' he asks Ian, the rangy husband.

Ian looks at Robin for a couple of seconds, as if he's deciding what to say. Then he looks at Angela, but she's still staring at the table, so he looks back at Robin. Someone tuts impatiently. I assume it's Keith, but Ian doesn't seem to have noticed. He swallows and takes a deep breath before he begins.

'My name is Ian, and the thing you might not be able to tell from looking at me is that my only child was killed in an accident when he was ten.'

There's a gasp. More than one, in fact, and after that we are entirely silent. Even Keith keeps his mouth closed.

'His name was Richard and he was playing on his skateboard on the road outside our house. He fell and banged his head and he never woke up.'

A tiny little sound comes from Angela. It's not quite a whimper, more like a choking noise, as if there's something in her throat that won't let her breathe. Nobody else speaks, but as the seconds tick by it's clear that someone is going to have to.

It's Grandma who breaks the silence.

'I'm so very sorry to hear that,' she says. 'I can't imagine how painful it must be for the two of you.'

Ian nods and gives Grandma a sad smile.

'Thank you,' he says. 'You know what they say about grief. It never gets any easier. You just get better at dealing with it.'

The old people all nod their heads, as if this is something they can all relate to. I've only had Grandad die, and that's been hard enough. I suppose the older you get, the more times you have to deal with someone you love leaving you behind. I've never thought of that before.

It's a relief when Robin turns to the next person to spill their secret, who is Grumpy Aisle Man Keith. He blows his cheeks out and make a noise a bit like a bull getting ready to charge.

'My name is Keith. I'm on this trip because I'm collecting cathedrals and I'm not going to tell you anything surprising about me because I think that's childish.'

He sits back in his chair with his arms folded, like he's ready to take on all comers. I assume Robin will just move things on, but he doesn't. I'm starting to appreciate Robin more and more.

'I'm afraid there's no escape, Keith,' he says with a polite smile. 'I can't let you be the only one that doesn't share something with the group. So, please tell us something we'd never guess about you.'

Keith gives Robin the kind of hard stare that Paddington would have been proud of, and for a minute I think he's going to refuse outright. But then he sighs and tuts.

'Well, if I must, although it's ridiculous.' He shakes his head to himself and harrumphs again. 'I keep fancy rats,' he says.

I shudder involuntarily. I hate all kinds of rats, fancy or otherwise.

'What's a fancy rat?' Mel asks him. 'Does it wear a bonnet and eat with a knife and fork?'

There is some mild sniggering from Cynthia, which she silences by stuffing her napkin into her mouth, looking round to make sure no one has seen.

Keith gives Mel a withering look. 'It just means that they are bred for their colouring. Mine are predominantly Siamese with red eyes.'

'Sounds very fancy indeed,' replies Mel.

Keith rolls his eyes and sits back in his chair to indicate that he's not going to tell us anything else.

Then it's my turn.

'Hi,' I begin. 'I'm Emma. I'm Phyllis's granddaughter.' I pause. I'm not sure whether Grandma wants me to explain about the golden wedding thing, so I decide not to. 'I'm here with my friend Mel. I work as a . . .' – I look at the assembled group and go for a more accessible description of my job – 'a window dresser for a large department store. And the thing you might not be able to guess is that . . .'

My heart is going like the clappers in my chest. Why is this such a difficult thing? Am I really so boring? I search my mind for something, anything than might make me sound less dull. I'm aware of Robin's eyes on me and I hate that I'm about to disappoint him, but there's nothing for it. 'I'm really badly organised,' I say weakly. 'So if I miss the coach, you'll have to forgive me.'

I give them a sheepish little smile, my insides scrunching with embarrassment, but they seem to love my confession.

'Oh, me too,' says Gloria loudly. 'We can miss the coach together!'

Everyone looks relieved that at least my surprising thing is neither traumatic nor complicated.

Arthur nods at me knowingly. 'Always good to keep your best surprises to yourself,' he says.

I send him a little smile. He doesn't need to know that that was my best surprise.

Next it's Mel's turn. Knowing that she's intending to lie, I feel uneasy about what might be coming.

'My name's Mel . . .'

'Carmel,' interrupts Gloria.

Mel throws her a look that might flatten the weak, but there's nothing weak about Gloria and so it rebounds off her like bullets off a shield.

'Mel,' she repeats. 'And I live with Emma.'

I wonder if they think we might be a couple and whether Mel has said that on purpose just to cause confusion. Obviously I wouldn't put that past her.

'I work for a double-glazing company, and my surprising thing is that . . .'

She pauses for dramatic effect. I see heads moving slightly closer to the centre of the table as if they don't want to miss what she's going to say.

'My great-uncle is Ringo Starr.'

My heart sinks. Is it the kind of lie that might actually be feasible? I have no idea. At least she didn't say he was her granddad, I suppose. That would be really easy to disprove.

There are various 'ooh's and 'really?'s around the table. Mel just sits there, basking in the attention. I don't know how she has the bare-faced cheek to pull it off, but she seems to be doing just that.

'Have you met him?' asks Cynthia, who looks quite overcome by the news. How old would she have been in the Swinging Sixties? I try to do the maths. A teenager, maybe. Certainly old enough to be in love with the Fab Four. I could kill Mel.

'Of course,' says Mel sweetly. 'Although the family didn't see as much of him after he married Barbara. That was before I was born. There was some falling-out over something or other. I have loads of cousins, though. Or cousins once removed or whatever. I'm never quite sure how that works.'

'They would be your third cousins,' says the man called Derek who matches his wife, but as his surprising thing was eating two burgers, I have kind of written him off.

'Is that right?' asks Mel, looking him straight in the eye. Honestly, the nerve of the girl.

There are questions coming at her thick and fast now, and she either bats them away delicately or makes a stab at answering them, depending on what they are. My insides are churning in horror. I just want it to stop. Why couldn't she just have said she won the triple jump at school? Or even at the Olympics!

Eventually the questions begin to die down. The man sitting next to Mel, Frank, who is married to Vivienne, is up next, and you can see from the way he's following the conversation with his mouth partially open that he's just waiting for a clear second so that he can leap in with his surprising fact.

'That's very interesting . . .' he begins. 'But we . . . If I could just . . . The funny thing . . .'

Robin lets him flounder like a fish out of water for a while and then brings us back to order.

'Your turn, I believe, Frank,' he says.

Frank sits up taller in his seat and shakes his head as if even he can't quite believe what we are about to be told.

'We are Frank and Vivienne Anderson,' he begins. 'This is our first coach trip. We usually go to Spain, but . . .'

Vivienne elbows him in the ribs and gives him a warning look, her eyes wide.

'Well,' Frank continues, neatly changing direction, 'things changed and we can't do that any longer.'

Vivienne stares at the ceiling, her jaw set tight.

'Anyway,' he continues, 'the thing you might not know about me from looking at me is that I whittle!'

He pauses for his amazing secret to sink in, but no one seems that impressed.

'Wood, I mean,' he continues, looking slightly thrown by the lack of a response. 'I make little birds and what have you. Whistles too. People say they're very nice, that I could sell them for quite a price if I put my mind to it.'

I'm starting to feel a bit sorry for him as the group leaves him thrashing about like a worm on a hook.

'That's an unusual hobby,' says Gloria. 'Have you been doing it long?'

I think at first that she's trying to rescue him, but then I see her face and realise that she's being entirely mischievous. This nuance seems to pass Frank by.

'Yes,' he says enthusiastically. 'I got my wood-turning badge in Scouts when I was a boy. Only one in my troop to get it.'

Gloria stifles a snort.

'But,' Frank continues, 'my wife, Vivienne. Now, she has a *really* interesting story. Tell them, love.'

Vivienne opens her mouth to speak, but before she can get a word out Frank is off again.

'She swam the Channel, didn't you? The English Channel. All twenty-one miles of it. Proper little mermaid, my Vivienne.'

When it becomes clear that Vivienne isn't to be permitted to tell us her surprising fact herself, she slumps back in her chair and lets Frank do the talking. I get the impression that this is how things generally work. Still, swimming the Channel is pretty impressive and deserves proper applause.

'Wow,' I say. 'That's amazing! How long did it take?'

I direct my question specifically at Vivienne, but Frank answers it.

'Eleven hours, forty-eight minutes and twenty seconds,' he says. 'Give or take.'

'Is that good?' asks Mel.

Frank looks at her as if she's asked if J. K. Rowling has sold a few books.

'Well, yes,' he says. 'It's an excellent time. For a woman.'

'Well done, Vivienne,' says Grandma, and Vivienne gives her a grateful smile.

Robin looks at his watch.

'Now then,' he says. 'That has all been totally fascinating, but I think it's time to wrap things up. We have all week to get to know each other better, and I'm sure we'll be best friends by Saturday.'

'Yeah, right,' mutters Mel, at exactly the same moment as Keith says, 'I very much doubt that.'

They eye one another darkly, each assessing the worthiness of their opponent. Robin ignores them pointedly and continues.

'You have a few hours at leisure now before we meet for dinner later. I will be around to answer any questions. The tables for dinner will be in groups of two to four, so you can choose to eat just with your travelling companion or with a few others. It's entirely up to you.'

Mel gives me a sidelong glance which I immediately interpret as meaning, 'Share a table with this lot? Absolutely no chance,' and I return it with the tiniest nod. We are on the same wavelength.

'Except your grandma, of course,' Mel adds, but I know she doesn't really want to eat with her either.

I look over to make sure that Grandma is okay, but she's already deep in conversation with Gloria. Grandma will be fine at dinner, I'm sure. If she's not we can invite her to join us, but otherwise it will be just me and Mel. This is supposed to be our holiday, after all, and we already have to spend all day with the old people. We don't want to eat with them as well.

There is a scraping of chairs as everyone stands to leave.

'We'll see you later then, Grandma,' I call to her.

'Will do,' she says, without really looking over. She really is fine without us.

It's only when we get back to the room that I realise that when we were going round the table Robin missed Grandma out.

14

RINGO STARR?! WHAT WERE YOU THINKING?

As we are on a holiday of sorts, and have brought most of the contents of our wardrobes with us despite our best intentions, Mel and I make an effort dressing for dinner. We may not be in Ibiza – we're in a hotel in York with a bunch of septuagenarians instead – but that's no excuse for letting standards slip.

We go the whole hog with the hair and make-up, and by the time we've finished we could have proudly graced a dining room anywhere in the world. We stand side by side and take in the results in the full-length mirror. We positively shimmer.

'Too much?' I ask doubtfully.

'Nah,' says Mel. 'Let's go and show them how coach trips should be done.'

When we get downstairs there are, not unpredictably, a few of the others hanging round near reception. The burger-eating man Derek and his wife, Rita, are there with Keith and Arthur. Robin is with them and I notice he's changed out of his red suit and into a pair of grey chinos that are an inch too short for him and an Argyle jumper. He looks as if his mum chooses his clothes.

'What are those two called again?' I whisper to Mel. They are truly so dull that I can't even get their names to stay in my head.

'Rita, is it?' she says. 'And David?'

'Derek!' The name comes to me in a flash of inspiration. 'Have they even got changed?' I add.

They're wearing walking trousers in a nice shade of dun and neatly pressed shirts that are buttoned almost to the top. They might be different items to what they've been wearing all day, but they are definitely following a similar theme.

The heads all turn to stare at us as we click across the tiled floor in our stilettos. Rita and Derek nudge each other, and Keith might have rolled his eyes, but I couldn't swear to it. Robin looks like a rabbit trapped in headlights. Only Arthur smiles.

'You two look as pretty as a picture,' he says. 'Are you going to go out after dinner?'

'That remains to be seen, Arthur,' replies Mel, giving him a radiant smile that borders on the suggestive.

I can sense that Keith is itching to pass judgement on our out-fits but has decided, wisely, to keep his opinion to himself.

Robin seems to recover himself, which is good because Mel has got him lined up between both barrels. She sidles over to him, stopping mere inches away. He can't back off because he's leaning against the reception desk, but I'm sure he would if he could.

'Don't you look lovely in your civvies,' she says to him. 'That jumper looks very snuggly.'

Robin's cheeks flare, but then he recovers himself.

'Well, it can get pretty chilly the further north we go,' he says. 'I like to come prepared.'

'Very wise,' agrees Mel. 'Not like me and Emma.' She smiles and gestures to our dresses, which would offer no protection what-soever against the cold.

'Er, no,' says Robin, not quite looking at us. 'But it's nice and warm in here so I'm probably a little overdressed.'

'You're certainly looking a bit hot under the collar,' she says, tilting her bare shoulder in his direction and smouldering at him over it à la Marilyn Monroe.

I need to step in and stop Mel before she gets too carried away. At this rate she'll terrify him into going for a drink with her, which isn't quite in keeping with the spirit of the bet.

'I think we could probably go straight through to the dining room,' I say. 'Unless anyone fancies a drink in the bar first?'

Rita and Derek shake their heads quickly, as if I've suggested something quite scandalous.

'I don't drink any more,' says Arthur ruefully. 'I find it helps to keep a clear head these days.' He taps his skull with his forefinger and I wonder briefly what he's getting at. What can he possibly need a clear head for?

Intriguing though Robin is, I'm not prepared to have a drink with him if it means dealing with Keith as well, so I move before Keith can take me up on the suggestion.

'Okay then. Let's go through, Mel.'

Mel leads the way and has a quick word with the head waiter before the rest of us have caught her up.

'It's those tables over there,' she says, pointing towards a selection in the far corner. 'The ones with the red napkins.'

Three more steps and she's laid claim to a table for two nearest the big bay window.

'Shall we sit here, Em?' she asks, and has pulled out a chair and is sitting before I have a chance to reply.

'Perfect,' I say, joining her quickly before there can be any debate from the others. There are four of them, after all. No one needs to be left on their own.

'That was close,' Mel says in a low voice when they have wandered to another table and are fussing over who sits where. 'Let's agree right now that we won't sit with any of the others at mealtimes. Except your grandma and Gloria,' she adds after a moment's thought.

'Agreed,' I say. 'But let's see how things go with Grandma and Gloria. They might not stick together all week, and I don't want Grandma being on her own.'

The waiter comes over and within seconds we've ordered a bottle of prosecco. When he returns with it and pops the cork, the others, all now seated, turn and stare. I can feel the disapproval snaking across the room towards us, but who cares? As I said, this is a holiday, despite all indications to the contrary, and we intend to enjoy it.

When the prosecco is poured, we begin the inevitable discussion about our fellow travellers.

'They're a peculiar bunch,' begins Mel. 'Typical old people. Fussy, stuck in their ways and a bit miserable.'

I have to agree.

'Frank and Vivienne are just awful,' I say. 'Him and his whittling. I mean, for God's sake. As if anyone cares. And did you see how he kept cutting Vivienne off? He didn't let her speak at all. Can you imagine being married to a man like that?'

Mel takes a slug of prosecco and shakes her head. 'And Keith! All that crap about telling us a surprising thing about himself being childish, when no one else had objected. What an idiot.'

'Robin did very well with them,' I say. Thinking about Robin does a peculiar thing to my stomach that I'm not feeling ready to share with Mel. She'll get all silly about it and make a fuss. It's not like I fancy him or anything. I mean, you just have to look at him to see that. But still, I hope she can't see it on my face. I try to hide behind my prosecco glass and add, 'He must have to deal with their sort every week. What a horrible job. Being nice to old people twenty-four seven.'

'Arthur's sweet, though. And Cynthia,' Mel concedes. 'And that couple who lost their kid. They seem okay. What were they called?'

'Angela and Ian,' I supply.

'Although,' continues Mel, dropping her voice lower still, 'I know it's sad, but their son died when he was ten. That must have been a good thirty years ago, at least. You'd think they'd have moved on by now. I mean, life keeps rolling and all that.'

I wince. Mel doesn't mean to be cruel, but sometimes she does it by accident. A friend of my mum's had a daughter who died, and it broke her completely. She carries on with her life, but she's never been the same. I know it's hard for me and Mel to imagine, though, not having any kids of our own.

'Maybe they were miserable before,' I suggest, trying to make light of it, and Mel laughs.

'What is it about old people?' she says. 'They're so . . .' She searches for the right word. 'So, well, boring, but it's not just that. It's like they can't remember what it's like to be young, like they aren't having any fun any more so they don't want anyone else to have any either. And all that rubbish about how we have it easy and they had it so hard. This lot must be Baby Boomers. They've had it easier than any other generation ever. They have houses that are paid for and the kind of pension funds that we can only dream of. And don't get me started on Brexit.'

'And they're so quick to moan and blame others,' I add, Mel nodding enthusiastically. 'All that "youth of today" rubbish, like we're a drain on society when, actually, we're the ones holding it all together. And then there's the casual racism and sexism, and most of them are probably anti-gay too. Anti pretty much anything, in fact. Climate change too, which they refuse to take any blame for.'

'Yeah,' says Mel. 'All of that,' she adds wryly. 'Remind me why we came again!'

Suddenly guilt shoots through me. Us being here is my fault. I'm the reason we came. Me and my many failings.

'It's okay, though, isn't it, Mel?' I ask anxiously. 'You're having a nice time, despite them?'

Mel gives me her brightest smile. 'Of course it's okay. It's a laugh. And remember that I have to deal with a moaning old person all day every day at work. It's like water off a duck's back to me. Let them fuss. We can listen to them, safe in the knowledge that we will never turn out like them. And if we do, we can agree here and now to administer fatal injections to one another before things get too bad.'

'Deal!' I say, and we clink glasses.

'But really, Mel,' I add. 'Ringo Starr?! What were you thinking?'

And then we're off again, laughing loud and long without caring what the rest of them think. Let them judge us. We just don't care.

15

TUESDAY

THESE YOUNG PEOPLE. WHAT CAN YOU DO?

I'm having a dream about being in York Minster. I'm stuck in the belfry. I can hear our fellow travellers standing down below shouting up at me about roses and rats. Then the bells start to toll and the room is filled with the sound of them chiming.

It gets louder and louder and the old people's shouting gets louder, and then there's a knocking sound too and I can't work out where it's coming from. My head is banging from all the prosecco – the third bottle was probably a mistake – and then the Minster starts to shake. It feels like an earthquake and . . .

I open my eyes. Mel is standing over me, shoving me hard on the shoulder. There is someone knocking on the door and the phone is ringing. I am totally confused, all my senses trying to grasp hold of reality at the same time . . . and failing.

'Whasss going on?' I slur at her.

I don't think I can have taken my mascara off before we fell into bed and my eyes won't open properly. I squint at her through what gap I can make.

'We've overslept,' she says. 'It's ten past ten.'

I groan.

'What time does the coach leave?' I ask her.

'Ten!'

She stops rousing me and lurches for the phone.

'Yes?' she snaps into the receiver. 'Yes, Robin. We know we're late. We're just coming now. We'll be there in two minutes.'

She slams the phone back down and goes to answer the door.

'Come on, Em!' she shouts at me as she tears around the room. 'Get up!'

It's Grandma at the door, standing there in her coat. Mel leaves her on the threshold and bounces back over the beds towards the en suite. The sudden motion of my mattress under her feet brings into sharp focus just how hungover I am. I groan again.

'Oh, Emma,' says Grandma in that disappointed tone that she reserves for when I've been particularly crap and which always stabs straight into my heart.

It's a struggle but I manage to sit up, then the sheer weight of my skull forces me back into the pillow. My eyes scan the scene of devastation that is the room. Despite us deciding not to unpack in each stop, most of the contents of our cases seem to have spewed out all over the floor and every surface is awash with make-up, dirty tissues and the empty cans of gin and tonic that Mel brought with her. The enormity of the task ahead of me suddenly becomes clear.

Grandma seems to click over into organising mode.

'You get dressed,' she orders. 'No time for a shower. I'll pack this stuff up. It might all end up in the wrong cases, but you can sort it out when we get to Durham.'

I nod, and then wish I hadn't as my eyeballs seem to have come loose from their sockets.

'Is everyone waiting for us?' I ask as I gingerly raise myself up from the bed like a patient who has been given a miracle cure but really can't quite believe it.

Grandma, who is now on the floor, bent over our cases, and thrusting things inside as if her life depends on it, makes a tutting sound.

'Yes. Most of them have been ready since eight o'clock!' she says sternly, but I think I can hear the slightest hint of humour in her voice.

Mel emerges from the bathroom. She looks like I feel. Her hair is matted to one side of her head like a toddler's and although she's taken last night's make-up off, it still looks as if it's run because of the huge black rings under her eyes. She is, at least, dressed.

I'd laugh, but the effort for it is more than I can currently muster. Instead, I prop myself up on the edge of the bed and touch my toes to the floor experimentally.

'Come on, Em,' Mel says. 'You're going to have to move faster than that or they'll go without us.'

'They can't go without all three of us,' pipes up Grandma, 'but they aren't going to be best pleased with you two.'

I'm about to share just how little I care, but then I think better of it. Actually, I do care and I do feel bad. There's no excuse for being late and holding everyone up.

'I'm sorry, Grandma,' I say. 'I can't believe that we forgot to set an alarm.'

Grandma looks up from her packing and gave me a look that makes it clear that she has no difficulty in believing this.

'I'm nearly finished here,' she says. 'Get dressed quickly and then we can go down. We might get away with being only twenty minutes late.'

'Okay,' I say sheepishly, and start to put on the clothes I travelled in the day before. Then something occurs to me.

'Shit, we've got a bar bill to pay before we can leave.'

'Already done,' says Grandma in a matter-of-fact tone. 'You owe me, but we can sort it out later.'

I barely feel like a grown-up as I finish getting ready. I'm twenty-eight and still being dug out of holes by my grandma. It's pathetic, whichever way you swing it.

Finally, everything is packed up and we leave the room with Grandma doing a last swoop round to make sure we haven't left anything behind. As we head towards the lift I catch Mel's eye. Her expression tells me that she's thinking what I'm thinking. We're going to be in bother when we get to the coach. The difference is whereas I'm feeling a bit ashamed of our behaviour and don't want to face the consequences, Mel really couldn't care less. I resolve to be more Mel.

My heart is beating hard in my chest when the lift doors ping open, but the first thing I see is Robin leaning against the desk chatting casually to the receptionist and looking as if he hasn't got a care in the world. Apparently late passengers don't worry him one iota. I immediately feel less anxious. I can face the wrath of the old folk, but for some reason that I don't want to unpick, I don't want to make Robin cross.

He looks over and when he sees the state of us – we are most definitely not looking at our best – he grins.

'Ready now?' he asks.

'Yeah. Sorry,' I say.

'See you next time,' he says to the receptionist, who I notice is blonde and pretty in an obvious, Instagram kind of way. This is clearly not the moment to work on the bet, but it appears that he might be open to a bit of mild flirting at another time.

I have rarely felt less like flirting right now, but I screw my face up by way of apology for our lateness.

'The others are going to have a field day, aren't they?' I say.

'I'm afraid so,' he agrees. 'You'd better get your flak jackets on. I think you two might be in for some enemy fire.'

Then he winks at me. That's not something you see every day, and it throws me for a moment, but then I rally and roll my eyes back at him.

He leads us to the coach. He doesn't offer to carry the bags, but I suppose we have forgone any such expectations by our behaviour. Dave the Driver is leaning against the side of the coach near the gaping luggage hole and smoking a cigarette, which he hastily drops to the ground and stamps out as we approach. He starts to break into a smile and then he sees it's us and the smile disappears. Mel must have blotted her copybook there when she was offhand with him yesterday.

'There's always one,' he says. And then adds, 'Or two. Good night, was it?'

I'd like to try and pretend that we just overslept because we work so hard the rest of the time that any time away from the daily grind is bound to result in episodes like this. But to be honest, you only have to look at us to see the extent of our hangovers.

Mel stays determinedly defiant, no mean feat in the circumstances, and sweeps past him and up the stairs to the coach.

'Sorry,' I say, stretching my mouth sideways into the vaguely frog-like expression that I always pull when I'm apologising. 'Really sorry.'

Even though I can't see her, I can imagine Grandma rolling her eyes at Dave as she brings up the rear. 'These young people. What can you do?' etc. And so, having stumbled my way over embarrassing moments with Grandma, Robin and now Dave, I brace myself for what is going to greet us when we get onboard.

16

IF IT'S TUESDAY, THIS MUST BE DURHAM.

My head is thumping as I climb the few short steps onto the coach. Each time I put my foot down it reverberates throughout my body, but I have to regather myself. Never let them see the soft bits underneath! That's what Grandad used to tell me. So, I do my best to pull my shoulders back and raise my chin, which works right up until I get to the top of the stairs and I see how many faces are scowling at me. Pretty much the entire coach.

Keith is the first to open his mouth.

'Nice of you to join us,' he says in a tone that reminds me of a particularly unpleasant boss that I used to have. It's sarcastic and mocking with undertones of deep menace.

I could just brazen it out, as I'm sure Mel is doing. But I'm not Mel, and my inner people-pleaser is panicking.

'Sorry we're late,' I say. 'We overslept.'

'I'm not surprised with the amount of alcohol they drank last night,' says a quiet female voice not quite quietly enough for me to miss. I think it's Vivienne, the submissive Channel swimmer. Not as submissive as we'd thought, then.

'You do realise that you're holding everyone up,' continues Keith. 'We have all been sitting here for almost an hour waiting for you two.'

It's not yet ten thirty, so if this is true then more fool them, I think, but instead I just mumble apologies again.

Mel, who has already sat down in 'our' place, because of course the old people have all sat in exactly the same seats they were in yesterday, pipes up. 'Keep your hair on, Keith. We're twenty minutes late. It's no biggy. Just chill.'

I'm not sure Keith is familiar with the concept, but I'm grateful to Mel for taking the heat off me. I slink into my seat next to her and slide down as low as I can without actually sitting on the floor.

'That's exactly the attitude I was talking about,' Keith announces to everyone, confirming that they have all been talking about us behind our backs. 'Irresponsible and thoughtless. Pure and simple. And they don't care either. As long as they get to do exactly as they please then that's all they're bothered about.'

'Yes,' agrees Vivienne, braver now with the shield of Keith to protect her. 'It's just so typical of young people today. They're all so selfish. They don't give two hoots about anyone else.'

Grandma has also climbed on to the coach now and is settling down in front of us. Robin brings up the rear and the big front door hisses as it closes behind him.

I feel Mel bristle next to me.

'Let it go,' I say. 'Who cares what they think?'

But Mel is having none of it, and she stands up and turns round so she can address the others.

'That, if I may say, Vivienne, is a ludicrous generalisation,' she says. 'Yes, we're late. We overslept by ten minutes.' She holds up both hands to indicate ten. 'It's hardly life and death, and to be frank I reckon we need to be congratulated on just how quickly we managed to get packed up and here, not strung up and shot. We're sorry we are late and that we've held the coach up a little. No more than Cynthia did yesterday,' she adds, and I wish she hadn't because I like Cynthia and it feels like a low blow. 'But you didn't all have a go at her, did you?'

This has all the makings of getting out of hand. Vivienne says, 'Well!' in that way that people do when they want everyone else to be aware of what just happened, but Robin intervenes, his hands raised in true peacekeeper style.

'The main thing is that you're here now,' he says. 'The schedule does have an element of slack built into it to cover eventualities like this, so there's no harm done. Although, if everyone could try to be ready for departure it does make things run a little more smoothly.'

I pull at Mel's top to get her to sit down, and she does.

'Sorry, Robin,' she says as she sits. 'We'll set an alarm tomorrow.' She holds his gaze for just a touch longer than is necessary and then drops her eyes modestly. Flirting? Now? Really? This is so obviously not the moment. However, Mel clearly reads the situation differently to me. Never a wasted opportunity with her.

Robin acknowledges her apology with a curt nod, and that should be the matter over and done with, but as the coach pulls away from the hotel I can still hear muttering voices behind us and I suspect it's not just Keith and Vivienne. We don't seem to be very popular.

I turn to look at Mel and grin. 'Oops,' I mouth at her, and she smirks back.

'I feel like shit,' she mouths back, and I nod my agreement and then wish I hadn't as my brain rattles around inside my skull. 'And I'd kill someone for some coffee,' she adds, a little louder.

'If you'd been up in time you could have had a proper breakfast,' says a voice behind us. They may be old but there is clearly nothing wrong with their hearing.

Gloria spins round and puts her face in the gap between the seats in front of us.

'Well done, girls,' she says with a broad smile. 'You two brighten things up no end.'

She winks at us and I feel myself forgiving her for monopolising Grandma.

◆ ◆ ◆

It's an hour and a half drive to Durham and, as if to punish us, Robin doesn't stop the coach once. Mel falls asleep almost immediately but my head is pounding too hard for that, so I stare out of the window and let the journey wash over me. After half an hour or so Robin takes a wander down the coach to check that his flock is okay. I hear snatches of the conversations behind me, something about trouser presses, but I'm not really listening.

As he wanders back to the front he stops alongside our seat. This would be the perfect opportunity to talk to him about his bee-keeping, especially as Mel is sound asleep and snoring gently at my elbow, but I just don't have it in me. So when he asks if everything is going okay for us I just smile wanly and nod and he leaves me to my hangover.

By the time we pull into the city I have a raging thirst, my head is still banging and I could really use some carbs to soak up what's left of the prosecco. But I slap a huge smile on my face – there's no way I'm going to give the old people yet more ammunition.

Mel nudges me and points out of the coach window, and there is the cathedral high on a hill, the distinctive three towers marking it out as a church, not a castle. I'm not particularly religious but my heart does a little skip at the magnificence of it and I shake my head in wonder.

'How on earth did they build them? I mean, with no machinery or cranes or anything?' I ask, speaking more to myself than anyone else, but a voice from behind me supplies an answer.

'With a lot of blood, sweat, tears and prayers. Actually, I'm something of an expert on Norman cathedrals, if you're really interested.'

It's Keith, of course, and I am actually quite interested and am about to turn around and tell him so when he adds, 'Which of course you won't be,' and so I stay where I am, fuming silently, determined to deploy Google and learn enough for myself to show him that I'm not the total airhead that he seems to think I am.

The coach pulls up outside what must be our next hotel. It's more modern-looking than the one in York, with lots of glass and chrome. In front of us Gloria is on her feet and retrieving her handbag from the overhead shelf.

'If it's Tuesday, this must be Durham,' she says with a twinkle in her voice.

Behind us I hear someone – Arthur I think – laugh gently.

'Should that not be Belgium?' he asks.

'It really should be, Arthur,' replies Gloria, 'but we'll just have to slum it.'

There is a general twittering around the coach and I look at Mel in confusion. It's like they are in a parallel universe that we have no portal into. Mel raises her palms skywards and shrugs, clearly as lost as me.

'It's a film,' says Gloria, who must have seen the mystification on our faces. 'About a bunch of Americans who take a whistle-stop coach tour around Europe.'

'It's very good,' adds Cynthia. 'Terribly funny.' She is standing at my shoulder, clearly keen to be off the coach. 'A little rude in places, though,' she adds coyly, and a pink bloom creeps across her cheeks. I had no idea that old people blushed, but she suddenly looks very pretty.

'I'll need to download it,' I say. Apparently this means nothing to Cynthia. 'So I can watch it,' I add, and her face lights up again.

'Oh yes,' she says. 'I'm sure you'd enjoy it very much. I haven't seen it for a very long time.' Doubt crosses her face again. 'Maybe it hasn't aged terribly well. Lots of these old films don't, do they?'

'It's a classic,' pipes in Gloria. 'It will have aged beautifully. Just like you, Cynthia.'

Cynthia blushes again.

Eventually we are all off the coach. By now my thirst is so raging that I could leap into the river that runs alongside the road and drink my fill. At least my hangover is abating just a little. My head is still pounding, but that's nothing some liquid and a couple of paracetamol won't fix. I could really use a shower, though, and I shudder at the thought of how I must smell.

'Now, you all know the drill,' calls Robin over the general hubbub.

It doesn't look like they know the drill at all. Rita and Derek, in their matching coats, throw worried glances at one another as if this is the very first time they have ever been to a hotel, and Arthur looks as if he's not quite sure where he is, which is fair. I'm not sure where I am either.

'We'll head into the hotel and then we can get your rooms allocated. After that we'll wander up to the cathedral for a tour and lunch in a very lovely café nearby. For those of you that want to make your own way today' – I'd swear he looks at us then, but I can't be certain – 'then dinner will be at seven in the hotel. Any questions?'

There are plenty of questions about the distance to the cathedral, the nature of the lunch menu etc., but Mel and I just queue and chat, letting the strife of the old people wash over us. It must be exhausting to be so fretful all the time.

'We're going on the tour, yeah?' I ask Mel.

'Hell yeah!' she replies. 'We need to get our money's worth, and there's too much comedy gold in this lot to miss a minute!'

Just as she says this, Frank's voice booms out. 'We never had all this queuing in Spain, did we, Vivienne?'

'If he likes Spain so much then what's he doing on this trip?' Mel asks me, and I shrug.

Something else to get to the bottom of, I think.

17

THE PLANTS WOULD ALL BE DEAD IN A WEEK.

It turns out that Dave is going to drive the coach as close to the cathedral as possible so the old people don't have too far to walk. However, not being old, Mel and I decide that we could use the exercise and the fresh air and make our way up there on foot.

'We'll be meeting in the café at one thirty,' Robin tells us with a distinct emphasis on the time, like we're teenagers who aren't to be trusted.

'Got it,' says Mel, and gives him a jovial thumbs-up sign. 'They'd better drop all this time-keeping rubbish,' she mutters as she turns away, 'or it's going to make me want to be late on purpose.'

'I don't think he means anything by it,' I say diplomatically. 'He's just checking we know the plan.'

Mel's probably right, though. I'm sure they all think we're incompetent fools and so far we're doing nothing to undo that particular prejudice.

There is a footbridge just outside the hotel that takes us across the river, and from there we just follow our noses up the hill. The streets are cobbled and get narrower the higher we go, and there are young people everywhere, all fresh-faced with glittering eyes and ready smiles. Students, I assume.

'Did we look like them when we were their age?' I ask Mel as yet another group of impossibly attractive girls passes by. 'And look how young they are to be living away from home.'

'They're not even twenty yet,' replies Mel. 'They know nothing.'

I try to remember myself as a student. I felt so grown-up. I'd left my parents behind and there was nothing you could tell me about how the world worked. I thought I knew it all.

But I remember seeing the concern on Mum's face when she dropped me off on that first day, her worried glances at Dad. At the time, I thought she was just making a fuss, but now, looking at how young and vulnerable these kids seem, I can understand why she was worried. This lot barely look old enough to tie their own shoelaces, and we all know how good I was at that.

'Yes,' I say to Mel. 'Wait until they're as old as us. Then they'll know it all.'

'What did Robin say the café was called?' she asks.

I tell her and we realise that we're standing right outside it. I look at the time on my phone. We're ten minutes early. We could wander off and look at something to fill the time, but we glance at each other and know instinctively what the other is thinking.

'Let's go in,' says Mel, and I nod my agreement.

The door to the café is up a short flight of steps, and I find myself worrying about how Rita will manage. I'm surprised at how quickly I've started thinking like an old person. It's hardly my problem.

There are more steps inside, the rises beautifully hand-painted with flowers and leaves, and there are plants with lush green foliage on shelves all the way up. My mind flicks to our scruffy little flat.

'This is how I'd like to live,' I say wistfully.

'Dream on,' replies Mel. 'The plants would all be dead in a week!'

She's probably right.

When we get to the top we explain to the girl who we are and she shows us to one of two large tables. I sit down with my back to the door, but Mel pulls me to my feet.

'Don't sit there,' she says. 'We need to be facing the entrance so we can see their faces when they spot us here already. And before them!'

I choose another seat and we wait, but not for long. Grandma appears first, with Gloria hot on her heels and the others following behind. The others are all so wrapped up in having arrived that they barely notice that we're already here.

Grandma and Gloria sit down with us, followed by Angela and Ian, which leaves one spare seat. I find myself praying that Keith doesn't take it, but Grandma calls out to Arthur, who is standing stock still and blocking everyone else from moving forward.

'Come and sit with us, Arthur,' she says to him.

Arthur looks up, smiles and then moves towards the space on our table so that everyone else can shuffle along.

'Well, this is all very nice,' he says to no one in particular as he sits down. 'Very nice indeed.'

There is the usual twittering as everyone comments on the café, how nice the artwork on the walls is, wonders about who waters the very many plants and finally turns their attention to the menu. It's not extensive but there is a Specials board which seems to throw them all into a spin. Even Grandma gets caught up in all the dithering and sounds just like the rest of them, which surprises me. I've always thought of her as completely competent, but maybe she's got old without me noticing.

The waitress comes and the orders are given. It takes an age and I've never heard so many questions about what is basically soup or sandwiches, but finally we get there and with all that out of the way we have to find something to talk about.

There is a momentary awkward silence. Knowing what we know about Angela and Ian's little boy seems to stain the air between us so that I can't think about anything else. I stare at a knot in the wooden table whilst I try desperately to come up with a conversation opener, but then Grandma saves the day.

'I'm very much looking forward to going into the cathedral again,' she says brightly. 'I haven't been since me and my husband Stan visited on our honeymoon.'

It's the first time I've heard her refer to Grandad and it brings a lump to my throat. I can't look at her because I'm sure I'll cry when I know she's being so brave.

'How lovely,' says Cynthia, with that smile she has that's so innocent and childlike. I notice that she doesn't ask about Grandad. I suppose there must be a kind of unspoken rule when you get to be old about treading carefully around absent people. Grandad used to worry about opening the local paper because of what he might discover between its pages.

'When you get to my age, Emma,' he'd say, 'they start dropping like flies. And then it's too late. You never get to go for that last pint because they're here one day and gone the next.'

I wonder if Grandad's friends felt the same when he died so suddenly.

'I've never been to Durham or the cathedral before,' Gloria says, moving us neatly away from Grandad's absence. 'How about you?' she asks, directing the question at the others, but they all shake their heads and the conversation dwindles.

Gloria tries again. 'So, I was interested in what you said yesterday, Angela . . .'

My chest tightens. She's not going to mention their son, is she?

'About being brought up on a sheep farm.'

I relax.

'How old were you when you came to England?'

Angela smiles and her whole face lights up. It's the first time I've seen her look anything other than terminally miserable and it completely alters her.

'I was eighteen,' she says proudly. 'I came to England to go to university. It was a big thing back then. Huge, really. No one in my family had even been to university, but I really wanted to be a doctor and I reckoned I could either travel thousands of miles across Australia to study or I could travel a few thousand more and come to Europe. So that's what I did.'

'Wow!' I say, genuinely in awe of that kind of decision. It makes the hour or so that I moved from home to go to uni look a bit feeble. 'And that was when?' Then I realise that questions about age can be seen as a bit indelicate by old people and so I add, 'If you don't mind my asking.'

Angela's smile broadens. 'I don't mind at all. It was 1966. I arrived in England just after you'd won the soccer World Cup. I didn't know much about soccer, but there was no avoiding it.'

Arthur pipes up then.

'I've never been keen on sport,' he says, gesturing to his rotund torso as proof, 'but you couldn't help but get caught up in all the football fever.'

Angela nods, enthusiastically agreeing with him.

'Yes! It was like the entire country was painted red and white,' she says. 'Such an exciting summer. Anyway, I studied in London and became a doctor, and then I met Ian . . .' She reaches over and takes her husband's hand. I can see him give it a reassuring squeeze. 'And I never went back. Well, other than to visit my family, of course.'

Having always lived within a couple of hundred miles of my family, I can't really imagine what this must have been like.

'Weren't you homesick?' I blurt out before I've thought about it. 'I mean, I don't suppose inner-city London has much in common with a sheep farm in the outback.'

She smiles again, but this time it's more wistful. 'More homesick than you can possibly imagine. When I arrived there wasn't a single thing that was familiar to me. Cars, shops, fashion, people, accents, weather. Everything was totally different from what I was used to. But I really wanted to qualify, so I just knuckled down and focused on that and eventually it began to feel more like I belonged.'

'Wow!' I say again, because it feels like the most appropriate word. She's right. I can't imagine it at all, but I'm massively impressed. 'You make me feel really inadequate,' I add, but Angela shakes her head.

'Not at all. We each have different challenges thrown at us in life. I'm sure yours have been just as daunting in their way.'

She's wrong. She's so wrong that I'm embarrassed by the smallness of my existence so far in comparison to hers. I try to justify myself by thinking that she's more than twice as old as me, but that doesn't help. She left Australia when she eighteen and she might have been married to Ian and had her son by the time she was my age.

What is it they say? Walk a mile in another's shoes and all that.

Sitting there, in a café in Durham with only my best friend's birthday to worry about, I suddenly feel very humble.

18

THE ICING ON A VERY ELABORATE CAKE.

'Nature calls, I'm afraid,' says Arthur, which cuts through my thinking and brings me straight back to the here and now. He gets to his feet and manoeuvres his way past the chairs to get to the door. 'Do excuse me,' he adds as he goes, and, 'Do you think I could just squeeze past?'

He's such a gentleman. I bet he was a country vicar in another life. He has that kind of vibe about him.

We finish our lunch, Robin makes an announcement about using the facilities before we leave and then it takes another fifteen minutes or so before we are all assembled outside the café and ready to walk the short distance up to the cathedral.

'Where's Arthur?' asks Mel, scanning the collected group. 'I can't see him.'

'Did he come back from the loo?' I wonder, but Mel shrugs.

'No idea. Maybe he's gone up to the cathedral and is waiting at the door.'

This seems logical, so when Robin does his headcount and discovers one of his flock to be missing, I offer it up as a likely explanation and Robin takes it as fact.

'I'm not one hundred per cent sure that's what's happened,' I add, but no one seems very interested.

We wander up to the cathedral and Robin hands out the headphones for the tour. More twittering.

'Oh, Emma, could you help me with this?' asks Cynthia. 'I seem to be all fingers and thumbs.'

She has got the wires in a knot and I see how twisted the joints of her hands are as she struggles to untie it.

'Here,' I say. 'Let me sort that out.'

I take it from her, untangle the wire and hand it back so that all she has to do is stick the headphones over her ears. She gives me a smile that is disproportionately grateful for the help I've given her.

'Oh, thank you,' she says. 'Thank you so much. I do struggle to manage these things.'

Bless her, I think, and then mouth to Mel. Mel raises an eyebrow. She doesn't appear to be quite as taken by Cynthia's charms.

Keith has his headphones in place with minimum fuss and is now parading them to everyone else as if they are all stupid. I really can't warm to him. I mean, he put some headphones on. What does he want? A medal?

We approach the main door and Robin starts telling us about the door knocker.

'The sanctuary knocker granted thirty-seven days of sanctuary to anyone who knocked, no matter how heinous their crime,' he says.

Mel nudges me.

'There you go,' she says under her breath. 'We can murder Keith and then claim sanctuary! Job done.'

To the right of the door is a tall thin cross set on a grassy knoll, and standing next to it is a small ball of a man who looks terribly familiar.

'Oh, there's Arthur,' I say, pointing over to him.

Robin's gaze follows my finger and then calls Arthur over.

'Thanks for waiting for us, Arthur,' he says when Arthur is close enough to hear him, 'but it makes my job a little simpler if we can all stick together.'

Arthur has that slightly bewildered expression that his face seems to settle into naturally.

'Sorry, sorry,' he says as Robin hands him his headphones, and then, without further ado, we head inside.

The cathedral is very different to York Minster. Where York felt light and bright and a little bit like the icing on a very elaborate cake, Durham is darker and heavier, more serious somehow.

Robin walks us round, pointing out interesting features, and after a while we find ourselves at the Shrine of St Cuthbert, who I discover was a pretty big deal in this part of the world.

'When the monks first opened his coffin eleven years after he died,' Robin tells us, his voice as heavy with intrigue as if he were telling a group of nine-year-olds a ghost story, 'his body was perfectly preserved and not in the slightest bit decomposed.'

'Eww,' says Mel. 'That's weird. But what were they doing opening his coffin anyway?'

'He was a saint,' sniffs Keith, as if this explains everything.

'So, is he still supposed to be, like, whole in there now?' Mel continues, her nose wrinkled in disgust.

It's a compelling idea, and I can see why the monks of old might have been tempted to keep opening the lid to take a peek, but Robin shakes his head.

'Sadly not. When they opened him up in the eighteen hundreds, all they found was a skeleton.'

'Well, thank Christ for that,' says Mel sarcastically. 'I was worried there for a minute.'

Matching-clothes Rita (today she and Derek are both dressed in navy blue) starts at this, as if she's expecting a lightning bolt to come down from the vaulted ceiling and strike Mel down for uttering something blasphemous. Mel, unsurprisingly, remains on her feet.

We continue our tour, finishing with the cloisters. The sky above our heads is a clear bright blue and sunbeams pierce through the Gothic windows that surround the grass courtyard, leaving sharp-edged shadows on the walls. It's beautiful and makes me choke up a bit, although I never thought I'd say that about stone and mortar.

'Just think of how many feet have walked on these stones,' I say to Mel.

'Do you think there are any of the undead floating around?' she asks me, raising her arms above her head and letting out a ghostly wail which echoes around us spookily.

Someone behind us tuts loudly and there is more muttering. Mel's head spins round to see who is being disapproving this time.

'I'm getting a bit sick of this,' she says to me, but loudly enough for the rest of the group to hear. 'Do none of them have a sense of humour?'

'There's a time and a place,' replies Keith stonily, 'and this is neither.'

I sense that Mel is reaching the end of her tether, but I really don't want her to get into a fight. As she bristles next to me, I shoot out a hand to warn her not to rise to him because he's just not worth the effort. But it's no good. Keith has been pushing Mel's buttons since we left Leeds. She spins round so that she is face to face with him and their eyes lock.

'Firstly,' she says, her voice low and menacing, 'I am not a child and I'm getting a bit tired of you treating me as if I am.'

Keith opens his mouth and I just know that he's going to say something about caps and them fitting, but Mel cuts over him.

'Secondly, I do understand the significance of a church and what might or might not be appropriate. I can respect the beliefs of other people, even if they don't tally with mine, and behave accordingly. But, in case you hadn't noticed' – she opens her arms wide and spins like Julie Andrews in *The Sound of Music* – 'this part of the building is basically outside and we're the only ones here.'

I'm squirming a little bit now. She's right, of course, but I don't want us to get any further on the wrong side of these people than we already are, or it's going to be a very long week. And there's Grandma to think about. We mustn't spoil her golden anniversary trip.

As I have this thought, my eyes flick over to Grandma, expecting to see shame and embarrassment in her expression, but actually, she looks like she's with Mel one hundred per cent, as do Gloria and a couple of the others.

'And thirdly,' continues Mel, who seems to be enjoying herself now, 'this is supposed to be a holiday. We are here to have fun. I imagine that concept means nothing to you, with your miserable attitude and your doom-and-gloom outlook on life. But for the rest of us' – she gestures to the group – 'it's kind of the main purpose of the trip. And you sticking in your snippy little digs at me and Emma every two seconds is making that pretty difficult.'

'Hear hear!' chips in Gloria, clapping her hands together joyfully.

'I know we're quite a lot younger than the rest of you,' Mel says, clearly reaching the zenith of her speech, 'but our age isn't a black mark against us, you know. We are just as interested in everything that Robin is showing us as you are, possibly more so because we have more to learn.'

She says this in a way that makes his know-it-all attitude even more unappealing and I'm suddenly filled with a warm glow that I recognise as pride. Go, Mel!

'So just lighten up, would you, and let us all get the most out of this fabulous trip.'

She throws her brightest smile at Robin at this point – how to win friends and influence people – and Robin stands a little taller in his shoes.

Everyone turns then to look at Keith to see how he is going to respond. I'm fully expecting him to fire back at her with both barrels, but instead he rolls his eyes and shrugs as if he couldn't be less interested in whatever Mel has to say. It's so infuriating, but what can she do? You can't force someone to rise to the bait.

It's Robin who breaks the tension.

'Right! I think we're just about finished here,' he says chirpily. 'The cathedral has a tea shop, which is that way' – he points to the opposite corner of the cloisters – 'for anyone who fancies refreshment, although that isn't part of your package and so will be at your own expense. We now have a couple of hours "at leisure"' – he does that dreadful air quotes thing with his fingers – 'so you can choose what you want to do for. Dave will be heading back to the hotel in the coach in twenty minutes. Anyone who would like to drive down with him, come with me. The rest of you, can you be back at the hotel in time for dinner at seven, please?'

I look at Mel questioningly.

'What do you want to do?' I ask her.

Mel redirects the question back to Robin. 'Well, let's ask our esteemed leader,' she says, shining the full beam of her smile on him. 'What would you recommend?'

His blush starts on his neck and works upwards, clashing hideously with his red jacket.

'Well, the castle is marvellous,' he says, without making eye contact with her, 'but if you've had enough of old relics and don't mind a bit of a walk then I'd suggest the Botanic Gardens, which are up near the university.'

His eyes might stray towards Keith when he says 'old relics', but I couldn't swear to it.

'Great,' I say. 'A bit of exercise would do no harm. Shall we see if we can find the gardens, Mel?'

I give Robin my own best smile. It's at a lower voltage than Mel's, and I can't quite manage the bold eye contact that is her speciality, but I think he notices. In any case, he definitely looks less uncomfortable than he did a moment ago. Softly softly might be my best approach here if I'm going to avoid a month of washing-up.

'Let's do it!' Mel replies, like someone in a motivational video.

'That's sounds great,' says Gloria. 'Mind if Phyllis and I tag along?'

It takes me a moment to realise that she means Grandma.

'Not at all,' I say. 'The more the merrier.'

19

YOU CAN'T KID A KIDDER.

We leave the cathedral and Mel locates the Botanic Gardens on her phone. It's a simple enough looking route so we set off, a merry little band of four.

Gloria is quick to congratulate Mel on her tirade against Keith.

'He definitely had it coming,' she says. 'I'm finding him very tiresome. The trip would be far more enjoyable without him and I'm sure some of the others would be less stand-offish if they didn't have him pouring criticism into their ears all the time.'

I think she's probably right, but I don't want this to turn into a 'them and us' situation so I don't get drawn in. Mel, however, still high on adrenaline, is well up for a little bit more fighting talk.

'He's such an arse,' she says. 'It's like he's decided that we're idiots because we're young, and nothing that we do or say will change that.'

Grandma clears her throat. 'Well,' she says, 'I could say much the same for you two.'

She looks at us meaningfully, her chin lowered and her eyebrows raised. Thinking about it, I suppose she might be right. We *have* decided that he is a grumpy old man and are seeing everything he says and does through that filter. And if I'm really honest, it's not just him. Mel and I haven't made much of an effort with any of them. But then that cuts both ways. Only Arthur, Cynthia and Gloria have spoken to us directly. The others have either ignored us or had a pop under their breath.

I see from her expression that Grandma's point has hit home with Mel too, but then she shrugs.

'The difference,' she says, 'is that we were prepared to give him the benefit of the doubt, but he thought badly of us as soon as he set eyes on us.'

Is that true? I'm not convinced. We had some pretty fixed ideas about what we expected from the elderly passengers before we even met them too, but I don't want to get into a row about it.

'How about we just ignore him, try not to let him spoil the trip,' I suggest diplomatically, and immediately hate myself for it. I hope that Mel will understand that I'm just trying to appease Grandma. When we're back in the safety of our room we can let Keith have it with everything we've got.

Luckily, Mel seems to get it, and we let the subject of Keith drift from our conversation.

It would be about a twenty-minute walk to the gardens at the pace that Mel and I usually walk, but, spritely though Grandma and Gloria are, we have to make allowances for them. There are also the obligatory pauses to look at the view from time to time.

'So, Gloria,' says Mel as we cross a slightly bouncy footbridge over the river and pause briefly to look up and downstream. 'Where do you live?'

It's an innocuous enough question, but I sense a reticence on Gloria's part to give much away.

'Oh, I'm between homes just at the moment,' she replies cagily.

'Interesting,' says Mel. 'Between jobs I've heard of, or between men. But between homes? Are you living in a tent?'

Gloria gives an odd little laugh. 'Good Lord, no,' she says. 'I . . .' She pauses.

'What she means,' says Grandma, eager to help out her new friend, 'is that she recently split up with her husband and is renting somewhere until the divorce settlement is sorted out.'

Grandma looks to Gloria for thanks, but for a second I think I see annoyance rather than gratitude on Gloria's face. It's fleeting, though, and gone as quickly as it appeared.

'That's right,' says Gloria. 'I'm renting a little flat south of Leeds just for the time being.'

'Whereabouts?' asks Mel. 'I mean, south of Leeds is quite a big area.'

Gloria waves a hand as if the details aren't important and answers with a question of her own. 'And Phyllis tells me that you two live north of Leeds?'

This is an equally vague description but somehow it doesn't sound at all mysterious.

'Yes. Not far from Phyllis,' replies Mel. 'We grew up there and then just kind of floated back after we made a not-that-successful bid for freedom.'

She grins and Gloria smiles back, but there's something not quite right about it. I'm not sure what is it, but I wonder if we've inadvertently hit yet another nerve with these old people.

When we finally reach the Botanic Gardens it turns out to be well worth the walk. The grassy banks are a sea of glorious daffodils and the blossom trees look like they've been washed pink with their buds all ready to burst into life. We stroll down various paths, following our noses rather than the signs, and end up in a wooded area where the birds are singing their hearts out. It feels very much like spring has arrived.

By then, the conversation has taken the inevitable turn towards our fellow travellers.

'What is it with Frank and Vivienne and Spain?' I ask. 'Have you noticed that whenever Frank mentions it, Vivienne gives him a dirty look?'

The others make vague noises and mutter that they haven't really noticed that, and I wonder whether I'm reading far too much into things. It wouldn't be the first time.

'I do like Cynthia,' says Grandma. 'I think she's one of those women who's spent her whole life being put in her place. That's what makes her so jumpy. But underneath that I'm certain there's bags of personality just desperate to sneak out.'

'Oh yes,' agrees Gloria. 'She's delicious. We definitely need to bring her out of her shell.'

'The ones who make me laugh are Rita and Derek,' chips in Mel. 'All those matching clothes! I wonder if they have a conversation about what they will wear each morning. Maybe it's a telepathic thing.' She laughs at this idea and we join in. 'I assumed they were train-spotters, but it's nothing as fascinating as that. Imagine if the most interesting thing you can think to say about yourself is that you once ate two beef burgers.'

Gloria hoots loudly, the sound ringing out through the woods and causing a blackbird to sound its alarm. I laugh with her, but I can't help but remember that my own interesting fact was that I was badly organised, and Mel lied about hers. We're hardly in the running for the world's most riveting people ourselves.

'So, tell me about Ringo,' says Gloria, her eyes twinkling mischievously.

I look over at Mel, wondering how's she's going to play this.

'Oh, I made that up,' she replies breezily.

Grandma's eyes widen and I feel my cheeks start to blush, but a lazy grin forms on Gloria's face.

'I knew that,' she says. 'You can't kid a kidder.'

At once I try to remember what Gloria's surprising thing was and whether she might have made hers up too.

'Haven't you put your hand up a cow then?' asks Grandma, sounding slightly nonplussed.

'Oh, I have. My grandad was a farmer. What I said was the gospel truth,' Gloria says, and Grandma looks relieved. I am too. It's not important, of course, but I'm feeling a bit at sea with all this uncertainty. 'But I had an inkling that Mel was fibbing,' Gloria adds, and winks at Mel.

'Do you think the others believed me?' Mel asks, and then adds, 'Not that I care.'

'Probably,' replies Gloria. 'I mean, why would you lie about who you are like that?'

Why indeed, I think.

We walk for a few paces in silence, just enjoying the birdsong and the peace.

'Arthur seems like a lovely man,' says Grandma next, moving on to more solid ground, and we all agree at once. There is definitely no edge to Arthur. He is one hundred per cent who he appears to be.

Our wanderings take us back up to the entrance and we call into the tearooms for a quick cuppa before we head to the hotel. Then we find an alternative path along the riverbank to get us back. As we turn a corner, we are stopped in our tracks first by a beautifully proportioned arched bridge that spans the river, and then by a spectacular view of the cathedral, its towers reflected in the still dark water.

'Oh,' says Grandma wistfully as she stares at the glorious building, glowing gold in the late afternoon sunlight. 'Stan would have loved that.'

She fumbles for a tissue from her coat pocket and then dabs at her eyes.

I feel a lump come into my throat too. Poor, poor Grandma. She should have been enjoying this trip with Grandad, not me. I keep forgetting, but he must be in her mind all the time. Thinking this makes me realise how very brave she is being, and I slip my arm around her shoulder and give her a squeeze.

'He really would,' I agree. 'Are you okay, Grandma?'

Grandma's shoulders give a little shiver and then she straightens up.

'I'm fine, thanks, Emma. Shall we keep going? We don't want to be late for dinner. I think Keith has had enough to have a go at for one day.'

We all share wry smiles for a moment, and then we press on, but Grandma keeps her eyes fixed on the view of the cathedral and its reflection until we turn a corner and can no longer see it.

20

I THINK I MIGHT BE THE TINIEST BIT TIPSY.

Mel and I decide to tone things down for dinner that night, although it's a bit of an unspoken agreement between us rather than a definite decision. We don't make quite so much effort getting ready as we did in York, and as a result most of the contents of our cases stay packed rather than scattered across the room. Even though oversleeping was accidental, we don't want to do it again.

But when we get down to the restaurant for dinner it seems like we're the only ones to be exercising any restraint. Most of the others are sitting round a table and I can see two open wine bottles and a couple of empty pint glasses in front of them. The old people seem to be letting their hair down.

'Looks like we started a trend!' says Mel in a low voice as we approach. 'At least they won't be able to have a go at us tonight.'

'That's true. I notice they didn't invite us to join them,' I say, trying not to sound put out.

I am put out, though. It isn't as if there are dozens of people on this trip. Making a plan to get together without involving everyone feels a bit off, and just goes to show how badly Mel and I are fitting in.

'Arthur isn't there either,' says Mel. 'Neither's Robin, or your grandma and Gloria.'

'They must be tainted by association,' I say bitterly.

It's Cynthia who sees us first.

'Yoo-hoo,' she calls, waving at us enthusiastically. 'Emma, Melanie. Over here.'

'For God's sake,' mutters Mel under her breath. 'They can't even get my name right. Let's pretend we didn't hear her.'

'We can't do that,' I say. 'We'll say hello, and then we can go and sit over there out of their way.'

I raise an acknowledging hand at Cynthia, and when we get close enough to be heard I say 'Hi,' which comes out in the kind of faux polite voice I reserve for difficult customers at work.

Cynthia is trying to push her chair away from the table to make space for us to join them, but I notice that none of the others do the same.

'We're just having an aperitif,' she says. Her cheeks are flushed and her eyes are bright and a little glazed.

'So we see,' says Mel, eyeing first the bottles that are empty and then Keith, who seems to be on his third pint. 'You've been here a while then?'

'Ages!' replies Cynthia. 'I think I might be the tiniest bit tipsy.' She lets out a little hiccup when she speaks and then she giggles like a schoolgirl. 'Oh dear,' she adds. 'Do excuse me.'

'Would you care to join us?' asks Keith. The words might be an olive branch but his tone suggests otherwise.

'No, thanks,' says Mel quickly before I have a chance to say anything different. 'It looks like this party has an exclusive guest list.'

It's a harsher reply than I would have given and I can see Frank and Vivienne drop their gaze, and Derek shuffles awkwardly in his seat.

112

Mel and I go straight through for dinner and are already tucking into our starters by the time the others wobble in. There's quite a kerfuffle as they try to decide where to sit and I see the heads of other diners turning curiously in their direction.

'Where's their precious sense of decorum now?' Mel asks. 'Just look at them! They're all over the place!'

I am sitting with my back to them, but I can hear their voices, their volume control stuck on loud because of the alcohol.

Suddenly Mel's jaw drops. 'Oh my God,' she says under her breath, and then she's up and out of her seat before I have time to ask her what's going on. I spin in my seat to see what she's up to. She darts towards the table that the others are all dithering around, picks something off the floor and is back at our table before anyone notices.

She sits down, a triumphant look on her face, and drops a keycard on the table.

'What's that?' I ask.

'Keith's room key,' she says, biting her bottom lip naughtily. 'I saw it fall out of his pocket just then.'

My mouth opens in surprise. 'After all that crap he gave us about having a system when we locked our key in the room,' I say.

'Precisely. And now look. He's lost his key and he hasn't got the foggiest idea what's happened. Great system, Keith.'

We both stare at the keycard on the table for a moment.

'We should probably give it back,' I say.

I meet Mel's eye and I see the familiar naughtiness twinkling there.

'Yes,' she replies solemnly. 'That would be the responsible thing to do.' She picks the card up, running her fingers along its straight edges. 'The trouble is, Em, we're just not that responsible. Keith said so himself. And, of course, he's always right.'

We finish dinner quickly. There's no need to rush. We're miles ahead of the others, but we want to make sure we have time to carry out our plan before the key is missed. Our fellow travellers are getting louder and louder. Keith is telling stories at the top of his voice, talking over the others and generally holding court, and the women shriek with laughter in a most un-old-people kind of way.

If we had been behaving like that someone would have trotted over and told us to pipe down by now. But instead of feeling vindicated, I actually like that they're having such a good time. It makes them seem more human, a bit like me and Mel but with less hair and more wrinkles.

No one notices as we slip away.

We run into the first problem when we get into the lift. We have the key but no idea what number his room is.

'Shit!' says Mel, her fingers hovering over the buttons. 'I didn't think of that. How are we going to find out? Do you think they'd tell us on reception?'

I shake my head, but something is tapping away at my memory. I press floor 3 and the lift starts to move.

'Lucky guess?' asks Mel.

'No. Remember when we locked ourselves out and you went to get another keycard? He said his room was on the third floor.'

I'm feeling very pleased with myself, right up until the moment Mel says, 'But that was in York, and we're in Durham.'

Damn.

'And I thought I was being so clever,' I say. 'Well, let's just try it on a few random doors. We might hit lucky.'

And we do! Halfway down the corridor on the third floor we show the key to the reader on room 324 and the little green light comes on. I look at Mel. She nods, eyes wide, and we push the door open.

21

You'll never guess what he's reading.

Inside room 324 it's dark and we can't see much. I have a sudden attack of conscience and I hover on the threshold without going in.

'Do you think we should be doing this?' I ask Mel doubtfully.

If she says no, then I'm totally ready to push the door shut and go back to our room.

But this is Mel.

'Hell, yeah! The man was a complete dick to us today. This is payback.'

She slots the keycard into the holder by the door and the room floods with light.

The en suite door is wide open, so that's where we go first. There are a few toiletries all neatly lined up next to the basin and it smells vaguely of aftershave.

'Very organised,' scoffs Mel.

She picks up a white bottle with a picture of a sailing ship on it and sprays a bit in the air.

'Is it driving you wiiiild?' she asks me.

'Put it back,' I hiss, but I can't help grinning at our naughtiness.

I see her eyeing the toothpaste, no doubt considering scrawling a message on the mirror, but she leaves everything as it is.

'Let's see what else we can find,' she says.

We move into the room proper. Keith's suitcase, also very neat and ordered, is open on the luggage stand and there's a pair of trousers in the Corby trouser press.

Mel sniggers. 'I didn't know anyone actually used those things.'

'I don't think there is one in our room,' I say.

'He must have put in a special request. Heaven forbid that Keith has to walk around in creased kecks.'

She peers inside his suitcase, lifting things up with one finger. More trousers, some neatly folded shirts and sweaters. I assume there is underwear in there somewhere but she doesn't search it out. You can say what you want about the man, but he packs a tidy case.

I can tell that Mel is growing disappointed in our discoveries and I worry that this means she'll make whatever she is planning to do even more spectacular. My insides squirm. I really don't like Keith, but I don't want to cut the legs off all his trousers.

Leaving Mel with the case, I walk round to the side of the bed to peruse his choice of bedside reading. There is a doorstop-sized hardback lying there without its dust jacket, and an old-fashioned alarm clock. I pick the clock up.

'Shall we make sure he doesn't miss the bus tomorrow?' I say, waving it aloft. 'What time shall I set it for? Three a.m.? Two?'

'I say three,' says Mel. 'That should give him plenty of time to sort out all this mess before we have to go.' She gestures at the pristine room, the sarcasm practically dripping off her.

I change the time of the alarm from six thirty to three and then put the clock back.

'It's a shame we don't have any cling film,' says Mel. 'For the toilet seat. We could put his toothbrush down the loo?'

116

We may like to think of ourselves as still young, but that is definitely a step too far for us. I wrinkle my nose and shake my head.

I pick up the book and open it to see what occupies Keith at night. When I see the title my jaw drops.

'Oh my God, Mel. You'll never guess what he's reading.'

'Plato's *Republic*?' she guesses. 'The biography of Winston Churchill?'

'*Riders!*' I say, my eyes wide.

Mel practically skips over to where I'm standing.

'What? *Riders* as in Jilly Cooper's *Riders*?'

'The very same!'

I offer her the book so she can confirm it for herself, which she does, not quite able to take such a ludicrous discovery on trust.

'Well, isn't he a dark horse?' she says. 'No wonder he's taken the cover off it. Why, though? Do you think it counts as porn in his world?'

We both start to laugh uncontrollably, the pressure of being in the room where we really shouldn't be making the discovery of the book far funnier than it actually is.

'Shhhh!' I splutter through my giggles. 'Someone will hear us. He could be back at any minute.'

'Pull the bookmark out,' says Mel, and I roll my eyes at the pettiness of the suggestion, but I do it anyway and relocate it later in the book.

Then Mel turns her attention to the desk. She stares for a moment and then calls me over.

'Come and look at this, Em.'

I put the book back down and go to join her. She's looking at a selection of photographs all laid out neatly on the glass surface. The pictures are all of rats, white ones with beady red eyes.

Instinctively I pull away.

'Ew. Gross,' I say. 'I really don't like rats, fancy or otherwise.'

'No, me neither,' agrees Mel. 'But look properly.'

I take a closer look. Keith is in a couple of the photos as well, holding the rats and looking at them with something close to adoration in his eyes. Some of the rats have rosettes with them.

I'm not quite sure what to make of it.

'It's weird that he's brought those with him,' I say. 'I assume it's so he can show off about how brilliant a breeder he is.'

Mel shakes her head slowly. 'I don't think so,' she says thoughtfully. 'If he was going to do that then he would have whipped them out at the cream tea.'

'Perhaps he's brought pictures of his rats because he doesn't like to be parted from them. It's like they're his children or something, you know, like some people are with their dogs. Having these photos means he can see them whenever he likes.'

I'm fully expecting Mel to take the piss out of this, but she doesn't.

'Aw, that's quite sweet,' she says instead. 'A bit like the Jilly Cooper too. I reckon our Mr Grumpy has a soft underbelly.'

From the corridor comes the ping of the lift. We stare at each other, frozen by panic.

'Shit. Do you think that's him?' Mel asks her eyes wide.

'I don't know. Could be. Let's go before we get caught in here.'

We take a last look round. The room looks exactly the same as it did when we arrived. So much for our schoolgirl tricks. Part of me thinks that it's a huge wasted opportunity to take our revenge on Keith when he has been so vile to us. But then again, we've learned far more about him in these few minutes than we thought we knew already, and maybe that's enough.

Plus, we have reset his alarm clock.

We scoot out of the door, pulling it behind us and leaving the key card in the power slot so it looks like he just left the room without it. The confusion that will give rise to will be very satisfying, not that Keith would ever admit to it.

We are just in the corridor when the people from the lift turn the corner. It isn't Keith or any of our party and our shoulders sag in relief.

'He's still an arse, though,' says Mel as we walk along, as if this needs restating in the light of our recent discoveries.

'Yeah,' I agree. 'Total arse.'

22

WEDNESDAY

It's obvious she's going to spill the beans.

To give them their due, the old people make a better stab at showing up on time than Mel and I did when we were hungover. They do look a little fragile, though, their movements even more snail-like than usual.

I catch Keith yawning widely and I give Mel a nudge. We bite back our smiles. It's such a shame that he's been up for so long. I love that we know secret things about him and he has no idea. It feels like a power of sorts. But what I love most is that he really isn't the person that he likes to present. A tiny part of me has shifted, knowing that he's not as dour as he makes out. It's only a tiny part, mind you.

The coach is very quiet. There's none of the usual background hum of morning chatter. When Robin gets on, he picks up on the subdued atmosphere straight away. He eyes us with something approaching concern and then, having decided that nothing is really wrong, he overcompensates by talking to us as if he's a presenter on children's television.

'Well, good morning, you lovely lot,' he says with an enthusiasm that could set your teeth on edge if you were that way inclined. 'And how are we all on this beautiful day?'

There is a general muttering that we are all very well, thank you, although it's apparent that some of us are more well than others.

'I think some people might have overindulged a little last night,' says Mel, unable to resist the opportunity to have a go.

'Oh, I did, Mel,' says Cynthia, immediately falling on her sword in her wavering voice. 'I only ever have a sherry or two at Christmas. I don't know what came over me.'

She shakes her head and gives a little shrug as if what made her drink more than usual really is one of the great mysteries of the world.

'It's good to let your hair down sometimes, Cynthia,' replies Mel kindly, all snippiness gone from her tone. 'We are on holiday, after all.'

'Well, yes,' agrees Cynthia, although she sounds far from convinced.

Nobody else seems ready to confess to anything, so Robin presses on.

'Today we'll be heading up to Alnwick,' he says. 'It's not far, less than an hour and a half door to door. When we get there there'll be the usual checking in, although we won't be able to get into our rooms until later due to cleaning and what have you.'

I hear Vivienne tut and mutter something to Frank that sounds like a complaint, and Mel throws me a look that says 'Here we go again.'

'But it doesn't matter because we will be busy,' Robin continues cheerily. 'We have a full day ahead at the castle and gardens. I'll tell you more when we get a little closer but, for now, sit back, relax and enjoy the ride.'

We leave Durham behind and soon we are pelting up the road towards Newcastle. Mel plugs herself into her music and closes her eyes, leaving me to my own devices. I don't mind. It's nice to have a little bit of time with my own thoughts.

I'm still wondering about Keith. He has been truly horrible to us, but what we saw in his room makes me think that maybe there's more to him than we've been getting so far. And, the thought dances across my mind, *maybe* Mel and I haven't been exactly easy to get on with thus far either. It's definitely not six of one and half a dozen of the other. But perhaps the split might be nine to three? I decide that I'm going to try a little bit harder with him.

We haven't been travelling for long when Gloria slips out of the seat next to Grandma and weaves her way down the aisle until she reaches Arthur. I can't hear what she says to him, but she sits down in the seat next to his and sinks down low.

I take advantage of the fact that Grandma is finally on her own and move into Gloria's seat.

'Hi, Grandma,' I say as I sit down, and I'm pleased to see her face light up at the sight of me.

'Oh, Emma, love,' she says. 'How are you? Are you having a nice time?' She gives me an anxious little smile as if she's not quite sure how I'll reply, but I realise as soon as she asks that yes, I'm having a lovely time, and I tell her so.

'I am pleased,' she replies. 'I was a bit worried, you know . . .' She drops her voice and rolls her eyes in Keith's direction. 'After yesterday.'

I wave her concerns away.

'All forgotten,' I say magnanimously. 'I'm sure he's a lovely bloke under all that gruff exterior.' And he reads Jilly Cooper and carries around pictures of his pets, I think but don't say.

Grandma looks a little taken aback by my show of forgiveness, but she says, 'Good. I don't like there to be any bad feeling.'

'Gloria's moved seats, I see,' I say, and Grandma shuffles a little in her seat and lets out a noise that might be a harrumph. 'You haven't fallen out, have you?' I add.

'No,' says Grandma quickly. 'No, it's not that.'

She seems reluctant to say anything else so I push her gently.

'Then what's up?' I ask quietly. 'Go on. You can tell me.'

Grandma shakes her head like everything is rosy in the garden, but it's obvious she's going to spill the beans.

'Oh, it's nothing really,' she says, and I wait for what it actually is. 'It's just that when I asked her about what her flat was like she was a bit off with me about it, like I'd overstepped the mark. So, to make up I told her about our house, mine and your grandad's. I told her how it's nothing special, what with that huge new estate that they built on those fields round the back of us.'

'That was thirty years ago, Grandma,' I laugh.

'I know that, but your grandad never forgave them. Those houses stole all our light. And our view. It used to be green as far as the eye could see at the end of our garden. The prices on our street fell through the floor when we got that estate on our back doorstep. Not that that matters. It's still our home and I'd never leave.'

I'm feeling a bit confused about where this is going and what it has to do with Gloria, but I've learned over the years with Grandma to be patient and that it will all make sense eventually, so I keep quiet and just listen.

'We don't have much, your grandad and I. There's no money to speak of. I hope you're not expecting a big inheritance, Emma.'

It upsets me when she talks like this, both that she's still using the present tense about Grandad and that she refers to when she will be gone too.

'No, Grandma. I'm not interested in any of that,' I say, brushing her comment safely away. 'I just want you to enjoy yourself.' The words 'while you can' pop into my mind but luckily they don't make it out of my mouth.

'Well, that's good, at least,' Grandma says. 'But I think I might be a bit lowly for Gloria. When I told her how small the house is she seemed to lose interest in me a bit. I mean, it's obvious that she's got a bob or two, but I didn't have her down as a snob. I suppose you can still be wrong about people, even when you're as old as I am.'

I take against Gloria instantly, even though she doesn't seem to have done anything but give off an impression to Grandma.

'Ignore her,' I say. 'If she wants to be like that, then let her. She's probably just jealous that you and Grandad were happily married for so long and she's about to be divorced.'

As I speak, I realise that what I'm saying sounds just like the kind of thing Grandma used to say to me when other girls were mean to me in the playground. 'Ignore them, Emma. They're probably just jealous of how lovely you are.'

'We haven't fallen out,' Grandma clarifies. 'Nothing like that. I just wonder if I shouldn't spend a bit more time with some of the others for the rest of the trip.'

'Yes! You can hang around with me and Mel,' I say, and Grandma gives me a little smile.

'Thank you, Emma,' she says. 'But I'd quite like to make some new friends too.'

Do old people still want to make friends? I wonder. Don't they have enough to be going on with already?

Just then Gloria lets out one of her ear-piercing hoots from behind us. Arthur seems to be getting the full Gloria treatment. I look at Grandma, eyebrows raised, and she gives me a grin back.

I think she's okay.

23

GHOSTS CAN BE TERRIBLY VINDICTIVE, YOU KNOW.

I have to say that so far I've been pretty impressed by the hotels that Odyssey Tours have picked for our trip. As the coach pulls up outside our home for the night in Alnwick, Rita lets out a little gasp. I look out of the window to see what all the fuss is about and see immediately. This one could actually be a real castle. It's got crenellations and a turret and everything.

'This place looks fun,' says Mel as she slots her headphones back into their case. 'I bet it's haunted.'

'Ooh, I hope not,' replies Cynthia, and then her hand shoots up to cover her mouth. 'I'm sorry, I didn't mean to eavesdrop.'

'Cynthia, you're sitting less than three feet from me,' says Mel kindly. 'That's not eavesdropping! That's being part of the conversation.'

Cynthia blushes and gives a modest little half-smile.

'Don't you like ghosts?' Mel adds.

Cynthia shudders. 'Oh no. Not since we had that poltergeist at home. I've never trusted the afterlife since then. Ghosts can be terribly vindictive, you know.'

Mel puts a hand up to silence her.

'Stop! Wait! Rewind. You had a poltergeist at home?' she says, eyes stretched with incredulity.

'Oh yes, dear,' replies Cynthia. 'It was dreadful. Mother had to get the priest to come and do one of those things. Now, what do they call it?'

'An exorcism?!'

'Yes, yes. One of those. Now, I assume we get off here.'

She stands up and bustles towards the front of the coach, leaving me and Mel staring at one another.

'We have to get to the bottom of that one,' Mel says.

Robin is directing the flow of old people traffic and Mel gives me a wink and then bounds off to stand next to him.

'You're being terribly masterful, Robin,' she jokes, gently nudging him on the arm and looking up at him like an actress out of a thirties movie.

I can see Robin's cheeks warming from where I am. He mumbles something that might be thanks and consults his checklist intently. I've noticed that he's totally at ease with the other passengers, able to navigate their whinges with aplomb and is never flustered or thrown. But as soon as Mel is within ten feet of him he seems to lose all his confidence and morphs into a bit of a buffoon.

I can think of only two reasons why this might be the case. One, he's scared of her – possible, but really, what is there to be scared of? It's not like she's going to do him any harm or get him into trouble.

I'm less keen on the second reason but, sadly, I suspect it's more likely to be the real one. Surely Robin is reduced to something approaching blancmange when Mel speaks to him because he finds her attractive. I know it's only a game and it really doesn't matter which one of us gets him to agree to a drink first. But I don't want it to be Mel. And now, I realise, I don't want it to be Mel quite badly.

Robin has got his cheeks under control and is fending off Mel whilst dealing with questions from our fellow passengers. I have to say, it's quite impressive to watch, and in the end Mel has to concede that this is not her moment and slinks back over to me. She raises an eyebrow and a finger simultaneously and draws a figure '1' in the air between us, like this is a strike in her favour.

I rally.

'Don't you be so confident there, young lady,' I say. 'He's not agreed to a drink yet!'

And he's not going to, I think, as it truly dawns on me how I'm feeling about it all. Not if I have anything to do with it. Things just got serious on the betting front!

We follow the crowd round to collect our cases from Dave and then into the reception area of the hotel. Mel slides over to talk to Grandma, leaving me next to Robin. Suddenly all ideas for conversation desert me. I wrack my brains, desperately trying to think of something intelligent to say, but without success.

But then he speaks.

'She's very full on, your friend, isn't she?' He cocks his head towards Mel and opens his eyes wide behind his glasses.

I grin, much happier talking about Mel than about myself.

'She is,' I agree. 'She's like a force of nature. We've been friends since we were at school and she's always been the same. I just follow along in her wake and watch her. She's like Hermione. I'm more of a Luna,' I add, then I think that Luna is actually far more impressive than I am and worry that he might think I'm bigging myself up.

'I've always preferred Luna,' he says quietly, and then moves off into the melee.

Then I remember the bee-keeping. Why didn't I ask him about that? He must think I'm so dull. I mean, Hermione and Luna. Honestly!

Inside the hotel the decor is very dark with lots of panelled wood everywhere, the scent of beeswax polish mingling with that smell you get in museums.

'They're really milking the whole castle vibe,' says Mel, who has reappeared at my side, nodding her head in the direction of a suit of armour that is standing sentry next to a blazing open fire.

'If you've got it, flaunt it,' I reply.

Mel smiles back but she seems a bit distracted and I can tell that an idea is blooming inside her head. It's always dangerous when that happens.

'What?' I ask suspiciously.

'Oh, nothing,' she says in an equally suspicious sing-songy tone. 'Just something we might do later.'

I let it go. She'll tell me when she's good and ready.

When I look across to see where we've got to in the checking-in process, I see Robin is now being hounded by Rita and Derek. Rita has taken her anorak off, probably because of the fire, and she's wearing an uncharacteristically bright pink top. It's all kinds of wrong seeing her and Derek not being dressed the same. Robin's face is stuck in that rictus grin that is becoming quite familiar. God, he must have the patience of a saint. I decide that he's more in control than I gave him credit for at the start. I thought he was a bumbling nerd on Monday, but having seen how he deals with all these old people and their interminable questions and complaints, my respect for him is growing. And there's something quite attractive about the way he rises above it all. In fact, I realise there's something quite attractive about him full stop. I'm not sure how I feel about this realisation, so I decide it would be best all round if I just park it for now until I have the bandwidth to think about it properly.

I notice that Gloria is stuck to Arthur like glue. She has her arm through his, which is vaguely comical as she is so tall and willowy and he is shaped like a ball. He's also a good foot shorter than her.

I think about what Grandma told me and wonder what she's up to. Is she trying to punish Grandma for something? That really would be primary-school behaviour, but maybe human beings don't really change as they grow up.

Arthur looks bemused by this new turn of events. Then again, he looks bemused most of the time, so that's nothing new. He's such a gentleman that I doubt he'd tell Gloria to sling her hook even if that's what he wants. All of a sudden, I feel quite protective of him and decide that I will try to spend some time with him today, just in case he does need rescuing from Gloria's clutches.

Robin gathers us together and explains the plan, which involves the castle and gardens. After two solid days of sightseeing, I'm feeling a little bit of old-building-exhaustion, but I can suck up one more for Grandma's sake. With Gloria's allegiances switched, I had worried that she might be on her own, but she's happily chatting to the couple whose child died, Angela and Ian, and doesn't look at all bothered, so I try not to be either.

Robin leads the way out of the hotel like the Pied Piper, with us all following behind like a little plague of rats. Did I mention that I really don't like rats? The thought of the Pied Piper makes me shudder, although it does bring the mysteries of Keith to mind again. I wonder if, now that I know he reads Jilly Cooper, I should make an effort to start again with him, but I'm not quite feeling strong enough just yet. The fact that his room revealed a softer side to him doesn't change the fact that he's been horrible to us every day so far. I won't be forgetting that overnight.

Rita and Derek are behind me, and whatever it is that they are unhappy about seems to be still bothering them. I can't hear what they're saying, but there's definitely some chuntering coming from their general direction. It's strange that for such boring, nondescript people they seem to get their knickers in a twist terribly easily.

Robin is speaking into my ears and I switch to listening to him.

'The earliest parts of the castle were erected in 1096,' he says. 'And it held a strong defensive position over the River Aln. If you look up, you will see that there are various statues adorning the gatehouse walls.'

He's right. They look like real people standing up there peering down on us. There's something a bit comical about them, like they're extras in a Mel Brooks film.

'Originally they were there to put off the enemy,' Robin continues, 'but then the first duchess added a few more when she made restorations to the castle in the mid-eighteenth century. Have a better look and pick your favourite.'

We all stand still, necks craned upwards as we stare at the gatehouse.

'I quite like him,' says Mel, pointing to a dumpy man in a frock coat and a crown. 'He looks friendly enough. Friendlier than some of this lot,' she mutters to me.

She's right, but I am starting to feel a bit bad about us constantly having a downer on the olds. But then again, they seem to have a constant downer on us so it's pretty evenly balanced.

Alnwick Castle is much like many other castles I've been to. I try to listen to Robin in my ear, but I find myself drifting off. I think about how much Grandad would have enjoyed this tour. He was always showing me interesting things when I was little. I can imagine him pointing out all these statues and making up a story or a joke to go with them all, and my throat starts to close. I miss him so much, but I can't think about that now, so I try to think about Cynthia's poltergeist instead.

'They filmed the first two Harry Potter films here,' says Derek suddenly.

He's standing right next to me, and it's feels like he's trying to find a connection with me, although he's a bit socially awkward and so doesn't make eye contact when he speaks. His comment is so unexpected that it takes me by surprise and I actually jump. I wonder if he's telling me this because he thinks it's the kind of thing I might be interested in as a young person. I probably would have been . . . if I'd been ten.

I'm about to reply when Mel gets in first.

'Yes. I knew that,' she says, completely taking the wind out of his sails, and Derek throws her a look that could curdle cream. I would have tried to soften my answer and been less abrupt, but he has already moved away from us and back to Rita.

'Well, really,' says Mel to me, because I think she can sense that I disapprove of her sharpness of tone. 'What is his problem? Am I supposed to pretend that I didn't already know his boring fact?'

Part of me wishes that Mel would make a bit more of an effort to fit in, but the rest of me is one hundred per cent with her. They seem to think that we're either delinquents, morons or children and can't find anything positive about us at all.

'Did you hear that?' Rita snips, and I see her looking around to check that someone, anyone, is listening to her. 'So rude! Derek was only telling them something they might find interesting. There was no need to be so unpleasant.'

We haven't been unpleasant, just uninterested, but after the row with Keith yesterday I'm really not up for another one. I turn round to Rita to explain.

'Look, Rita,' I say. 'We seem to be getting off on the wrong foot here. I'm sorry that we're not more enthusiastic about the Harry Potter thing, but we're not kids. And I did actually know that they'd filmed here because I did some research before we came. They filmed parts of *Downton Abbey* here too . . .'

I can see Rita struggling between wanting to be angry with me but at the same time consumed by a desire to know my *Downton Abbey* trivia. Her curiosity wins out.

'Really? I do love that programme. Which parts were filmed here?'

'They used it as Brancaster Castle,' I say, racking my memory for the details of what I'd read. *Downton's* not really my kind of thing, but I've clearly hit on something as Rita is more animated than I've seen her all week. She looks at me expectantly, waiting for me to furnish her with more *Downton* facts, but I've reached the limits of my knowledge.

Luckily, Robin, who must have seen that he no longer had our undivided attention, comes to my rescue. I remember, with a slight tightening in my gut, that I have just used Harry Potter as a reference in my feeble flirtation with Robin and now here I am making out to Derek that I'm not interested. I hope Robin didn't hear. He takes off his headset so that he's talking directly to us and so I do the same.

'I was just telling Rita what I know about *Downton*,' I say to him. 'Which is next to nothing. I'm sure you know far more, Robin.'

I try a little smile and he winks back at me. Again! That's twice now. What does it mean? Has he winked at Mel too? Questions whirl round my head as he gives Rita the benefit of his not inconsiderable knowledge.

'Ah yes. Alnwick and Downton,' he says, steering her towards the main gates. 'When we get inside, you'll see the state rooms where they did some of the filming.'

Rita matches her pace to his and at once I am relieved of my tour manager duties, although I'd quite like to be party to their conversation. I might even be a little bit miffed that all his attention is being directed elsewhere.

But that's just ridiculous. Isn't it?

24

I REMEMBERED WHAT TO DO. AND I DID IT.

We all troop through the castle, following the signs and listening to Robin's dulcet tones through our headphones. To be fair, the stuff he tells us is very interesting and quite detailed. I wonder if he has to mug up the night before or if all these dates and facts are just lodged in his memory. My self-esteem bows its head, defeated as I think about how I struggle to remember what day it is most of the time.

Also, I must stop thinking about Robin.

After the castle, we head out into the gardens. Spring has only just begun and the plants haven't got very far, but there will be some incredible cherry blossom later on in the year, judging by the number of trees.

I find myself drawn to the spectacular waterfalls. The water trickles from pool to pool and then shoots up skywards in mesmerising patterns. It's absolutely beautiful and definitely my favourite sight of the tour so far.

There is something so healing about the sound of falling water, and I'm quite lost in its cadences when I become aware of someone shouting. I can't quite make out what they're saying, but it sounds urgent.

There's no one else nearby. Mel has gone to the loo and the others have wandered off somewhere. I start walking in the direction of the voice.

'Hello?' I call out. 'Is everything okay?'

'No! Help me. Please help!'

I'm not certain, but it sounds like Rita. I have no idea where she is, though, and as I move closer towards the fountains her voice gets lost behind the falling water.

'Where are you?' I shout. 'I can't see you.'

'Over here. Behind the hedge. Quick! Help. It's Derek! Derek!'

The voice is getting shriller and more panicked.

There are box hedges to either side of the cascade of waterfalls, and I make for the one nearest to me, moving faster now, almost running.

'Rita? Is that you?' I shout as I move.

'Yes. We're here. Help me.'

I turn a corner and there she is on the floor, kneeling over Derek, who is lying flat out on the paving stones, half-hidden by the tall box hedges. Even from this distance I can see that his skin has gone a weird grey colour. He isn't moving.

My heart jolts in my chest and adrenaline prickles my scalp. I've sometimes wondered how I would react in a medical emergency. Until it happens to you, you never know if you'll stay calm or fall apart, but it seems that I'm about to find out.

I reach them and drop to my knees next to Derek. His face is creased in pain and his eyes are tight shut, and I'm not sure he's breathing.

'What happened?' I ask. My fingers reach for the zip on his anorak and begin to yank it down.

Rita's eyes are wide and her mouth is open, but she can't seem to get any words out.

'Help me,' she says again, but now her words are a whisper. 'Help me.'

I lower my head and rest it on Derek's chest, listening for any sign of breathing. He is ominously still. I fish my phone from my pocket, ring 999 and then pass it to Rita.

'Speak to them,' I say. 'Tell them we need an ambulance and answer their questions.'

Then I begin CPR. It's been a while since I did the training. Gavin from work and I went because the classes were during the working day and it meant that we could skive off. An added bonus was that it would annoy Suki, as she could hardly object when the store had set up the sessions and it's such an important life skill. Even though I'd thought we'd been mainly messing about, what they told us must have sunk in because now it almost feels like muscle memory.

My hands find their way to the right place on Derek's chest, and, resting one on top of the other, I begin to press. Under my breath I'm singing 'Stayin' Alive' because that's what the instructor told us to do. As I pump, I hear Rita talking to the emergency services.

'He just collapsed,' she says. 'No. I don't think so. Yes. A girl. She's doing it. No. I don't know. Where are we?' she asks me, her voice desperate.

'Alnwick Gardens,' I say quickly, still trying to keep the counting going in my head.

'We're in Alnwick Gardens,' Rita repeats. 'Near the fountains.'

I've done thirty compressions and now it's time to breathe into his mouth. This was the part that felt a bit icky in training. Even though we were practising on a dummy, I kept thinking how I'd cope with having to put my mouth on a stranger's. I'm not surprised to discover that it feels just as off-putting in real life as I thought it would. But that's okay. I can overcome it. I just have to keep going until help comes.

I stop breathing and go back to the chest compressions. A crowd is gathering around us. One of the castle guides is there, I think, and then I hear Mel's voice, but I don't focus on what she's saying. I've got one job to do and I'm going to do it the best I can.

I pump for what feels like for ever.

'Look!' I hear someone say. 'He's getting some colour back.'

I turn my head and see that it's true. The grey pallor has left him and he does have a flush to his cheeks. We're not out of the woods yet, though. I have to keep going until the ambulance gets here. I keep pumping and breathing, the Bee Gees sounding in my head like a third-rate disco. My hands and arms are tired and my shoulders are starting to feel tight but I just keep at it.

Then I'm aware of someone at my back, gently moving me to one side.

'You've done a fantastic job,' she says. 'Thank you. We can take it from here.'

The woman, dressed in the familiar bottle-green uniform of a paramedic, takes over, calling instructions out to her colleague. An oxygen mask is fitted over Derek's nose and mouth and they lift him on to a gurney and wheel him away, Rita at their side.

I sit back on my heels. I feel completely numb. I'm aware of someone rubbing me on the back, of someone saying, 'Well done' and the general buzz of a crowd around me, but all I can think is that I did it. I remembered what to do and I did it.

25

It's a very special talent you have there.

There are people all around me, pushing in close, in my space. Some of them are talking, but it's just sound. I can't make out any words. Someone slips an arm across my shoulder.

'Let's go and get you a nice cup of tea,' they say. I have no idea who it is.

I nod and let myself be led along. Then Mel is at my other side. She's all questions, but I can't answer them. I just keep putting my feet one in front of another until we reach a table and chairs. Then I let myself drop.

'Where is he? Where's Derek? Is he okay?' I ask the questions hardly daring to hear the answers. What if he didn't make it? I'm not sure I can bear to know, but I have to.

'They've taken him in the ambulance,' says Mel gently. 'Rita has gone with him. The paramedic said you saved his life, Em.'

I saved his life.

Me.

I feel the emotion bubbling up in my chest and then my face screws up and tears trickle down my cheeks. All of me is shaking.

I feel Mel wrap her arms tight around me and I cry into her collarbone.

'You were amazing,' she says. 'And so calm. I'm incredibly proud of you.'

I don't feel very calm now, I have to say, but that doesn't matter. The main thing is that I held it together when it counted.

'There she is,' says someone else, Gloria I think, although I'm not with it enough to know for sure. 'The champion of the hour. Well done, Emma.'

'Yes, very impressive,' says a male voice.

I stay buried in Mel's hair, not wanting to come out. I need time to process what just happened. But it doesn't look like I'm going to get it. The questions come at me thick and fast until Mel leaps to my defence.

'I'm sure she'll tell us all about it later,' she says, 'but for now can we give her a bit of space, please?'

I hear Robin ushering the group away and I stay where I am, with Mel's arms holding me tight.

After a few minutes I stop shaking and feel in control enough to emerge. Mel's hair sticks to my hot face and I pull the salty strands away as she laughs at me.

'Look at the state of you!' she says, running her thumb under my eyelashes to wipe away my decimated mascara. 'Drink this tea. I've put a gazillion sugars in it because if you can't have something that will rot your teeth in the aftermath of an emergency, then when can you?'

The tea is hot and distressingly sweet, but there is a strange comfort in it and by the time I get to the bottom of the cup I'm feeling more like myself.

'Do you think he's going to be all right?' I ask. 'Derek, I mean.'

'Well, he stands a much better chance than he would have done without you. You were amazing,' she says again. 'Well done, Em!'

Then Grandma is there too.

'Oh, Emma,' she says, and her voice is so kind and familiar, touching the secret places deep in my heart, that it starts me crying all over again. 'My lovely girl,' she says. 'Your grandad would have been so proud of you. And I am too. Just wait until I tell your mum and dad what you've done. They're saying you saved his life, you know. If you hadn't been so calm and known exactly what to do, well . . .' She lets what might have happened hang in the air.

It's not often that I get stuff right, and it's hard to process. I picture Grandma telling Mum and Dad, Dad's face as he hears that I've saved someone's life. Me! Who can't tie my own shoelaces the way he'd like me to. For the first time in as long as I can remember I allow myself to feel proud of me. It feels good.

◆ ◆ ◆

We don't find out anything else about how Derek is doing until dinner that evening. Robin gathers us in the bar to give us an update.

'You'll be glad to know that the news is good,' he tells us. His smile is a little jaded and there are tiny lines around his eyes that I swear weren't there before. 'I've spoken to Rita and the doctors say that, due to Emma's quick reactions and expertise, the damage to his heart is treatable. He'll be in hospital for a few days but then he'll be safe to go back home. Rita wanted me to pass on their sincere thanks, Emma,' he adds and there is so much gratitude in his smile that I wonder if the thanks are partly from him too. I suppose no one wants a dead guest on their watch. 'Now, what will you have to drink?' he asks. 'I bet you could use one.'

'She'll have a glass of Pinot Grigio,' replies Mel. 'A large one. And so will I!'

'I'll get those,' says a voice from behind me. It's Keith, and he already has his wallet in his hand.

'Two large glasses of Pinot Grigio,' he calls over our heads, 'and whatever the rest of them are having as well,' he adds. 'I think we could all do with a little steadier.'

'Thank you,' I say to him. My voice comes out very small and quiet.

'No more than you deserve,' he says gruffly. 'That was a marvellous thing you did today.'

There's no accompanying smile so I assume that's all I'm going to get from him, but it's enough. There is an understanding of sorts between us now, a kind of taciturn respect.

The others all buzz around me as the barman serves the drinks. When the questions get too intense, Mel steps in to save me, like a bouncer with a celebrity.

We seem to float from bar to seats, and for the first time we are all sitting together by choice. Grandma keeps looking over at me and smiling. She doesn't make a fuss, but I know she's proud and I get a warm buzz in the pit of my stomach.

'Have you ever thought about training to be a paramedic?' Ian asks me.

'God, no,' I reply, brushing his question away, embarrassed. 'I'm not sure I'd be any good at that.'

'I think you would,' counters Ian immediately. 'You were so calm today, focused on what you needed to do. When Richard had his accident that was one of the things that stayed with us, how wonderful the paramedics were. Not just with Richard, but with us too. Calm and kind, in control when our world felt anything but. It's a very special talent you have there, Emma. You should use it.'

There's a murmuring agreement around the table and lots of nodding heads. I take a big swig of wine, anxious for the attention to fall away from me, but it does feel amazing to know that I did something so important, and I did it well.

26

AND THEN IT STARTED ON THE CHINA.

After Cynthia's comments this morning, I know Mel has been planning our evening's conversation all day, so I'm not surprised when she casually brings up the subject of ghosts.

We've finished dinner, and now that our numbers are down by two we fit better around a single, albeit quite large, table. Everyone has a drink in front of them, but no one is drunk tonight. We all seem to have learned our lessons on that score.

'So, Cynthia . . .' Mel begins.

Cynthia jumps at being addressed directly, but then her face slides into something approaching glee that she is the centre of the group's attention. I don't think she often has all eyes on her.

'Tell us about your poltergeist.'

Mel's eyes twinkle with mischievous delight, and I struggle not to roll mine. I can see exactly where this is going. Mel loves ghost stories and anything paranormal. She makes us watch all those celebrity-in-a-haunted-place programmes and laughs at their terrified faces in the night vision cameras. I tell her that we'd be scared too if we'd been wound up as much as they have beforehand, but she just says that she likes being scared.

I wonder briefly if it might be a bit crass to talk about the afterlife when one of us so nearly met their maker today, but then again, maybe that's exactly the time to discuss it.

'What's this?' asks Gloria, sitting forward in her seat.

I notice that her manicured hand is resting on Arthur's corduroy trouser leg. Arthur is staring at it as if he's not quite sure what it is or why it is there.

'When we arrived, I said the place looked haunted, and Cynthia started to tell us about a ghost she once met.'

'Ooh! How exciting,' says Gloria. 'Please tell all, Cynthia.'

Keith makes a little hmmm sound and sits back in his chair, like he's saying that this is going to have to be good to convince him. Frank rubs his hands together.

'Oh, I love a good ghost story, don't I, Vivienne?'

'You do, Frank,' replies Vivienne dutifully. 'We both do actually.' She pulls her chair a little closer to the table.

Cynthia is blushing at all the attention now, but that doesn't seem to be putting her off.

'Well, it was when I was a child,' she begins. 'We had this problem in the house. Things used to move about, you know, all by themselves. Quite big things sometimes. Like Father's mantelpiece clock. That was terribly heavy. And I saw it floating across the room like it was light as a feather.'

'Really?' asks Vivienne. Her eyes are like saucers. 'What else?'

'There was door-slamming. Locked doors, mind you, that were mysteriously opened and then banged shut. And the lights. It was always messing with the lights. On and off all night long. It was impossible to get any sleep.'

'Draughts and faulty electrics,' says Keith. 'All easily explained.'

Cynthia turns to him. Her face is completely guileless, like a child's.

'Well, yes. That's just what my father said too. But we had everything checked and they couldn't find anything wrong. And then it started on the china. That's what really upset my mother. It had been her mother's, you see. And it was getting smashed piece by piece. When there was only the tea service left, my mother said, "Enough is enough," and she stormed straight up to the church and got the priest.'

'And what happened then?' asks Vivienne, who is hanging on every word, positively agog.

Cynthia crosses her arms across her chest and takes a deep breath. There's the flicker of an excited smile and I can see that she's quite enjoying herself.

'The priest came that evening, which was good because by then we were down to the teapot, the milk jug and four cups and saucers. The sugar bowl smashed to smithereens when it got hurled at the fireplace.'

'And that was the poltergeist, was it?' asks Vivienne.

Cynthia looks at her as if she is stupid.

'Well, it wasn't me,' she says.

'Poltergeists usually turn out to be a prank, though,' says Keith, with that air of authority that he gives to everything that comes out of his mouth. 'I mean, there's no actual scientific proof that ghosts exist.'

Ian clears his throat and shifts in his seat. He looks quite uncomfortable and I wonder what's rattled his cage. Maybe he has a ghost story to tell as well. Angela opens her mouth to speak, but then seems to think better of it and closes it again.

'I don't know about the science side of things,' replies Cynthia, 'but we couldn't work out what was going on. All we knew was that Mother's precious crockery collection was decreasing by the day.' Cynthia gives a little sniff and I worry that Keith's scepticism has put her off her stride and that she's about to take her bat home.

Mel must sense the same because she speaks, her voice gentle and encouraging.

'It must have been terrifying,' she says.

Cynthia gives her an appreciative smile. 'Oh, it was, Mel,' she says. 'I didn't dare sleep at night. There was no telling what might happen.'

'So, the priest came . . .' Mel prompts.

'Yes. The priest came, and he brought salt and holy water.'

'What? No crucifixes and garlic?' scoffs Keith.

'That's for vampires, I believe,' says Arthur quietly.

'And he made us all stand in the best room and hold hands, and then we said the Lord's Prayer together, and he said some other prayers.'

'And did that work?' asks Vivienne breathlessly. 'Did the poltergeist leave?'

Cynthia beams at her. 'It did! And I still have the tea service, although a saucer got broken when it slid off the draining board one time.'

'Well, thank the Lord,' says Keith, taking a mouthful of his pint. 'We shall all rest easy in our beds tonight.'

I can't help feeling a sneaking sympathy with Keith on this one. I mean, I'm growing quite fond of Cynthia, but this poltergeist business really is far-fetched.

'I'm glad you got it all sorted out,' I say diplomatically. There's no point pouring fuel on Keith's fire, fun though that might be.

Vivienne looks almost disappointed at the happy outcome of the story. She slumps back in her seat.

'Anyone else got any good ghost stories?' Mel asks, looking round the group, that naughty smile of hers dancing on her lips.

I see Angela look at Ian. He is shaking his head, but it's such a subtle movement that it's barely noticeable. Angela turns her head from him deliberately and says, 'I once went to a séance.'

27

OH, I DO LOVE A SÉANCE.

Angela has our undivided attention but, unlike Cynthia, she really doesn't look like she welcomes the attention. Her gaze stays firmly on the table, and she twists her wedding ring round her finger, turning it first this way and then that as if she doesn't know what to do with her hands.

Ian reaches out and touches her knee.

'Angela,' he says. 'I'm not sure that this is quite the moment.'

He looks genuinely uncomfortable, and I actually feel quite sorry for him. But I want to hear about Angela's séance more. I'm not the only one.

'Oh, I do love a séance. And a Ouija board too,' says Vivienne with unmistakable delight. 'So what happened at yours? Did they manage to summon anyone?'

'Yes,' chips in Mel. 'Start at the beginning, Angela. Tell us everything. Who did you go with?'

'I went with my friend Liz,' she says. 'We saw it advertised in the local paper and Liz said she knew some people who'd been before, so we thought we'd pop along.'

'What an adventure,' says Cynthia, her eyes shining. 'So brave of you.'

God bless Cynthia. She's such a trooper, but her world must be tiny.

'It was in the upstairs room of a pub near where we live,' continues Angela. 'There were six there, including me and Liz. And then the medium, of course. His name was Luca.'

'That's an unusual name,' says Vivienne. She looks at Frank for confirmation of this fact, like she can't hold any opinions of her own, and he nods his approval.

'So, Luca welcomed us all in and we sat around his table and did the introductions.'

'Was it dark?' asks Mel. 'You always picture these things in the dark, don't you?'

Vivienne and Cynthia nod enthusiastically.

'Actually, it wasn't dark,' says Angela. 'Not that first time. It was June and it was still light outside. Luca told us to hold hands and that his job was to be the conduit between the spirit world and us. He said there were no guarantees that the spirits would come, but that there was usually someone around.'

'That's true,' says Cynthia. 'That's what the priest said to my mother. He told us that lost souls were far more common than people thought, and it was just that most people weren't sensitive enough to be aware of them.'

Keith coughs into his hand, clearly smothering a laugh.

'Sorry,' he says, when everyone turns to look. 'Drink went down the wrong way.'

He catches my eye and I think he winks at me, but I wouldn't like to swear to it.

'Carry on, Angela,' urges Vivienne, giving Keith a disdainful look.

'So then the others told Luca who they were hoping to contact. They all had someone and they called the names out one by one.'

A cold sense of dread creeps up my spine as I suddenly realise where this is going. I shoot a glance over at Ian. He looks dejected, broken almost, his head hanging and his shoulders drooped.

This is going to be about their son, the little boy that they lost. Richard. Here we are, trying to orchestrate a silly night telling ghost stories, and Angela is about to share something so very personal and poignant and not the tiniest bit funny. No wonder Ian doesn't seem that keen.

I don't know what to do. I can hardly change the subject. Mel and I started this, and Vivienne and Gloria are totally rapt. They would never stand for it if I tried to stop Angela telling her story.

I realise that I'm just going to have to let it all come out and hope it doesn't get too morbid.

'And then Luca started,' Angela continues. 'There was nothing very dramatic about it, no wailing or moaning. He just closed his eyes and let the spirits run through him. Not everyone had a visitation that time. There was a man who was trying to speak to his identical twin brother. He was lucky. His twin appeared pretty quickly, and Luca gave him the messages. The man seemed pleased.'

Maybe not that hard to divine some information about a person when you know they want to hear from someone who looks just like them, I think.

'There was a lady who needed to know where her husband had hidden the spare key to their car because she'd lost the other one.'

Mel laughs. 'That's funny,' she says. 'Handy too. Did he come up with the goods?'

'Well, she never came back so we didn't find out,' says Angela. 'Another woman wanted to contact her mother, but she didn't appear. Liz was just there with me, so she didn't really have anyone. And then I had Richard.'

She pauses and takes a little swallow as she says this, as if just saying her son's name out loud takes a huge amount of her strength.

'Your son, of course,' says Grandma kindly, and Angela nods once.

There is something unsavoury about the way the group seems to want to hear the story even though we can all see how painful it is for Angela to tell it. Vivienne and Gloria are hanging on her every word. Only Cynthia has the grace to look a little ashamed.

I catch Mel's eye and raise an eyebrow as discreetly as I can.

'Shit,' she mouths at me, and pulls a face. I don't need to pull a face back. Mel and I know each other so well that tiny little gestures are all it takes to know what the other one is thinking.

'I wasn't lucky that time, though,' says Angela.

She says this so breezily, as if she missed out on a win on the tombola.

'So, did you go back?' asks Vivienne.

'I did. I went back a lot, actually,' replies Angela.

Ian sits up a little and leans towards her. 'Angela, I really don't think they want to hear . . .' he says in a low voice.

'Oh, but we do!' interrupts Gloria. 'Did Richard ever show up for you?'

Angela has gone very still and even though the lighting is pretty dim I can see she's gone so pale that she almost looks like a ghost herself.

'Just once,' she says, her voice so soft now that we all have to lean in to hear her.

28

THANK GOD FOR THIS SMALL SPECK OF HUMAN DECENCY.

The whole group falls still. Even Keith, who has been merrily splut-tering his way through the conversation thus far, keeps his mouth shut. The atmosphere is electric as we wait to hear what Angela is going to say next.

'It was on my fourth visit,' she says. 'It was winter by then, so it was dark outside.' She says this to Mel, who had asked about the light before.

Mel presses her lips together. It's not often that I see her look-ing uncomfortable, but she does now.

'There was only me and Liz left from the original group. The others had got what they wanted or just stopped coming. New people came each time,' she said. 'Luca has a brilliant reputation. He can always fill a room.'

I think of all the documentaries Mel and I have laughed our way through where mediums are proved to be charlatans. It's just clever observation and manipulation combined with gullible people made desperate by grief. We haven't really had much to do with Angela and Ian on this trip, but now, looking at them through the filter of this evening, I see a man worn down by tragedy who is struggling to support his increasingly unstable wife. I had interpreted their lack of involvement with the group as rudeness, but maybe they were just trying to hold on.

I look over to Ian. I want to signal to him somehow that I've got it, that I understand what is going on here, how difficult it must be for him to see his wife like this, but his eyes are firmly on his feet. He's not even looking at Angela any more. My heart aches for him. It's decades since their son was killed. Has he been living like this for all that time?

'Anyway, that day I'd got a bit upset,' Angela is saying. 'It's sometimes overwhelming, all that energy in the room. It can knock you for six. Luca could see that and so he made an extra effort to contact Richard. And it worked. He told me that he could hear Richard loud and clear.'

Tears are trickling down her cheeks now, settling in the creases on her face. She makes no effort to wipe them away. It's as if she hasn't even noticed that she's crying at all.

'Richard said that he was so happy where he was. He said that there were lots of other little boys and girls to play with and he was having the time of his life. He said that he loved me and his daddy very much and that we weren't to worry about him any more. And then he said that he wouldn't be able to visit Luca again so I should stop going to see him.'

Luca wasn't a total charlatan then, I think. Thank God for this small speck of human decency.

From the expressions on everyone's faces, it's obvious that they finally understand that this isn't just a piece of juicy gossip, a good story. This is Angela and Ian's life – these unrealistic hopes and dreams are what they have been living with for thirty odd years. There are tears in Cynthia's eyes and I see Arthur get out his handkerchief and offer it to Vivienne.

Ian stands up. He puts his arms round his wife.

'I think that's enough now,' he says. 'We'll head up to bed. Goodnight, everyone.'

He helps Angela to her feet. It's like she's in a trance, not really aware of where she is but being carried along on the memory and her grief.

'We'll see you all in the morning,' Ian adds, and then he leads Angela away, her head on his shoulder and her back bowed, suddenly looking twenty years older than she had done at dinner.

There's a stunned silence around the table. I don't think anyone wants to be the first to pass comment on what just happened. Gloria and Vivienne, who didn't appear to have worked out what was going on at the start, look a little sheepish, but no one is blaming them. How is anyone supposed to know the depths of another's desperation until they show you?

Keith speaks first. When I hear him draw breath, I'm immediately worried that he will say something crass about what we've just witnessed, and I'm ready to leap in to defend Angela. But there's no need.

'That poor woman,' he says. It's the first time I've heard him say anything without barking it. Now his voice is genuinely sympathetic, gentle, with all its sharp edges gone. 'I can't even begin to imagine the pain she's been through. Is apparently still going through. And Ian as well. You can see what supporting her is taking out of him. You wouldn't wish it on your worst enemy.'

It's such a kind and thoughtful response to what we've just witnessed and yet from such an unlikely source.

Grandma speaks up then. She's been so quiet that I'd almost forgotten she was there.

'There's no pain like losing a loved one,' she says. 'I think we can all agree on that.'

We nod solemnly. Everyone is touched by death at some time. It's inescapable, a part of being alive.

'I think we might turn in as well,' says Frank.

He looks drained, like it's all been a bit much for him. Vivienne looks reluctant to leave the group, her FOMO shining through. She doesn't get up for a moment, but then, when it's clear that Frank will leave without her, she stands too.

'We'll see you in the morning,' she says in a slightly grudging tone.

And then they are gone.

The group breaks up pretty quickly after that and within ten minutes or so we have all drifted back to our rooms. Mel and I walk along the corridor with Grandma to see her to her door.

'Are you okay?' I ask her, conscious that she must be thinking of Grandad and hoping that he isn't far away.

She takes my hand in hers and squeezes it. 'I am, Emma. Your grandad dying was a shock, but he went when he should have. He'd had a good life and it was his time. When you compare that to Angela and Ian . . . well, you can't, can you?'

'No,' I agree. 'You can't.'

◆ ◆ ◆

Mel and I lie in our beds in the dark.

'Well, I didn't see that coming,' says Mel. 'I feel really crap that I set us off down that track. I just thought it would be funny, you know, telling ghost stories, lighten the mood a bit. Got that wrong, didn't I?'

'It wasn't your fault,' I say, keen to reassure her. 'I don't see how anyone could have known what was going to happen.'

Neither of us makes the obvious joke about psychics.

We lie in silence for a moment. I'm not sure what's running through Mel's head, but I'm feeling grateful. My life definitely has its ups and downs, but nothing that comes anywhere close to this. I'd assumed the old people on the coach were just rude and grumpy. I hadn't really thought about what they might have had to deal with until this point, how that might colour their outlook on life. I mean, some of them are rude and grumpy, but maybe we should cut them a bit of slack.

'I'm thinking this evening might have done some good, though,' Mel adds. 'You know, been cathartic in a way.'

'Yes,' I say, trying to make it sound as if it's a really good point well made. 'I'm sure it'll bring us all a bit closer together from now on.'

But as I lie there staring up at the inky ceiling, I'm not sure.

How can it ever be good for someone to be in so much pain?

29

THURSDAY

Did the house burn down?

'We have a real treat in store today,' says Robin as we clamber aboard the coach.

He wasn't at our ghost-story-telling session – better things to do with his time than hang around with his guests – so he isn't aware of how things have changed between us all. I wondered if he'd sense a kind of lightening in the atmosphere, but if he does then he doesn't let on.

We wait, like children at a birthday party, to be told what the treat is to be. He is grinning at us as if he might burst with the excitement of it all.

'The tides are in our favour, which means that we will manage to squeeze in a few hours on the Holy Island of Lindisfarne.'

Shoulders slump collectively around the coach. It hadn't occurred to me that there was a chance we *wouldn't* get to Holy Island, and from the response of the others I assume it's the same with them.

Picking up on the lack of buzz, Robin raises his microphone again.

'We're very lucky,' he confirms with the tone of a man who protests too much. 'The last tour I did on this route missed their chance because the tides were all wrong. But for us they're perfect. So, right now we're heading for our hotel in Bamburgh. There'll just be time for a brief explore before we come back to the coach ready to cross over to the island. We can then visit the castle and have a wander round the priory on Holy Island before coming back to Bamburgh for dinner.'

'Great,' says Gloria. 'Sounds like you have it all worked out, Robin.'

Her cheerfulness is starting to grate on me a little. Not the cheerfulness per se, but the fact that it always sounds just a little bit forced, like it's not really real.

'I do indeed,' replies Robin, matching her cheerful tone and raising her. 'So, sit back and enjoy the trip.'

There has been a switching of seats this morning, like some unspoken changing of the rules. Gloria has abandoned Arthur, who looks much happier without her stuck to his side, and is now sitting with Keith. Cynthia has slipped in next to Grandma, which is great. It's nice for her to have some company, and I've decided that there's more to Cynthia than I first thought.

I stand up and lean over the seats so I can say hello to them both. Grandma beams when she sees me.

'Good morning, Emma,' she says. 'I'm still so proud of you, you know, after yesterday.'

She looks at me expectantly. For a moment I'm confused, thinking she's talking about the ghost conversation, and then I remember. I saved Derek's life. Me! I give her what I hope is a modest smile.

'Come and sit with us,' says Grandma, inclining her head at the pair of seats on the opposite side of her table.

I slide out of my seat and slide back in opposite Cynthia, who is still nodding in response to Grandma's praise of me.

'Terribly brave,' she says. 'To do what you did, Emma. Terribly brave. I would have been scared that I would do something wrong and make matters worse.'

'I'm not sure how it could have been any worse, for Derek, at least,' says Grandma. 'He was lucky you were there.'

'And you stayed so calm,' added Cynthia. 'I'd have been all of a tizzy. I've never been much use in a crisis. I remember when I accidentally set fire to my house.'

It's such a surprising sentence that I almost giggle, but I manage to hold it in and concentrate on making sure that my face doesn't give me away. Luckily Grandma steps in to pick up the slack.

'That sounds very dramatic, Cynthia,' she says. 'What happened?'

'Well, I'm awfully fond of dried flower arranging,' says Cynthia. 'And I'd hung some allium heads over my stove to dry out. But then I was frying an egg for my tea and somehow the fat got too hot and set alight and then the flames touched the dried flowers and before I knew it the whole kitchen was ablaze.'

'Good gracious,' said Grandma. 'What did you do?'

'Well, that's the point,' replied Cynthia. 'I didn't do anything. I was in too much of a tizzy. I just stood there as the flames caught hold of more and more of my things.'

I can picture the scene so clearly. A kitchen ablaze and tiny Cynthia standing in the middle saying 'Ooh' and not doing anything. I hardly dare ask how it turned out, but I need to know.

'What happened?' I ask. 'Did the house burn down?' I appreciate that this isn't the most sensitive question, but I'm really curious.

'Oh no, dear,' replies Cynthia, shaking her head. 'That's the point. There were two lovely ladies living next door to me. Quite elderly. Older than I was, at any rate. And they smelled the smoke and came round to see what was happening. They came straight in and before I could say Jack Robinson they'd got the whole thing under control. Fire out in no time. The kitchen was in a terrible state. I had to replace everything. But the house didn't burn to the ground.'

'Thank goodness for that,' I say.

'Indeed. But my point is that it was their quick and calm thinking that saved the day. Just like you yesterday, Emma. Not everyone can stay calm in a crisis. It's a talent. You shouldn't forget that.'

Grandma nods her agreement. 'We had a couple of old ladies living in our street too,' she muses. 'I always thought it was lovely that even though they'd never found the right man, they were great friends and could keep each other company.'

Cynthia gives Grandma a pitying look.

'Oh no, dear,' she says. 'They were a couple. As good as married, really. I expect your ladies were too.' She says this in such a matter-of-fact way, as if it must have been obvious to everyone other than the very dimmest.

Grandma's hand shoots to her mouth.

'Well I never!' she says. 'That never occurred to me.' She's blushing slightly. 'All those years and I never once thought they were anything other than nice companions for one another.'

It would never have occurred to me that a couple like that weren't gay, but it's clearly come as a huge surprise to Grandma. But not to Cynthia, it seems. I like Cynthia more and more.

I go back to my seat, and Mel and I hunker down. Mel is quiet this morning, but I know her well enough to understand that it's nothing I've done and to give her the space she needs. I watch the countryside go by as the coach wends its way ever further north.

Behind us, I can hear every word of Gloria and Keith's conversation. She's definitely lost her shine for me because of the way she ditched first Grandma and now Arthur. She is talking at Keith, and Keith is making humming noises to show that he's listening. They seem to be talking about money.

'Of course, my ex-husband left me terribly well provided for,' Gloria is saying. 'He was generous like that, even after the divorce. I mean, he was rich as Croesus so it was no skin off his nose to make sure that I'm set up for the rest of my life, but he didn't have to do it.'

I'm sure this isn't the story she gave Grandma.

'I've always been a saver,' I hear Keith say. 'My father used to tell me, Keith, neither a lender nor a borrower be and you'll not go far wrong.'

'Very sound advice,' agrees Gloria. 'And I bet you've got quite the nest egg built up by now, a successful chap like you.'

'I don't do too badly,' says Keith. 'I'd have been a fool to be at the top of my game as I was and not to have put a pretty penny away for a rainy day.'

'Financially independent. I like that in a man. A woman in my position can't be too careful. There are some real rogues out there. They'd clear out your savings as soon as look at you.'

'Yes. You can't be too careful,' agrees Keith. 'Just take all this online banking. That's a recipe for disaster if ever I saw one. Who knows who is merrily clicking their way through your money? People giving out their bank details willy-nilly. That's never going to end well.'

'No. I quite agree,' says Gloria.

She sounds to me as if she's just agreeing with Keith to butter him up. I can't believe she doesn't use online banking. She's far too savvy not to.

'I try to avoid using banks altogether,' Keith continues. 'Cash. That's what you need. Cash will always be king. You know where you are with it. I always carry plenty with me. No need for cards then. I've got around . . .'

Then he drops his voice so I don't hear just how much cash he's brought with him. I can't help but think that carrying large amounts of money on your person and then telling people about it is probably just as dangerous as the online banking that he's seeking to avoid, but what do I know?

I am saved from any more of Keith's archaic views by Mel.

'So, what's the plan for Saturday?' she asks. 'Bars then a club? Shall we have food or not bother? Is eating first a really grown-up thing to do? We never used to think about food on nights out. I can't actually believe I'm going to be twenty-nine. Nearly the big three-oh. God, it feels so old.'

My stomach lurches. I still haven't done anything ab0ut Mel's birthday.

'Food first, I think,' I say, trying to sound more confident than I feel. 'I'm just finalising the details. And thirty isn't that bad.' I tip my head discreetly in the direction of Frank and Vivienne, who are sitting across the aisle. 'Things could be worse!'

'True enough,' replies Mel under her breath. 'True enough. Although I have to say that one or two of the old codgers are starting to grow on me.'

She shrugs as if this fact is hard to believe, but I have to agree.

'Yeah, me too. I'm not sure the feeling's mutual, though,' I say.

'Oh, I don't know. I think we're growing on them as well. You're definitely flavour of the month after your lifesaving antics yesterday.'

'I hope he's okay,' I say. 'Do you think Robin would tell us if he wasn't?'

Mel pulls a face. 'I doubt it,' she says. 'It'd be a bit of a downer on the trip. But he said yesterday that Derek was going to be fine, so let's hang on to that, shall we?'

I hope she's right.

30

DO YOU THINK THEY'LL SEE THE FUNNY SIDE?

The hotel in Bamburgh is nice enough and there's nothing about it that makes us think of ghosts or ghoulies, so that's good. I don't think we need any more of those.

Mel and I wait in the queue with Grandma. She's quieter than usual and it makes me worry that she's not enjoying the trip as much as she'd hoped. Hard though I try, I'm no substitute for Grandad.

'Is everything okay?' I ask her.

'I think I might scatter your grandad's ashes today,' she says. Her voice cracks a tiny bit. 'He loved Holy Island. It feels fitting.'

A lump rises in my throat. I'm not sure what to say. Do I offer to go with her, or is this a private moment? There's been no talk of Mum and Dad being there, so I guess she wants to do it on her own.

'Would you like me to come too?' I ask.

Her gaze rests on the middle distance for a moment, as if she's considering. And then she gives the tiniest nod of her head. I take her hand in mine and squeeze it.

Before I can ask what she has in mind, Arthur swoops in from behind and strikes up a conversation with her about the British and queues. Grandma makes a joke or two and I conclude that she's all right with everything. She can tell me her plan later.

We reach the desk and give our names to the receptionist. When I tell her mine, her face lights up in recognition.

'We have something for you.'

I throw a look at Mel, the corners of my mouth pulled down as I try to imagine what can possibly have been sent here. No one knows where I am. My head races from speeding tickets to Amazon deliveries, but nothing makes sense.

'What've you done now?' asks Mel as the receptionist disappears into a back room. 'Honestly, I can't take you anywhere!'

'Is this one of your jokes?' I ask her, narrowing my eyes suspiciously.

Mel shakes her head and looks convincingly confused.

The receptionist emerges seconds later and is totally engulfed by an enormous bouquet, a glorious confection of pinks, purples and blues. She hands it to me.

'They're in water already,' she points out. 'Which was very thoughtful of someone, when you're moving on so quickly.'

She's right. It is.

'Who's got a secret admirer, then?' asks Keith as Mel does that annoying *woooo* noise that teenage girls make when they want to draw attention to something and embarrass someone at the same time.

'Come on then, Em,' she says when she's finished *woo*ing. 'Don't keep us in suspenders. Who are they from?'

'Not a clue,' I say, genuinely flummoxed.

I put the flowers down on the counter and riffle through the foliage until I find a little envelope stuck to a wooden stick. I lift the flap, pull the card out and read.

161

To Emma, with our heartfelt thanks. We will always be in your debt. Kindest regards, Derek and Rita.

'Oh!' I breathe. I'm quite lost for any other words.

I pass the card to Mel, who reads it out loud for everyone to hear. There are murmurs of 'How lovely' and 'No more than she deserves' around me. My eyes well up with tears and Mel throws her arm around my shoulder and gives me a little squeeze.

'Aw, that's cute, mate,' she says. 'Nice touch.'

'Isn't it?' I manage.

'And when she had so many other things to think about too,' Grandma points out.

This is true. In and amongst all the fear, and being bombarded with information from the paramedics and doctors, and all those horrible 'what if's that haunt you at times like that, Rita was thoughtful enough to arrange this beautiful bouquet to be sent to me.

I feel kind of bad. I had Rita pegged as a dull and whingey woman, but I hold in my hands the evidence of how wrong I was. Again.

The main thing, though, is that Derek is all right.

'I know. We should set up an Insta page for the bus,' says Mel. 'We can post pictures and stories of where we are, and then Derek and Rita can see what we get up to so they're not missing out.'

'A what?' asks Keith, but I notice that his tone isn't as dismissive as it might have been if she'd suggested that a couple of days ago.

Mel replies with more patience than I might have expected. A rapprochement, maybe?

'Instagram,' she says. 'It's social media, where you share photos with your friends.'

Keith looks as if he might not hold with sharing photos with anyone, but then Robin steps in.

'That's a great idea, Mel,' he says. 'I can get a message to Rita to tell her, if you like.'

Mel throws him a truly blistering smile. She's clearly serious about winning this bet.

'Right. You're on,' she says. 'Leave it with me.'

Robin wasn't joking when he said that our look around Bamburgh would be brief. By the time we've checked in and I've got over the shock of the flower delivery there's barely half an hour left before we need to be back to set off for Holy Island.

'Have we got time to go to the beach?' asks Mel. 'Is it nearby?'

'Bamburgh's not that big a place,' I say. 'I think everything is nearby.'

The receptionist points us in the right direction and soon enough we are standing on the biggest, emptiest beach that I've ever set foot on.

'Wow!' says Mel as we take in the vast expanse of golden sand with barely anyone else on it.

As if we're suddenly teenagers again, we set off at a run, unable to resist such a huge open space. We race to where the sand has been touched by the sea and is firmer underfoot, a darker shade of gold. The wind is a bit sneaky and it whips our hair up around us, but the air is crisp and smells of salt and seaweed and the sky is a perfect blue, the kind of colour you see in holiday brochures for Greece.

'God, how perfect is this?' asks Mel, reaching for her phone and clicking a quick selfie of us laughing and living our best life. 'There's one for the Insta.'

I spin on the spot, my head thrown back and my arms wide. The space feels so liberating after the confines of the coach.

'Who knew beaches like this were even here?' says Mel. 'If the weather behaved itself, you could come for your summer holiday.'

You could come here on your summer holiday even if the weather didn't behave, I think, but I know what she means. This beach would put many others in our more usual holiday destinations in the shade.

Behind us Bamburgh Castle looms large, rising straight up from the grassy dunes.

'Imagine if you lived in there,' I say. 'How cool would that be? All those rooms to explore, and the beach as your back garden.'

'Our flat just pips it to the post, though,' Mel replies, grinning at me.

I think of our grotty little home with its threadbare carpets and peeling paintwork. Mel's grin slips a bit and is replaced by something more thoughtful. 'You know, when we get back, how about we start looking for a slightly nicer place?'

She eyes me, her head cocked to one side as she waits for my response.

For a moment I'm thrown, not sure of what I think or how to reply. Moving isn't something we've ever discussed, and whilst the flat isn't the most salubrious gaff in town, we've made it ours over the years.

And it's cheap.

Mel can see that I'm not immediately warming to her idea. She links her arm through mine and we start walking back the way we came, the wind twisting our hair together.

'Go with me on this for a minute,' she says. 'We're nearly thirty and we're still living like students. If this trip is teaching me anything, it's that you need to make the most of life. Look at Angela, still stuck in the past. Or Cynthia, jumping at her own shadow and apologising for everything. We need to take life by the throat and give it a good shake, see what falls out, otherwise before we know it, we'll be old too and taking coach trips to pass the time.'

This idea is hardly new. Who hasn't thought that their life is passing by too quickly at some point? But she's right that spending a few days with our fellow passengers is making me think about life a little differently. I don't know what my future holds, but when I reach my seventies I don't want to look back and think of all the things I wish I'd done. That makes me think about saving Derek, and what Cynthia said earlier too.

'I don't want to still be living in a dump when I'm thirty,' says Mel as we reach the path back to the hotel. 'I think we need to trade up a bit, invest in ourselves.'

She's right. And not just about that. There are a few other things that could do with changing too.

'Okay!' I say, surprising myself with how enthusiastic I suddenly am at the idea. 'Let's do it!'

◆ ◆ ◆

Mel and I are last back to the coach, but we're still fifteen minutes earlier than the advertised departure time, so no one complains. There seems to have been yet another switching of seats. Rita and Derek's absence has left a big gap between us and Angela and Ian, so they have moved to fill it. Gloria is still sitting with Keith but everyone else has shuffled up so that we're all at the front end of the coach. It's a good job it's not a boat or we might topple over.

Mel is on her phone, setting up the new Insta account. She's taken a photo of the coach for the profile photo and she turns the screen towards me for my approval.

'Shall I call it "The Coach Potatoes"?' she asks. 'Do you think they'll see the funny side?'

I have no idea. She does it anyway and then posts our beach photo.

'You do know you're going to have to give them all Instagram tutorials,' I laugh. 'I'm not sure half of them have even got smartphones.'

Mel shrugs. 'Well, the important thing is that we're trying,' she says, and I have to agree.

The coach pulls out of the car park and Robin leaps to his feet, microphone in hand, although we're all now so close to the front there's really no need for it. Unless your hearing is a bit dodgy, I suppose. Am I starting to empathise with my fellow passengers?

'So, some notes about the rest of today,' he begins, with his trademark smile firmly plastered on to his face. His cheeks must ache by bedtime. 'As I'm sure you know, Lindisfarne, also known as Holy Island, is an island.'

'Well, not exactly . . .' begins Frank, but Robin speaks over him.

'It's joined to the mainland by a causeway which is drivable for parts of each day. However, when the tide comes in, the causeway is submerged and the island is cut off until the tide goes out again.'

Mel nudges me and rolls her eyes.

'Well, duh!' she says.

Robin must have heard her, but he pretends he hasn't and presses on. I'm secretly pleased. If she annoys him, she's less likely to get him to go for a drink with her. For Mel this is literally just a bet. She has no real interest in him, whereas I've surprised myself by finding him increasingly attractive as the days go on.

'So, today, the tide will cover the causeway at five thirty. Obviously, we're checked into the hotel in Bamburgh so that's where we're going to spend the night. The coach will leave Holy Island at 5 p.m. If you're not on it, then I'm afraid you'll be sleeping under the stars.'

'I think I might quite like that,' says Vivienne quietly, and I register my own surprise at her daring.

'Oh, I don't think you would,' says Frank at once. 'You know how your chest gets.'

I want to lean across the aisle and tell Frank to stop controlling his wife, but I restrain myself.

'Now, I will be running a tour of the priory and the castle. It'll be a little bit whistle-stop but nothing that a fit bunch like you can't cope with.'

The coach fills with approving noises, as if they do really all believe that they're fit as fleas.

'Lunch will be sandwiches and soup in the pub near the car park. But as always, if you want to do your own thing, then that's fine, on the proviso that you're back here in your seat at five o'clock.'

I look at Mel. 'Shall we go with them or do our own thing?'

'Go with them?' she says, a question in her tone. 'I like Robin's tours.'

'Me too!' I agree with far more enthusiasm than is required, although my motivation is obviously coloured by how much I also like Robin. 'They're very educational!' I add in case my enthusiasm is suspicious. 'And I'd like to stick with Grandma. I think she's going to scatter Grandad's ashes today.'

My chest tightens as I say this and Mel must see something in my face because she gives my hand a little squeeze.

'Aww,' she says and looks at me sympathetically. 'That'll be lovely. I'm sure your grandad would have loved that.'

I nod, not quite trusting my voice, but I'm sure she's right.

31

Youth is wasted on the young, and all that.

I'm not sure what I was expecting the causeway to Holy Island to look like, but I can't help but be a bit disappointed. It's basically just a tarmacked road that cuts across the mud flats with stumpy white posts marking the way on either side.

As we approach, an ominous yellow sign warns us not to cross if the water has reached the tarmac, but the only water we can see is a few benign-looking puddles to either side of the road with ducks floating on them.

Halfway along there's a little hut on stilts that looks a bit like a lifeguard platform from *Baywatch*, but less glamorous.

'Cute place,' says Mel. 'Is it on Airbnb?'

Robin gives her one of his 'I'm tolerating you because I have to' looks. One point to me, I think, remembering Mel's finger-in-the-air strike the day before.

'That's a refuge for the stupid souls who they think they can outrun the North Sea,' he says. 'It's climb up there or die of hyperthermia. Or drown.'

Mel gives me an 'oops' look followed by a grin.

'It's a serious business,' Robin continues. 'Every year around ten cars have to be rescued. Drivers who think they can make it despite all the warnings. That's ten expensive call-outs to the coast-guard. When the water starts to come in it moves very fast. People don't realise. They think they can just drive through it, but you can't make it from one end to the other once the waves start to roll across.'

We peer out of the window at the mud flats and dunes and try to imagine what it must look like when the tide is in, but it's impossible. We'll have to take Robin's word for it.

'I could swim it,' says Vivienne.

I have rarely heard a less likely suggestion. I glance at Vivienne, stick-thin and stooped over in her seat like she's never stood up straight in her life. She looks as if she'd have difficulty climbing out of a bath, let alone swimming against a raging current.

And then I remember that very first day. Vivienne's interesting fact was that she had once swum the English Channel. Looking at her now, it's hard to imagine, but, unlike Mel, most people don't lie about stuff like that, so I assume it's true.

'Yes, of course,' I say brightly. 'I'd forgotten that you are a swimmer, Vivienne.'

'Was,' she corrects. 'I was a swimmer.' She looks out of the window across the sands that shimmer in the sunshine, her eyes wistful.

'Don't you swim any more?' I ask. I can't imagine having a passion like that and then just giving it up, but at the same time it's hard to picture Vivienne doing lengths.

'No,' she says sorrowfully. 'My knees went and then my back, and I have a weak chest these days. In the end, I just had to let it go. I still miss it every day, though, that feeling of cutting through the water, meeting no resistance. The power of it.'

'That must be hard,' says Mel, with rare empathy.

'It's shit,' replies Vivienne, and I start, almost jumping in my seat. The word sounds so jarring coming out of her mouth. I don't think I've heard any of them use bad language all week. And she says it with such force, as if it's harbouring decades of resentment.

'Getting old is shit,' she continues. 'Everything starts to let you down. Nothing works like it used to. It gets so that every day is a struggle. Just getting out of a chair can be hard.'

There's a general murmuring of agreement around us.

'Remember when you could see properly?' says Keith. 'When you weren't having to search round for your glasses just to read a label?'

'Oh yes,' says Ian. 'And hearing. I swear Angela has to say everything to me twice.'

'I do!' confirms Angela. 'Everything.'

'And don't get me started on my memory,' slips in Arthur. 'I used to be able to remember anything you told me. I could recite whole chunks of Shelley and Wordsworth. I didn't have a diary. Didn't need one. It was all just there . . .' He taps the side of his head. 'Now I can't remember what I'm supposed to be doing most of the time. I can't find anything to hold on to.'

He lets out a sad little sigh as the others all agree enthusiastically. Arthur doesn't seem buoyed by this sense of solidarity, however. As I watch, he drifts away from this conversation on the coach and into a private place in his head.

'Every day I think about what I used to be able to do, and then I look at the state of me now,' continues Vivienne. 'I wish I'd known what was going to happen when I was your age,' she says, pointing a finger at us. 'I'd have made more effort to hang on to what I had.'

'You're not wrong,' says Keith. 'Youth is wasted on the young, and all that.'

They all laugh, and the mood lightens a little as they continue to cite yet more examples of their decrepitude.

Mel throws me a sideways look.

'Cheerful,' she mouths, and rolls her eyes.

I hadn't thought about any of that, though, what it must be like for them. I've been impatient when Robin has had to tell them the plans over and over again. But what I saw as fussing was maybe just confirming to compensate for a shaky memory. And I had just assumed that they walked so slowly because they couldn't go any faster, but I'd never thought how that must *feel*. To be reminded every day of how much you have lost. That must be really difficult. I suppose it's not surprising that they get a bit grumpy. I would, too, in their shoes.

And then I remember. This is just the ageing process. I will be in their shoes one day.

◆ ◆ ◆

The coach makes it across the causeway in one piece and we park up and head to the pub for the lunch. Even though it's only March I can feel spring in the air. The sunshine is warm on our backs and there are people sitting at wooden tables outside the pub, their faces raised towards the light like flowers.

We are almost there when Grandma stops in her tracks. Her mouth opens and she stares at one of the tables.

'No!' she says. 'I can't believe it. It can't be.'

I follow her gaze and see a man dressed head to foot in black leather sitting at one of the picnic tables. A black motorbike helmet decorated with a white skull and a wreath of red roses rests at his elbow.

'Digger Hawkins as I live and breathe,' she says, more to herself than us.

'Who?' I ask, but Grandma isn't listening. She's picked up her pace and is heading directly for the leather-clad man.

As we get closer, I see that despite the biker's garb and the menacing black helmet, the man that Grandma seems to recognise must be around the same age as her. His hair is pulled back in a ponytail and he has a sharply cut goatee and a waxed handlebar moustache, but his hair is as white as Santa's.

When we're almost at his table and he stands, I see that although the leathers are straining a little around his midriff, he's in remarkably good shape.

'Phyllis Potter!' he says. 'That is you, isn't it, Phyll?'

Grandma is laughing now.

'It is. Digger! I can't believe it. How are you? What are you doing here?'

'I've come to spend the night on the island. I've ridden across so many times, but I've never seen the tide come in from this side. So, today's the day. What about you? Where's Stan the Man?'

Digger looks over Grandma's shoulder to see where Grandad is and then back at Grandma. He must work out from her expression what has happened.

'Oh, Phyll, I'm so sorry. He was a good man. The best.'

'He was,' Grandma agrees. 'And this is my granddaughter, Emma, and her friend Mel. We're just here for the day.'

Digger nods at us. 'Nice to meet you both.'

Then he sees that we seem to be in a larger group.

'Oh my God! Tell me it isn't true. You are never here on a coach tour for old people!' His face breaks into a wide smile and he starts to laugh, a generous round sound that makes his whole torso shake.

Grandma is laughing too.

'I am!' she says a little sheepishly, and shakes her head slowly. 'What has become of me?!'

Digger turns to me. 'We used to knock around together, me and your grandma and grandad. Raising hell and generally misbehaving.'

'Digger, shush,' Grandma interrupts, giving him a mock warning glare. 'Don't tell Emma all about our misspent youth!'

'No, do tell us!' I say. 'Misbehaving how?'

'Get the drinks in and I'll spill the beans,' says Digger. 'Mine's a pint!'

We order drinks and our soup and sandwiches from the bar and get them delivered to Digger's table.

'You know your grandad rode a bike, I assume?' he says, looking to Grandma for confirmation that he's not revealing any secrets.

I nod. 'Yes. Of course. A big black one. I always wanted him to take me on the back of it, but Mum wouldn't let me go.'

'Nothing bad would have happened to you,' Digger says. 'Stan was the best rider I knew. Could handle anything on that bike. Always could. Do you remember when we rode the Scottish coast path that summer, Phyll? He took those corners like he was suspended on a wire from the heavens.'

'And where were you, Phyllis?' Mel asks.

'I was on the back, of course,' says Grandma. 'I was always on the back. I just fitted there, tucked into Stan.'

'Are you still riding?' asks Digger.

I cannot imagine my grandma on a motorbike. Not now, not then, not ever.

She shakes her head. 'No, not for a long time now. Still got the bike, though. Locked in the garage. She runs like a dream.'

My head whips round to look at her.

'What? How come I didn't know that?' I ask, incredulous.

Grandma throws me a sly smile. 'You don't know everything, Emma,' she says, and I feel my cheeks go a bit pink.

'I'd take you for a spin,' says Digger, 'but I'm already a couple of pints in. She's just over there, though.'

He nods at a line of motorbikes all parked up against the wall. Grandma gets to her feet and makes her way straight to one of them as if she's greeting a long-lost friend. The bike, low and black with gleaming chrome, has a vintage look to it, not that I know the first thing about motorbikes.

'That's not the one you rode with Grandma and Grandad back in the day?' I ask.

'It sure is,' Digger replies. 'I've looked after her and she's never let me down.'

Grandma is running a hand across what I assume is the fuel tank. She strokes it as if it has feelings, and her lips are moving, although I can't hear what she's saying.

'She's still got it,' Digger shouts over to her.

'Oh yes,' replies Grandma. 'She always was a beauty.'

She comes back to the table and sits down. 'Would you mind awfully, girls, if I skip the tour and just spend the time here with Digger? Is that okay with you?' she adds, giving Digger a questioning look.

'You need to ask?' he says.

'Yes, of course that's fine,' I reply. 'Shall we see you back at the coach at five?' I wonder if I should mention Grandad's ashes but decide against it. Grandma is smiling. I don't want to spoil that.

Grandma nods and then turns to face her old friend and their conversation starts up at once, as if there isn't a second to waste.

32

I'm aiming for nonchalance, but I'm not quite sure I'm pulling it off.

We leave Grandma and Digger chatting away and follow Robin and the rest of the group towards the castle. We follow a path along the coastline that takes us past some sheds that are basically upturned boats. They're just crying out for an arty photo.

Mel obliges.

'Let's have a shot of all of us,' she says. 'For the Insta feed.'

The rest of the group look taken aback and then a bit suspicious, as if they don't quite trust Mel's motives. But after some gentle persuasion, we manage to corral them all together in front of the boat/shed.

'Say cheese!' says Mel as she clicks.

They all comply.

Mel checks what she's got and makes an appreciative noise. 'Nice.' She slips her phone into her jeans pocket and starts to walk towards the castle.

Cynthia clears her throat apologetically as she does each time she wants to say something.

'Mel, do you think you could take one of those for me, please?' she asks.

'Of course,' says Mel, turning back to the group. 'Pass me your phone.'

Cynthia rummages in her bag.

'Actually, it's a camera,' she says.

I can't remember the last time I saw someone use an actual camera.

'I just need to make sure I wound it on properly,' she says as she takes it out of its case and fiddles with a lever on the top.

'Ah, real film,' says Keith appreciatively. 'None of your digital rubbish.'

Cynthia throws him a muddled look, as if she's not quite sure what he's talking about. The camera being ready to her satisfaction, she passes it to Mel. Mel doesn't look entirely sure.

'It's just that big button on the top,' Cynthia explains. 'Just point and press.'

We all resume our positions, and Mel does the honours.

Then they're all at it.

'Mel. Could you . . .'

'Would you just . . .'

Cameras and phones are thrust at her from all angles, and it's a good ten minutes before everyone has the photos they want.

'We could just have airdropped mine,' Mel says as she hands the last phone back to Ian, but I get the impression that they are all happier having their own photos safely in their own devices.

'That was a nice thing to do,' I say to her under my breath as we continue to walk.

'Well, we need to have something to remember the old goats by,' she says, and winks at me as she uploads the photo on to the Coach Potatoes feed.

The path up to the castle gets a bit steep towards the end and the pace drops to Vivienne's, she being the slowest among us. I find that I don't mind. It's quite nice to dawdle rather than race for a change, and the conversation from the coach is still in my head as I think about how much of a challenge the hill might be for some of them. As we walk, I try to start up a conversation with her.

'You've mentioned Spain a few times,' I begin. 'Is that somewhere you and Frank like to visit?'

I might have said 'I hear Frank eats small children for breakfast', given the reaction I get.

'No!' she replies quickly. 'No, no, no. Absolutely not.'

And then she shuts up. There's not really anywhere to go from that.

Inside the castle the rooms are quite cosy and not at all palatial. The ceilings are low, cut across by rustic-looking beams and arches shaped like more upturned boats, and all the furniture is simple and practical.

'Maybe we could move somewhere like this?' Mel says with a grin.

'Not sure there are that many castles down our way,' I reply.

'Then we're living in the wrong place. They're two a penny round here.'

As we make our way through the rooms, Robin supplies us with his cheery mixture of facts and jokes, which really brings the place alive. I can see other people trying to listen in to him, and a couple even attach themselves to our group, until Keith gives them an accusatory scowl and they slink away.

'Cheeky blighters,' he says to Gloria.

'Aren't people incorrigible?' she says, rolling her eyes playfully.

When the castle has shared all its secrets with us, we head back down to the priory, which is reassuringly close to where the coach is parked, given that time is of the essence.

'It's almost as if he had a plan,' quips Mel.

Robin rolls his eyes at her good-naturedly. 'I don't just make this up as we go along, you know!' he says.

'I'm teasing, Robin, dearest,' Mel says, tucking her arm into Robin's and squeezing up to him. 'You are the best tour guide I've ever had.'

'And the only one, no doubt,' Robin says wryly.

'Well, that too,' she admits. 'Listen, Robin . . .' she begins.

I can see exactly where this is going. I think of my overworked Marigolds and dive straight in.

'What's that bird over there?' I say, pointing wildly towards the sea.

Robin turns to look.

'Not sure where you mean,' he says, scanning the horizon.

'Oh, it's gone now,' I say, trying to sound disappointed. Mel throws me her best fake dirty look, and I grin back. Foiled!

'Right, everyone,' Robin says, turning his attention back to the group. 'It's around forty-five minutes until the coach leaves, so that's just time to pick up a last-minute souvenir or two. You'll find lots of galleries selling work from local artists and potters on the main street, which is just over there. And don't miss the mead. I'll see you all back at the coach for departure at five.'

Mel and I pick our way over the ruins of the priory and go to the top of the hill to look at the view.

'That was a near miss back there,' says Mel. 'I so nearly had him on the hook.'

'Ah, but not quite nearly enough,' I reply. 'There's still every-thing to play for.'

Mel stops where she is and turns to eye me, brows knotted. 'Have you been trying to win behind my back?' she asks.

'Of course! It's a bet,' I say. 'I'm hardly going to roll over and let you snatch victory from me. Not with those seriously high stakes.'

I'm aiming for nonchalance, but I'm not quite sure I'm pulling it off. Mel holds my gaze for a moment longer, her eyes narrowed. I can almost hear her brain working, and then she releases me and starts back down the hill.

'Last one back's a sissy!' she laughs. 'And also possibly cut off by the tide.'

When we get back down Cynthia is standing on the path looking highly distressed, even for her.

'Oh, girls,' she says. 'I'm so glad you're here. I don't know what to do. I can't find Robin and the others have all gone to the shops.' Her eyes are wide and she's wringing her hands, rubbing hard at her swollen knuckles.

'Oh, Cynthia,' I say as we get closer. 'Don't look so worried. What on earth is the matter?'

She looks up and down the street, her eyes darting this way and that. Then she looks back at us.

'It's Arthur,' she says. 'He's disappeared.'

33

I SPOT A FAMILIAR PAIR OF HOUNDSTOOTH SLACKS.

'He can't have disappeared, Cynthia,' Mel says reasonably. 'The island is tiny. He must be around here somewhere.'

'It's not that tiny,' I reply, which makes Cynthia look even more panicked. 'But I'm sure he can't be far away,' I add quickly. 'We'll have a scout around, see if we can see him. Don't you worry, Cynthia.'

'He might be at the coach already,' Mel suggests. 'We'll start there. Is that okay?'

Cynthia nods. 'Oh, thank you, girls. Thank you. I didn't know what to do. The tide is coming in and we have to leave with Robin. What if we can't find him in time and he gets trapped here?'

She starts to flap again, the hand-wringing getting even more violent.

Mel uses her gentle voice, which I think is a first for this week. 'There's plenty of time, Cynthia. Don't worry. Why don't you go and have a quick look at the shops with the others? Me and Em will track him down.'

Cynthia nods again. She's biting her lip and I feel bad leaving her, but if we start the search with her in tow we'll still be on this spot when we need to leave.

'I'll go to the coach,' says Mel to me as we walk away. 'You start with the village. Text me if you find him.'

'Can you remember where we saw him last?' I ask, but Mel shakes her head.

'He was there when I took the photo, I think, but I'm not sure after that.'

Mel heads off towards the coach and I head towards the pub. I don't think of Arthur as a drinker, but this trip is turning into one long surprise.

Grandma and Digger are still sitting at the outside table, deep in conversation.

'You haven't seen Arthur, have you?' I call over as I pass by.

Grandma looks up. 'No. Why?'

'Cynthia says he's disappeared. She's worried about him missing the coach.'

'Do you need some help?' Grandma asks.

'No. You finish up with Digger. I'll see you back in the car park.'

I don't know where to start. Arthur could be anywhere, although most likely he's already back at the coach, as Mel suggested. Just as I think this my phone pings with a text from her.

He's not here. Going to find Robin.

I send a thumbs-up emoji back.

Arthur is the quietest of the group and, whilst he's always been a complete gentleman, I don't feel like I know him at all. Is he more likely to be looking at ruins or views? I really have no idea.

But I can't cover everywhere in . . . I look at my watch . . . thirty-seven minutes. I need a strategy.

I decide to head back towards the castle, which is where I think I saw him last, and I set off at a run. I'm hardly a gym bunny, but I find that I settle into a gentle pace quite quickly. Maybe I should take up running?

The light is starting to drop. It won't be properly dark for an hour yet, but the sun is very low in the sky and the clouds are beginning to turn a pretty pinky-orange. If I weren't under pressure I'd stop and take some photos, but there isn't time. I keep running across the grassland back towards the castle.

What will happen if we don't find him? I wonder as I jog along. Robin has been very clear about the arrangements. The coach would have to go and leave Arthur behind. Would he even realise that we'd gone? He has this perpetually bewildered look about him. I picture him wandering the streets of Lindisfarne, few though they are, trying to find us like a puppy that can't find its litter, and tears spring to the corners of my eyes.

I have to find him.

The problem is that the further I run, the longer it's going to take me to get back. I can only keep going for five more minutes or so and then I'm going to have to turn round or I'll miss the coach myself.

'Arthur!' I shout. 'Arthur!!'

It's pointless. There are only a few seagulls to hear me and they don't look interested.

He could be anywhere. I'm retracing the group's steps, but there are loads of paths all over the island. He could have wandered off down any of them. I might even be running in entirely the wrong direction.

My chest is starting to feel tight now and my legs are aching. I can't keep this up any longer. I look at my watch. It's twenty to five. Time's up. I take one more desperate look round, call out his name, and then set off in the direction I've come from.

The sky is incredible now, huge swathes of deep orange and red as far as the eye can see. I wish Mel were here so we could enjoy it together, although I suppose she can see it from where she is too.

And then, as I reach the point where the track I'm on joins the path back to the village, a noise cuts through the quiet. An engine.

I look up and see a motorbike coming towards me. Thank God. They can cover the ground so much more quickly than I can. If I flag them down, I can explain the situation and maybe they can find Arthur whilst I go back to the coach.

I wave my arms wildly and then watch as the bike pulls to a halt. I recognise the helmet with the skull and roses. It's Digger's. But the rider isn't wearing leathers. Then I spot a familiar pair of houndstooth slacks and a blue quilted jacket. The rider lifts the visor just as I say, 'Grandma?!'

This is my grandma on a massive motorbike! It takes a second for this to sink in. My grandma!

'The others are all on the coach,' she says briskly. 'You get back there, and I'll find him.'

'You'll miss the coach!' I say, but she doesn't seem to hear me. She revs the engine, does one of those wheel-spin-turn things that Steve McQueen does in *The Great Escape* and then she's gone, leaving me slack-jawed.

My grandma!

By the time I get back to the coach I'm a sweaty mess. I climb the steps and am greeted by anxious questioning faces.

'Is he here?' I ask, my voice breathless.

Robin shakes his head. 'And we have to leave. Tide and time, and all that.'

'But what about Arthur and Grandma?' I say.

Robin shrugs and shakes his head. 'They knew the arrangements. I'm afraid I can't hold up the coach. We have no accommodation on the island, and I need to do what's in the best interests of the group as a whole. Now, is everyone else here?'

He leaves me to walk down the aisle counting heads as if we're a bunch of kids on a school outing.

'But we can't just abandon them,' I say, more to myself than anyone else because I know there isn't really any other option. Robin has to decide between having all of us with nowhere to stay and leaving just two of us behind. It's Hobson's choice and he needs to pick the lesser of the two evils.

Dave starts the engine and the coach pulls slowly away. My eyes scan the area around us, desperately hoping to catch sight of them before it's too late, but there's no sign of either of them. We really are going to leave them behind.

When we get to the end of the road and on to the causeway the water is already very high. Those mud flats and sand dunes that we could see when we came in have already been submerged. The orange light from the spectacular sunset shimmers in the water and bounces back up, casting everything with a warm glow. It would be breathtaking, if my breath weren't already taken by worrying about Grandma.

What will she do? Does she have any money with her? Will there be any rooms free? How long will the island be cut off for? Will we go back and pick her up tomorrow? My head is a whirl of questions.

'At least she's got Digger,' says Mel, reading my mind. I'd forgotten all about him. Immediately I feel a bit better.

'Yes,' I say. 'Yes. That's good. He won't let anything happen to her.'

The water is really close to the sides of the causeway now. I imagine it won't be long before it's lapping over the edges. I'm sure

Robin's timetable has some flex in it, but it doesn't look like there's much.

Then I remember I haven't told Mel the most important thing.

'Grandma was riding Digger's bike! On her own. Just her.'

'Oh my God! No way!'

'Yes. I couldn't believe it when the bike pulled over and it was her. She looked so cool. She even did a wheel-spin thing. I had no idea she could do that. I mean, I knew she and Grandad rode around on a motorbike, but I assumed that it was Grandad who did the driving.'

Mel twists her face into something a bit sheepish, which is unusual for her.

'These assumptions,' she says. 'They just keep on tripping us up.'

She's not wrong.

But then, despite everything that I've been worrying about, a huge wave of pride rushes over me.

My grandma the Hells Angel.

Who knew?

34

OH, I'M SURE I WOULD HAVE MANAGED.

Dave gets us across the causeway and then parks the coach on high ground so that we can watch the water engulf the road. There's no way Grandma is getting back now, but at least she has Digger. I imagine them lying top to toe in his bed at the pub like children, but then that's too weird so I stop. Still, it's no weirder than seeing my grandma riding a huge black motorbike, I suppose.

And what about Arthur, who caused all this bother in the first place? What if she can't find him before it goes really dark and he has to spend all night outside? But he's a grown man. I'm sure he can make his own way to some shelter, but it's only March and the island is very exposed. Thoughts of hyperthermia cram my mind.

'It'll be okay,' Mel says, immediately understanding my worries without me having to explain them. 'Don't worry, Em. The people in the pub will know what to do. I bet it happens all the time. And when your grandma explains to them that she was only left behind because of her Good Samaritan act . . .'

'I know,' I say. 'But I shouldn't have got her involved in the first place. If anyone should've missed the bus, it should have been me.'

'I don't know how you work that one out,' Mel replies indignantly. 'It should have been Arthur. I mean, what an idiot, wandering off like that. He knew the deal. It wasn't like Robin didn't give us plenty of warning!'

She's right, and I don't understand what Arthur was playing at either, but he's not here to ask. We'll just have to wait until we're all in the same room again. Whenever that may be.

Then there's a shout from the back of the bus.

'That's not . . . Do you know, I think it is. Well, would you look at that.'

We stand up to see who's making all the fuss. It's Ian. He'd wandered down to the back seat to watch the sea through the big rear windscreen, but now he's bouncing on the spot and pointing wildly at the causeway.

'I think they're coming!'

Who's coming? And coming from where? It makes no sense, but I stand up to look anyway, and that's when I see a black motorbike powering through the breakers. There seem to be two people on it. Someone with grey hair at the front and a bigger person wearing a helmet riding pillion. I know what I'm seeing, but my brain is having difficulties processing it.

'It's Phyllis!' Mel shouts. 'It's only bloody Phyllis. Quick! Get outside!'

Mel and I leap to our feet and race to the steps and off the coach, the others following behind rather less speedily. Dave jumps out of the driver's side after us.

'Well, I'll be blowed,' he says. 'I've seen some sights in my time . . .'

And it is an incredible sight. The causeway is now completely submerged in a thin layer of water and the sky above us is entirely orange. And there, in the middle of it all, is my grandma on a black motorbike, riding as if she has the devil snapping at her heels.

We all start jumping up and down on the spot and cheering like there's no tomorrow. Mel does a few of her world-famous wolf whistles, and then Keith outdoes her by whistling even louder.

They are off the causeway now and racing up the road towards us. When they reach us, Grandma brings the bike to a stop with a little skid of her back wheel. She's grinning from ear to ear, and when Arthur takes Digger's helmet off, so is he. They are both covered in sea spray, especially Grandma, whose clothes and face are dripping wet. She doesn't seem to mind, though.

'Bravo, bravo!' shouts Gloria. 'You go, girl!'

'Talk about travelling in style,' says Ian. 'That was very impressive, Phyllis.'

'Hidden talents indeed,' says Keith, who is still clapping loudly.

I rush over to them both and grab hold of Grandma, not caring how soggy she is.

'Are you okay?' I ask her desperately, even though it's more than apparent that she hasn't had this much fun in years.

'I'm fine, Emma,' she says, and I detect the teeniest bit of irritation in her tone. 'It's not like I haven't ridden a motorbike before,' she adds.

I want to say that she wasn't seventy then, but I realise that actually it doesn't matter how old she is. She's just a woman riding a motorbike, and there really oughtn't to be anything surprising about that, so I shut up.

Arthur doesn't pass comment on how he is, but as it was his fault that all this happened in the first place, I don't actually care what he's feeling right now.

'When I said we all had to get to Bamburgh for the night,' says Robin, raising his voice to be heard over the general hubbub, 'I didn't expect it to be anywhere near as dramatic as that!'

He looks a bit pale. I imagine he'd get in bother if he lost two of his passengers to the waves. He's already Derek down.

'Sorry, Robin,' says Grandma. 'But sometimes, needs must.'

She turns to Arthur and speaks to him in quieter voice. It reminds me of how she used to speak to me when I got upset as a little girl.

'Now, Arthur. Shall we get you on to the coach and back to the hotel? You need to change out of those wet things.'

She puts an arm around his shoulder and ushers him towards the coach and up the steps, but she turns back and pulls a face at Robin. Clearly there's something not quite right, but we'll have to wait to hear what it is.

'What's she going to do with the bike?' Mel asks just as Grandma reappears.

'Give me two minutes to ride it up to the café.' She nods at the building on the other side of the road. 'Digger rang them, and they will look after the keys until he can walk over tomorrow and collect it.'

'Bless him, that's kind,' I say. 'What would you have done if the water had been too deep to drive across?'

I'm expecting her to look slightly panic-stricken at the thought, just like she usually does when she thinks about how things might have gone wrong, but she beams at me, her eyes all twinkly.

'Oh, I'm sure I would have managed,' she says.

35

IT REALLY WAS MOST INVIGORATING.

We only have one set of towels in our hotel room and, as Mel is in the shower when we realise, I volunteer to nip down to reception and get some more.

This hotel has a touch of faded glamour about it, I think as I traipse down the wide staircase to the ground floor. The carpet is woven with an intricate paisley design that must have been expensive once but is now threadbare on the stair treads, and the wallpaper in the corridors is linen or maybe even silk, but there are pale rectangles where pictures have been moved. It feels a bit like a Hollywood movie star whose beauty has lost its lustre.

If you'd asked me which kind of hotel I prefer before we set off on this trip, I'd have mentioned bougie little boutiques, all crushed velvet and quirky lighting, or the fluffy white towels of the big corporate chains. But actually, these slightly down-at-heel places have an unexpected charm all of their own. You can't help but wonder about the conversations the walls must have heard over the decades.

I add this to the ever-growing list of things that have surprised me this week as I hurry down to get the towels.

As I cross reception, I notice Arthur. He is sitting on his own, staring into the roaring log fire. I'm still ever so slightly annoyed with him for getting lost, but he looks so sad that I find I can't really hold on to my irritation.

Towels forgotten, I stop next to his chair, expecting him to look up. When he doesn't, I say his name. He turns towards the sound and then, when he sees that it's me, he smiles, but it's a doleful expression, as if he's only doing it to be polite.

'Ah, Emma,' he says. 'How are you?'

He seems like such a gentle man, docile and good-natured and, despite the thoughts that are clearly occupying him just now, he is still extremely polite.

'I'm fine, thanks,' I say. 'Have you recovered from your adventure today?'

I'm expecting him to make a joke at his own expense, and then apologise for all the bother he caused, but instead his face crumples.

'Oh, don't worry,' I say brightly. 'It doesn't matter. All's well that ends well, and all that. And I think Grandma loved riding that bike, which she wouldn't have done otherwise.'

'I was very lucky that your grandma was there. And I gather I have you to thank for that.'

'It was actually Cynthia who noticed you were missing,' I say, hoping that that doesn't make me sound uncaring. 'But I can move a bit faster than she can so I went to look for you. Then Grandma was faster still.'

'I really am most terribly grateful,' he says. 'I don't know what I'd have done without you all.' His shoulders sag and he looks as if he might cry.

'Hey, hey,' I say, kneeling down so we are eye to eye. 'It really doesn't matter. Just a silly little mistake. There's no need to get upset about it.'

Arthur looks back into the fire and shakes his head.

'You don't understand,' he says, and he's right. I don't have a clue. I can't see what can possibly be so bad it's making him cry.

'Then explain it to me,' I say, as gently as I can. 'Shall I sit down?'

I pull a tweed-upholstered armchair up next to his so that we can talk without being overheard.

Arthur takes a couple of deep breaths, looks as if he's going to start telling me and then closes his mouth tightly. Whatever it is, it's clearly not that easy to discuss. I just wait. If he wants to tell me, he will. There's no point trying to push him on anything.

After what feels like for ever, he has another go.

'The thing is,' he begins, 'this trip is something of an experiment.'

I'm not with him, but I don't interrupt.

'A month or so ago, I noticed that I was forgetting things. To put the bins out, or whether I'd paid the milkman. Nothing serious. The kind of thing that everyone forgets from time to time. Except I never used to. I'm quite a particular person, you see. I don't tend to make mistakes.'

This much would be obvious to a blind man in a dark room, but I don't say so.

'But then one day I went to the library to return my books and I couldn't find my way home. I stood on the streets that I've walked all my life and I didn't have the first idea where I was. It was so frightening, Emma. I didn't know where to go or what I was supposed to be doing. I found a bench and just sat there while I tried to work out what to do next. I think I sat there for a couple of hours, but I couldn't be sure.'

'Oh, Arthur,' I say. 'That must have been so scary.'

His eyes meet mine and he nods hard. 'Yes! Exactly so. After that I took myself off to the doctor and they did some tests and it turns out I have dementia. I know there's nothing unusual in that for people of my age, but I just never thought it would happen to me. You don't, do you?'

I'm with him on that one. I look at the statistics for all the bad things that could possibly happen, but I always assume that the one in three, or whatever, will be the other people and not me.

'So, as I say, this trip was a kind of experiment,' he continues. 'To see just what I can manage by myself. I thought that if I could cope with a holiday like this on my own, and without anyone else realising that I'm not well, then things couldn't be all that bad.'

It dawns on me then. He has just failed his own test. I blink my eyes slowly as I try to work out what I should say next, but when I open them again, I still have no idea.

'It happened again today,' he continues, although there really is no need to explain. I'm with him. 'I got separated from the group and then I got confused. I had to be rescued.' His eyes brim with tears and he takes a checked handkerchief out of his pocket and wipes them away. 'Do excuse me, Emma. A quite unacceptable display.'

'No,' I reply. 'It's not. It's a big thing, huge. It's only natural that you'd find it upsetting. Anybody would. So, what are you going to do?'

He sits forward in his chair and warms his hands in front of the flames.

'Well, I suppose now that it is apparent that I can't be trusted on my own, I shall have to confess all and tell the group that I'm a liability. I imagine it might be quite cathartic, letting my secret out. I've been carrying it around with me for a while now. I didn't want to be a burden, you see. I don't have much family, just a nephew and a niece. And they both have young families of their own. They won't want to be bothered with troublesome old Uncle Arthur.'

I want to contradict him, but then what do I know? His relations might not be interested in helping at all. But what I can do is speak for our group. After four days on a coach with them, I think I can safely say that they'll be there for Arthur.

'I think everyone will be really supportive,' I say. 'They're all such nice people.' I wince a little as I think of how much bitching Mel and I have done during the course of the week.

'I totally agree,' says Arthur. 'I will explain my quite indefensible behaviour over dinner this evening, throw myself on the mercy of the group.'

He smiles then, some of the twinkle returning to his eyes.

'And do you know, that was my first ever ride on a motorcycle. It really was most invigorating.'

36

I HAVE SOMETHING I NEED TO TELL YOU.

Somehow, we seem to have subconsciously decided to sit together at mealtimes now. It happens without discussion. We find ourselves asking waiters to rearrange the tables as if it's the most natural thing in the world, and they do our bidding with full apologies that they had inadvertently tried to split us up. Even Robin decides to eat with us, keen not to miss out on the buzz of the day, I assume.

Mel and I exchange quizzical glances as we all take a seat, trying to work out where we'd like to be in this new arrangement. There are still some places that would be preferable to others. I haven't quite made my mind up about Frank and Vivienne, and Gloria is a little domineering for my tastes. I try to loiter near Robin, hoping that maybe he will end up next to me, but Vivienne seems determined to monopolise him and I end up sitting between Angela and Mel with Arthur sitting directly opposite me, so that's fine.

I wonder when Arthur is going to make his confession, but he sits there meekly without making any attempt to command the attention of the table. Grandma, however, is a very different matter. She has barely sat down and I can already see that she's bursting to talk about the great rescue.

It's Ian who asks the first question.

'Well, Phyllis,' he begins. 'Where on earth did you learn to ride like that?'

There's a murmuring of approval around the table and Grandma sits a little taller in her seat.

'My husband, Stan, taught me when we were courting,' she says. 'He had a bike and he used to pick me up when we went out. My mother hated it, said I was making a show of myself in front of the whole street. Stan offered to go round the back so the neighbours wouldn't see, but I wasn't having any of it. I was proud of his bike. It was a beautiful machine. And Stan was such a lovely young man that my mother came round in the end. I didn't tell her that he was teaching me, though. It wasn't the kind of thing that young ladies did.'

She glances round the table a little shyly.

'Well, it's a good job you did learn,' says Frank. 'Or poor Arthur here would still be on Lindisfarne. What were you up to anyway, Arthur? Did time just run away from you?'

There's no particular edge to Frank's question, but knowing what I do I can't help but feel a bit defensive on Arthur's behalf. Arthur himself just waves at Frank and pulls a 'silly me' kind of face.

I'm keen to move the focus of attention away from Arthur until he's ready to receive it, so I ask Grandma a question instead.

'So, exactly what happened, Grandma?' I ask. 'Take us through it step by step.'

Grandma gets herself comfortable in her seat and sucks in a deep breath.

'Well, I knew that Arthur wasn't with everyone else,' she begins, 'because Emma and Mel told me they were going to look for him. Then Mel came back telling me that Emma had gone off to find him. And Digger, he's my old biker pal, the one I met in the pub . . .' She looks round for acknowledgement that we know who Digger is and I see something cross her face – pride, maybe, that she has such unexpected friends. 'He said it would be much faster to take the bike. Well, I wasn't sure at first. I mean, it's been a long time. But Digger'd been drinking so he couldn't go and it looked like Arthur might miss the bus. So I just decided to do it.'

'And what was it like?' asks Angela. 'Being back in the saddle after all that time?'

Grandma's eyes are shining now. In fact, all of her is shining. She's almost glowing.

'Do you know,' she says, 'it was just like riding a bike.'

Everyone laughs.

'Well, not exactly,' Grandma clarifies a little sheepishly. 'It felt far heavier than I remember. I thought as I rode off that if it tipped over I wouldn't be strong enough to pull her back up. And I was a bit wobbly at the start until I found my balance again. But after that it was fine.'

'I couldn't believe it when I turned round and it was my grandma on that massive bike,' I say.

'It's not that hard to believe,' says Mel. 'She's always been a pretty special lady.'

She winks at Grandma, who grins back at her.

'And how did you find Arthur?' asks Keith.

'I just retraced our steps,' says Grandma. 'And there he was.'

Frank opens his mouth, no doubt to make another comment about Arthur's inadequacies, but Grandma cuts him off. 'So you hopped on the back, didn't you, Arthur . . .'

'I'm not so sure about "hopped",' Arthur replies. 'I can't remember the last time I had to lift a leg as high as that. I'm surprised my hips could still manage it.'

'Well, manage it they did. And once we'd had a quick lesson on how to ride pillion we were off. We had a tide to beat!'

'I don't think I'll ever forget the sight of you both riding through that water,' says Ian, his voice brimming over with admiration. 'The sky looked like it was on fire. And the spray coming up from your wheels with the water all round. It really looked like you were riding on the surface of the sea, like a scene from a Hollywood movie. Incredible.'

Grandma twinkles first at him and then Arthur.

'Indeed it was,' she says. 'Indeed it was.'

The conversation finally drifts away from Grandma's heroic escape from Holy Island. Robin tells us a bit about the itinerary for the next day in Berwick-upon-Tweed. I can't quite believe it'll be our last stop. At the start of the week, Mel and I couldn't get to Edinburgh fast enough, but now that the trip is almost over I find myself wishing that we still had a couple more days.

Gloria and Keith still seem to be getting along very well. Maybe romance is what she's been after all the time, although if that's true then I'm not sure why she started with Grandma.

'Oh, Keith,' she says now in a voice loud enough that people on the neighbouring tables turn their heads in our direction. 'You are such a naughty boy. What a suggestion!'

I didn't catch what Keith had suggested, but from the raised eyebrow and mischievous grin I'm sure it wasn't entirely wholesome.

'Ew,' says Mel, laughing under her breath. 'Old-people sex. Get a room!'

Grandma is still glowing – her eyes shine and she looks a good ten years younger than she did this morning, although I can't identify what it is that's changed. The high that she must have got from riding that bike is coming off her in waves, though.

Ian seems fascinated by the whole incident and brings the conversation back to it.

'And will you carry on riding a bike?' he asks. 'Now that you know that you still can.'

Grandma looks thoughtful for a moment. The other conversations seem to drift away and now everyone turns towards her to hear what she has to say.

'I still have the bike,' she says. 'We talked about selling it, me and Stan, but somehow we never quite did. So I could have it serviced, I suppose . . .'

'You definitely should,' says Keith. 'It's a waste to let it just sit there, rotting away.'

The others all seem to agree, and there is much nodding and 'Oh you should'ing around the table.

'But . . .' Grandma continues, tapping a finger against her lips thoughtfully. 'I don't think I will. It's lovely to discover that I can still ride, and today was such a thrill, but just because you can do something doesn't always mean that you should. Being on a motorbike is wonderful. That sensation of freedom and power is hard to beat. But I'm not looking for that in my life any more. My needs have changed. And I don't need to hang on to the past. There are some things in life that you need to let go.'

I might be imagining it, but I think she's speaking to Angela here, although she's still looking at Ian.

'I think I'll get the bike checked over, but then I'll probably sell it. There's no point it rusting in my garage when someone could be getting joy out of it like we did.'

There's a moment or two of silence as everyone lets this sink in. I suppose letting things go from your life is something that our fellow passengers have had to deal with, being aware that they are doing something for the last time, that soon it will be beyond what they are capable of. Better then to choose the last time, rather than let whatever it is just float out of your life unintentionally.

It's hard to get my head round, to be honest. But I'm trying.

And then this is the moment Arthur chooses to tell us his secret. He clears his throat and it looks as if he might actually stand to address the group, but fortunately he thinks better of it and just draws his chair a little closer to the table.

'If I may . . .' he begins.

His eyes cast round for something to focus on and then land on me, maybe because I've already heard what he's about to say. I give him an encouraging smile.

The group switches focus from Grandma to Arthur. Cynthia raises her glass, assuming I suppose that we're heading for a vote of thanks, and then lowers it again awkwardly when no one else does the same.

'I have something I need to tell you,' Arthur continues. 'A small wrong that I need to right.'

The atmosphere becomes very hushed.

'I have been deceiving you all,' Arthur continues. 'It wasn't entirely intentional, but with the benefit of hindsight I can see now that I should have been more honest from the outset.'

Gloria throws Keith a sidelong glance, arched eyebrows arched even higher.

'I have recently received a difficult medical diagnosis. It has taken me a while to come to terms with what I was told. I think our young friends would say "process" it.' He throws me and Mel a fond smile. 'Also, I was a little ashamed about sharing the information, as if it were a kind of disgrace that I ought to be keeping to myself. And so that is what I've been doing.'

There's a warmth about the group now. You can see in the expressions around the table that as well as a fair smattering of curiosity about what is coming next, there's also concern and support for Arthur.

'But today,' he continues, 'all that went awry. I put one of the loveliest ladies I have met in a long time in danger. That was unforgivable. It was never my intention, but it was unforgivable anyway.'

I'm sure Grandma wants to point out that no one was in any danger, and least of all her, but she bites her tongue. This is not the moment to be blowing her own trumpet.

'And it has made me realise,' Arthur goes on, 'that no matter what my personal qualms, I have to be honest, if nothing else for those around me.'

He looks to his glass, but it's empty. He looks back up at me and sucks in a deep breath through his nostrils.

'I have dementia,' he says.

37

But we're not strangers, are we?

The silence around the table feels suspended in the air, fragile as spun sugar. There's a sense that no one wants to be the first to speak, but someone has to say something. We can't just leave him hanging there.

I'm about to pipe up, but then Arthur presses on.

'The condition is not very advanced, but I have had a few episodes which have given me cause for concern. I decided that if I came away on this trip I could show myself that my dementia wasn't yet life-limiting, that I was in control.'

He pauses, swallowing hard.

'It's apparent that I was wrong. I have no control over it. It strikes when it wants, and I cannot go about putting others in peril just because I am too much of a coward to face my future.'

The silence breaks now. Everyone joins in, denying that things are as bleak as he believes, making supportive noises. I wonder how genuine they really are, though. I bet Arthur wasn't that wide of the mark when he assumed that people would respond to him differently if he told them about his diagnosis. People don't like illnesses of the mind. Even now, in the twenty-first century, they still frighten us. We don't know how to deal with them, or what to say or do.

That's what it feels like now. Although there's a lot of 'Poor you' and 'I'm sure it will be okay' buzzing around the table, no one has said anything practical or even particularly honest.

Then Cynthia speaks.

'I think you're very brave, Arthur. I can't imagine how frightening it must be for you, knowing that at any moment you might lose a grip on the things you've always taken for granted. And of course, I understand why you might not want to share it. That's only natural. But you're amongst friends now. We've got you. We won't let you fall.'

This isn't entirely true – we have only known each other for four days and only have one day left to look after him in – but somehow Cynthia makes her words feel sincere. It's because she is so guileless herself. There is no side to her at all. When she speaks it is with total honesty and integrity and, as I think this, it occurs to me just how very rare that is in a person.

'Hear, hear,' says Keith, clapping his hands loudly. 'Well done, Arthur. But you'd better hold someone's hand in Berwick tomorrow. Can't be losing you again.'

My hackles rise at once, but before I have a chance to reply Mel is there, almost spitting in her fury.

'For God's sake, Keith. Show a bit of empathy, would you? You can be such a dick sometimes.'

Keith opens his mouth to defend himself, but then seems to think better of it.

'Sorry,' he says, and almost sounds as if he means it. 'That was a bit off-colour.'

Well, blow me! An apology from Keith! Aren't we all on some kind of journey all of a sudden? I almost feel the need to confess something myself!

'My brother had Alzheimer's,' says Vivienne in a quiet voice. 'It was so difficult watching him lose himself, knowing that every day another little part of the person I knew and loved was gone for ever.'

Tears prick my eyes. I didn't even know Vivienne's brother, but this is such a universal fear that I'm with her without too much of a stretch of my imagination.

'My gran has dementia too,' says Robin. 'It's been really hard on my mum. But actually, my gran seems so happy. She's given up trying to remember things. It's like she lives completely in the moment, appreciating the stuff she can see, like cut flowers, or the blue tits on the bird table. Even just the clouds. Obviously, it's still difficult caring for her when she can't do the simplest things for herself, but the fact that she smiles makes it easier for everyone cope.'

There's a murmuring of agreement around the table. I worry that all these sad stories will make Arthur feel worse, but there is such a warmth in the group now that he looks like he's taking comfort from that. And there is a sense of inevitability that the old people seem to accept, have come to terms with even. Maybe that's partly what they mean about getting older and wiser.

'The important thing is that you're well now,' says Ian. 'None of us know what's around the corner and so dwelling on what might be gets us nowhere. We should live in the moment. And with help I'm sure you'll be able to come up with strategies for the rare occasions when you get a bit muddled. I can't see any reason to stop going on trips like this, either.'

'And they're coming up with new treatments all the time,' Mel adds.

Arthur nods bravely, even though he must be thinking that there won't be a cure in time to improve things for him.

'But what you need to remember,' Mel continues, 'is that you aren't on your own. When I get scared about something, the very worst thing I could do is to try and deal with it by myself. That's why I have this one.'

She snakes an arm around my shoulders and gives me a squeeze, and my insides heat up instantly.

'She's always there for me, no matter how bad things seem. She always has been, and I like to think that she always will. Of course, she's not perfect . . .' she adds, grinning.

I'm most definitely not that, I think.

'But she listens and tries hard to understand. And when I tell her what I'm scared of it suddenly seems less scary. And that's how you should feel, Arthur. Even though we aren't your best buddies, I hope that just telling us, saying the words out loud, has made you feel a bit less frightened. Because if there's one thing I know it's that hiding from what scares you is never going to turn out well.'

'She's right,' says Cynthia, nodding her head sagely.

I see Grandma touch Angela's hand under the table. Angela flinches at the contact, but then she gives Grandma a tiny smile. Arthur is smiling too, a sad smile, but a smile nonetheless.

'Thank you, Mel,' he says. 'And to all of you for being so kind. I should have told you about it from the outset, especially you, Robin. I can see that now.'

He shrugs at Robin, who pulls a face that suggests that he agrees. He must be thinking about his public liability insurance.

'And I'll hold on to your hand tightly tomorrow, Keith. I promise,' says Arthur with a wink.

At least Keith has the good grace to look embarrassed.

◆ ◆ ◆

By the time we start to drift off to bed I'm absolutely wrung out. What a day!

'Bloody hell,' says Mel as we stumble into our room and collapse on the beds. 'Who knew that going on holiday with a bunch of grey-tops would be such an emotional roller coaster?! Can you imagine carrying all that angst on your own and not telling a soul? I couldn't do it. I'd have been texting you on the way out of the doctor's surgery.'

'I know, right! Poor bloke. I hope he feels better now that he's told everyone. Easier, maybe, to start the process with a group of strangers.'

Mel stares up at the ceiling and doesn't speak for a moment. I wonder if she's fallen straight to sleep in her clothes, but then she says, 'But we're not strangers, are we? Not any more. We're his friends.'

38

FRIDAY

THIS TRIP JUST GETS WEIRDER AND WEIRDER.

I wake up with a start.

You know what it's like when you have that feeling of dread in the pit of your stomach but you don't quite know why.

I run through all the things that might be wrong in my head, but it takes me a minute or two until I work out what's gnawing away at me.

Mel's birthday!

It's tomorrow, and I haven't done anything to prepare for it yet. I promised her a birthday to trump all birthdays to make up for my Valentine's Day disaster, and so far I've done nothing.

I need to get my shit together.

And fast.

I can hear her breathing on the other side of the room, deep and regular. She's still asleep. Well, that's something at least. I have some time to get things arranged. I reach for my phone and start googling.

We'll be starting her birthday in Berwick. I'll need streamers and balloons to decorate our room, or maybe Robin will let me string some around the coach. That might be better, as we'll see them for longer.

As I search for 'party shops in Berwick' I curse my stupidity at not bringing what I need with us, but of course that didn't occur to me until now, and so we are where we are.

Berwick doesn't seem to have a party shop as such, but surely there'll be a stationer's or something. They must have birthdays in Berwick.

I put that to one side for now. More important than the decorations is the actual night out in Edinburgh. We'd been talking about it the other day, whether we were going to go for dinner before we hit the clubs, but I don't think we reached a conclusion. That said, our drinking-all-night days are probably behind us. It would be folly to think otherwise. I should find somewhere nice to eat and then we can take it from there.

Mel stirs in her sleep and a pang of guilt runs through me. If this were the other way round and it was my birthday tomorrow, Mel would have the whole night organised already. She'd probably have made a spreadsheet and everything.

And here I am without a single balloon.

What a crap friend I am.

But it's not too late.

I can still redeem myself.

I just need to focus.

There seems to be a kerfuffle going on in the corridor outside. There's some shouting, but I can't make out what they're saying. It wakes Mel.

'What's going on?' she asks as she claws her hair off her face and struggles to open her eyes.

'Not a clue,' I reply. 'Hang on.'

I hop out of bed, open the door and peer out into the corridor just as the fire door at the end closes. Whoever it was has gone.

'Whatever it was, it's all over,' I say. 'Right. Shall I have a shower first?'

I've no sooner stepped under the water when I hear a knock at the bedroom door and then voices. My first thought is that we're late again and this is Grandma telling us to get our backsides into gear, but even though I can't see a clock I know that it can't be that. I've been awake since sparrow's fart, worrying about Mel's birthday and my lack of planning therefor. There's no way we could be late.

I try to listen through the sound of running water, edging closer to the door and straining to make out any words. I might be wrong, but it sounds like Keith. Weird. I can't hear what he's saying, though. Nothing important, I don't suppose. Perhaps some change of arrangement for later, although why that couldn't wait until we're all assembled downstairs I don't know.

Then the door closes and he's gone. I assume.

I speed through the rest of my shower, dying to know what he wanted, and am soon dripping on to the carpet in the bedroom.

'Was that Keith at the door?' I ask.

Mel is back under the duvet. 'Yeah. He wanted to know if we'd seen Gloria.'

'It's seven thirty!' I say. 'We've barely even seen daylight. Why was he looking for her?'

'I don't know,' replies Mel with a shrug. 'I told him we hadn't, and he left.'

'This trip just gets weirder and weirder,' I say, going back into the bathroom to dry off.

As I put my moisturiser on, peering into the steamy bathroom mirror, I almost ask her if she's thought about what she wants to do tomorrow, but then I decide that that will reveal how paltry my birthday planning has been thus far so decide against it. I just need to keep thinking and pull something spectacular out of the bag at the last minute.

No pressure.

◆ ◆ ◆

We're packed with our suitcases downstairs when we next see Keith. He's looking far more dishevelled than usual. His usually neatly combed hair is sticking up and I think he's still wearing yesterday's shirt, although I couldn't swear to it.

'Walk of shame,' Mel whispers to me, and I stifle a giggle.

'She's not in her room and she hasn't been down for breakfast,' he's saying to the woman on reception.

'Has Gloria really gone missing?' I whisper back. 'She's not got dementia too, has she?'

'Mrs Smith has checked out,' the receptionist says.

'Yes, yes,' says Keith. 'We're all checking out. We move on this morning.'

The receptionist eyes him and gives a little sniff.

'Yes, sir,' she says with exaggerated politeness. 'I understand that. But Mrs Smith checked out earlier. Much earlier. She has left.'

'But she can't have.' Keith looks quite manic now, his eyes darting around as if Gloria is hiding behind the pot plants.

'I can assure you, sir, that she did. I called her a taxi myself.'

Keith groans and runs his hands through his sticky-up hair, making it even messier.

'I think we may need to call the police,' he says.

I look at Mel, eyes and mouth open wide. What has gone on here?

The receptionist looks a little more interested now.

'Oh yes?' she asks. 'Has something happened?'

Keith's face twists so much that he looks as if he's in actual pain.

'No,' he says, in such an anguished tone that I'm almost prompted to go and give him a hug. 'No, thank you. Forget that.' He seems to gather himself. 'Thank you for your help,' he says, and then half-strolls, half-staggers back towards the lifts.

'Something has definitely occurred there,' says Mel. 'Shall we go and see if he's all right?'

There's a twinkle in her eye that definitely isn't born of sympathy for whatever predicament Keith finds himself in. Before I can stop her, she's followed him to the lift and is standing next to him. I dither on the spot for the moment, and then, just as the lift doors are opening, race across the foyer to join them.

The three of us step into the lift and the door swooshes closed behind us.

39

THAT'S NOTHING TO DO WITH BEING OLD.

We stand in silence. We're only going up two floors, but the lift is old and moves at a snail's pace. The idea that it might give up the ghost entirely, leaving us trapped in here, scuds gently across my mind, but I ignore it.

Mel speaks first. Of course she does. She's like a heat-seeking missile sometimes.

'Is everything okay, Keith?' she begins. 'It's just that I couldn't help overhearing your conversation at reception. Has something happened?'

All of Keith's numerous natural defences are down. He seems small and vulnerable. Getting information out of him now feels a bit like shooting fish in a barrel. I don't like it much, but my eagerness to find out what's going on overrides my qualms.

'She's taken everything,' he says, his hand clamped to his forehead and his gaze on his feet.

Mel throws me a glance that says 'I didn't see that coming,' and presses on.

'Who has?' she asks in the voice she reserves for dire emotional emergencies only. 'Gloria?'

He nods. 'I fell asleep and when I woke up it was all gone.'

I'm assuming he doesn't mean the pictures of his fancy rats. Then I remember him telling Gloria on the bus that he didn't trust banks and was a cash-carrying man.

From Mel's expression I can tell that she's stuck on the 'Keith and Gloria asleep in the same room' part of what he's said. That is intriguing in its own right, but this is not the moment to focus on it.

'Did she steal from you?' I ask as the lift door opens, revealing the shabby-chic corridor beyond.

Keith nods, such a small gesture that it would be easy to miss. I actually feel sorry for him, which I never thought I'd say at the start of the week.

'She went through my things and found where I keep my cash,' he continues. 'I'm travelling on through Scotland for a few weeks after this trip ends. Or I was. I had money with me to cover that.'

I hardly dare ask how much.

'It was in the safe until last night,' he carries on. 'But I was packing ready to leave when she knocked on my door. I have a laminated checklist, you see, so I don't ever leave anything behind, and I'd just reached "Contents of the safe".'

I feel Mel's body tighten next to me as she stifles a giggle, and I studiously ignore her.

'And then she was so . . .'

He doesn't finish this sentence, leaving us to imagine what Gloria had done to distract his attention from his laminated list, but it doesn't take that much effort. We've seen his Jilly Cooper novel and his photos. For all that Keith comes across as rude and blustering, underneath there seems to be a gentle and possibly quite lonely man. And this is what Gloria has exploited.

We reach his bedroom door. It stands wide, as if he just rushed straight out. So much for his security systems, I think.

We follow him inside. His case lies open on the bed, all neatly packed like it was when we saw it in Durham on Tuesday. The safe in the wardrobe is gaping, and as empty as a nest in December.

'We should call the police,' I say. 'Report it. They might catch her before she gets too far.'

I'm thinking APBs and roadblocks like you see on the telly, but Keith is shaking his head.

'And have the world see what a foolish, gullible, vain old man I am? No. Let her have the money, if that's all she wanted.'

He slumps on to the bed, holds his head in his hands.

'I should have known,' he says. 'It's my own stupid fault. I should have known that someone like her wouldn't be interested in someone like me. I let my ego cloud my judgement.'

Well, we've all been there, I think, and it's nothing to do with being old. It's to do with being human.

'And it wasn't the first time she'd tried,' he adds. 'I'm sure someone was in my room earlier in the week, but the money was safely locked away then. She had to bide her time, pick her moment.'

Our childish pranks of Tuesday night seem pathetic now, but I'm not going to let on that it was us and not Gloria who had been nosing around his private space.

'Shall we tell Robin?' I ask.

Keith jerks upright, apparently horrified by the idea.

'No!' he almost shouts. And then, 'Please don't. I'd rather the others didn't know what an idiot I've been. I do have a modicum of pride.'

I nod. I get this. I've made a fool of myself often enough to recognise the need to keep it to yourself.

'Why don't we tell Robin that she had a family emergency and had to leave in a rush?' Mel suggests. 'We can say that she knocked on our door early to tell us and asked us to tell him.'

Keith lets out a little sigh of relief.

'Yes,' he says. 'That would be good. As long as you don't mind telling a lie.'

Mel grins and rolls her eyes. 'Well, it wouldn't be the first time, would it?' she says.

But this feels all kind of wrong to me and I can't help but intervene.

'If we do that, though, she'll be able to do it again to someone else,' I say. 'She's been working her way through the coach. She's clearly a pro.'

Keith raises his head, interested in what I'm saying despite his misery.

'What do you mean?' he says.

Now I've said this out loud, I'm less sure of myself, but Keith's expression is telling me that he needs to be able to salvage something here, something that will make what he has allowed to happen appear less foolish.

'Well,' I begin, 'I may be wrong, but it looked to me that she started with Grandma. But then Grandma told her that her house was only small and that she didn't really have much money. Gloria seemed to lose interest in her after that. We thought she was just a snob, but maybe this is a better explanation.'

Keith is nodding, considering what I'm saying, and it starts to sound less far-fetched as a theory. I press on.

'And then there was Arthur. Did you notice how she kept stroking his knee? Arthur looked like he hated every second. And then she suddenly ditched him too. I don't know why, but maybe he said something that made her doubt he was worth going for. And then . . .'

I look up at Keith, my face settling into something I hope looks sympathetic.

'And then she settled on me,' he says sadly. 'And I made it so easy for her. I told her I carried cash. It never occurred to me that she might want to steal it.'

I shrug. 'I overheard that conversation,' I say. 'And she told you that her ex-husband had left her well provided for, whereas she gave Grandma the impression that she was a bit on her uppers following her divorce.'

Mel speaks now, clearly warming to my theme. 'Yes. And she was really odd when we asked where she lived. Do you remember, Em? Vague when there was no reason to be. Looking back, that was a bit suspicious too.'

'So you see,' I conclude, 'I think she must be a professional thief, which means there's no reason for you to be embarrassed that she fleeced you, and plenty of reason to get her stopped before she steals from anyone else.'

Keith lets his eyes stray from me to Mel and back again as he weighs up his options. Then he sniffs and sits up purposefully.

'You're right,' he says. 'I have to report her to the police. It's my public duty. Let's go and tell them at reception.'

The receptionist is most helpful. I think this might be the most exciting thing to have happened to her in a while. She rings the local police station and a couple of officers turn up ten minutes later, like they don't have much crime to deal with and are just waiting for someone to misbehave. They take a statement from Keith and then from me because of my 'pattern of behaviour' ideas. Finally Robin talks to them too. They don't seem that hopeful of getting Keith's money back, but Keith says that he just wants to stop her stealing from anyone else, and they seem to think that that's commendable.

◆　◆　◆

The coach is late leaving Bamburgh after all the business with the police. Mel and I decide not to pass on what we know about what happened to Keith, even though it is A1 gossip.

'I feel a bit sorry for him,' says Mel. 'He's got enough to deal with without being made to feel like a laughing stock on top.'

I'm not sure the others would make him feel like that. We're getting to be quite a tight little band now, what with all these confidences being shared night by night, but I agree it's not our place to tell.

However, we needn't have worried because Keith decides to inform everyone himself and soon the bus is all atwitter with the gossip.

'I always thought there was something a bit off about her,' says Vivienne, who has suddenly been blessed with second sight, it seems. Strangely, it didn't manage to save Keith in the first place.

'You can't always tell that someone is dishonest,' says Frank. 'They can hide it very well.'

'And we should know,' agrees Vivienne, and then blushes furiously.

'Some of the things she told me didn't ring true,' agrees Grandma. 'I should have realised she wasn't who she said she was.'

Arthur is too much of a gentleman to say anything rude about Gloria, but when Mel suggests that he might have had a narrow escape he looks quite relieved.

'You read about things like this in the paper,' says Cynthia, not quite able to keep the excitement out of her voice. 'But you never think it will happen to someone you know. Ooh,' she adds, 'do you think we should tell Rita and Derek? It seems only right. They would have been here, after all, if it hadn't been for the heart attack. Perhaps we could use your Insta whatsit, Mel?'

So Mel takes a staged photo of Keith looking outraged, which we post on the thread with some funny hashtags.

Then Robin arrives back on the coach. His curls are even more wayward than usual and I wonder for a moment about how it would feel to smooth them down with my hand. It's a short hop from that to imagining stroking his face with the tips of my fingers, and then touching his lips, and then . . . I pull myself back into focus.

'I have news,' he says, thankfully totally oblivious to what's going on in my head.

'I've spoken to a few of my fellow tour guides and it seems she's well known on the European circuit. She stole from someone on a tour of the Amalfi coast and again on Castles of Bavaria, both run by different companies, so that no one recognised her.'

'Well, of all the cheek . . .' begins Vivienne, as if she takes Gloria's behaviour as a personal affront.

Gloria and her exploits keep the coach humming all the way to Berwick-upon-Tweed. Mel and I discuss the scandal, too, in hushed voices, hunkered well down in our seats.

'How much do you reckon she took from Keith?' I ask.

Mel shrugs. 'A few grand, maybe. He said he was planning on being away for a while yet, and he'd need to pay for accommodation and food.'

'He's lucky she just took what was there. She could have played the long game, taken him for everything he'd got.'

'But that would have meant building up a relationship with him. I mean, could you do that?'

I think of all our encounters with Keith over the last week.

'Maybe not,' I admit, 'but he's not as bad as I thought he was on Monday.'

Mel sniffs, but then she has to agree. 'Yeah. They're all right really, aren't they?'

40

It would be our privilege.

It feels like we're entering a different country as the coach rolls into Berwick. Gone are the chocolate-box houses of Bamburgh. Here the architecture is more structured and severe, and the mousey-grey of the stone feels sombre and grown-up.

Robin is telling us about the border history, how the town has shifted between England and Scotland at least thirteen times over the years. I'm sure it's fascinating, but I'm not really listening. All I can think about is how I could possibly have failed to arrange anything for Mel's birthday and how I am going to fix it. The trouble is that as my feeling of inadequacy grows, it's becoming harder and harder to focus on the matter in hand. In fact, I'm almost entirely overcome by a blinding panic that is proving totally counterproductive.

'So, we'll be following the Lowry Trail this morning, for those of you that are interested,' Robin continues. 'As always, if you don't want to come with me, you are more than welcome to do your own thing.'

'I fancy the Lowry Trail, don't you?' asks Mel, and my focus snaps back to the here and now.

If truth be told, I fancy spending the time in a coffee shop and using their Wi-Fi to sort out a killer birthday plan, but I can't tell Mel that, so instead I smile and nod.

'That sounds good,' I say. 'But I thought Lowry came from Manchester.'

She raises an eyebrow at me.

'Who wasn't listening?'

◆ ◆ ◆

We get off the coach in the car park. With the departure of Gloria, our numbers are down to a nice round ten, which is a good size for a walking group. However, as usual there is a great deal of fuss about who wants to do what and with whom. Mel and I stand close to Robin to indicate our intentions and wait patiently whilst the rest of them go round the houses about their various options.

'I think I'd better stay with Robin,' says Arthur with a mischievous twinkle that melts my heart just a little bit.

'Sounds good to me,' replies Robin.

He pats Arthur on the back and then gives him a little squeeze on the shoulder as if to say, 'I've got you.' It's quite touching. Robin really is lovely.

Cynthia always sticks to our guide like glue, and eventually all the others decide to follow along too. Keith still looks totally distracted. I think Robin could have said that he was going to march everyone off the end of the pier and Keith wouldn't have noticed. Only Grandma doesn't look sure. She's glancing about her, as if she's trying to get her bearings. I forget that she's been to all these places before on her honeymoon with Grandad and probably knows where she is.

'Is everything okay, Phyllis?' Robin asks.

Grandma nods. 'It's just that . . . does your route go anywhere near the big bridge? The one that George Stephenson's lad built.'

Robin pulls a face. 'Not really,' he says. 'You can see it from various parts of our walk, though.'

'What about the lighthouse?' Grandma asks.

Robin's face lights up. He clearly doesn't like to disappoint his guests.

'Ah yes,' he says. 'We'll be walking along there to see Lowry's picture of the sea.'

Grandma looks thoughtful, as if she's weighing up a decision.

'I'm not sure what to do,' she begins, more thinking aloud than asking us for our opinions. 'Stan loved that bridge, but the end of the pier feels more fitting somehow.'

'Fitting for what?' I ask her.

Grandma digs about in her handbag and brings out a pale green urn, the one with Grandad's ashes in it. There's a collective drawing in of breath.

I'd forgotten all about the urn and seeing it makes me wince, but now my insides clench tighter still as I realise that Grandma must have been carrying it around with her all week and I haven't even noticed.

Grandma holds Grandad's urn to her chest and squeezes it tight.

'Today would have been our golden wedding anniversary, mine and Stan's,' she begins, and tears instantly spring to my eyes. I bite my lip as I try to stop myself from crying. I don't want to make this about me, but it's not easy to keep myself in check.

'Oh, Phyllis,' says Cynthia. 'Are you all right?'

Grandma holds her head up high and sniffs.

'I'm fine, thank you, Cynthia. You see, we were going to do this trip together to celebrate. But then Stan couldn't be here in the end, and Emma and Mel very kindly agreed to come with me so I wasn't on my own.'

Mel and I shrug and try to look like this wasn't a big deal. It occurs to me that this is the first time that the reason for our presence has been explained. Angela smiles at me in approval, such a tiny gesture that I might have missed it, but definitely there. There is a collective lightbulb moment around the whole group, in fact, as it dawns on them that Mel and I are here purely to support Grandma and not, as they might have thought, to disrupt their holiday. I think I sense a shift in atmosphere, although it could just be wishful thinking.

'As it turns out, you are all so lovely that it wouldn't have mattered,' Grandma continues, 'but I'm very glad to have Emma and Mel here too. Anyway, as this is our last day by the sea, I want to scatter Stan's ashes before we leave. I meant to do it yesterday, but what with one thing and another . . .'

Arthur raises a hand to acknowledge his part in all that, and Grandma smiles at him affectionately.

'I just need to decide where to do it, what would be best, what Stan would want.'

There's a pause whilst everyone decides whether it's appropriate to offer an opinion.

Grandma is stroking Grandad's urn, and that's too much for me. I let out a shuddering sob.

'Oh, Emma, love,' says Grandma. Her eyes are dry. She's so very brave.

'I'm sorry,' I sniff. 'It's just so sad. I miss him so much. And he'd have loved this trip.'

'He would,' Grandma agrees with a melancholic smile. 'I bet he's up there now, telling terrible urn jokes.' She is quiet for a moment and then says, 'You know, I think I'll come with you, Robin. Then we can scatter the ashes off the end of the pier.'

Robin nods and pulls the kind of face you might expect from a sympathetic vicar.

'We can make ourselves scarce and give you a little time, if you'd like,' he says, but Grandma shakes her head.

'I actually can't think of a nicer way to say goodbye to Stan than with the new friends I've met on this trip,' she says, smiling in turn at Angela, Arthur and then Keith.

'Well, it would be our privilege. And honour,' says Keith, his own troubles seemingly forgotten for a moment.

We pause. I wipe my nose on a tissue that Mel has discreetly stuffed into my hand.

'Right then,' says Robin. 'Let's go. Now, as I was telling you, L. S. Lowry liked to come to this area on his holidays . . .'

We saunter along at the pace of the slowest, but it's no longer as irritating as it was at the start of the week. Robin points interesting things out as we pass them, things I probably would never have spotted if I'd been walking at a more reasonable pace.

After twenty minutes or so, we pass a shop that might have birthday fare inside.

'I'm just going to pop into here,' I say. 'I'll catch you up.'

Mel gives me a questioning look, but I wave a hand.

'Two minutes. That's all. You carry on.'

I slip into the shop on my own.

41

A NICE BAG OF PICK AND MIX.

The bell above the door jangles as I enter the shop and I immediately feel like I've stepped back in time. It's a proper paper shop, the kind I remember from when I was a girl, with the newspapers and magazines displayed on shelves up one wall.

On another wall are row after row of glass jars all containing different kinds of sweets. Some I recognise – cola bottles, white chocolate mice, fudge. But many of the others have fascinating names that seem to bear no relation to their contents – dolly mixture, chewing nuts, poor Bens. I stand and stare, mesmerised by choice.

'Can I help you?' comes a quavering voice from behind the counter, although I can't see anyone there. Then a tiny old woman, blue rinse just peeping out from under a spotted headscarf, shuffles out. She's wearing a matching blue polyester housecoat, and on her feet are a pair of those slippers that look like they're made of carpet remnants.

'I'm sure you could,' I reply, 'if I knew what I wanted.'

This is exactly the kind of customer that I loathe when I'm at work in the department store. They wander in, stare at the displays, touch a few things and even ask the odd question, and then wander off without buying anything at all. But the old lady doesn't look at all bothered by my lack of direction. She just eyes me enquiringly.

'The thing is,' I begin, 'I've got myself into a bit of a mess.'

The most minuscule change in the woman's expression suggests that she's not at all surprised by this, but she waits patiently for me to explain.

I don't know if it's the stress of realising that I'm on the verge of cocking up again, or all the stuff about Grandad's ashes, but suddenly everything is just too much and I burst into tears.

'It's my best friend Mel's birthday tomorrow,' I start to explain through my sobs, 'and I've forgotten to bring anything to decorate our hotel room with. We're just here for a night and then we go to Edinburgh. I promised to give her the best birthday ever because . . . well, because I haven't been a great friend. But I've messed up again. And now I don't know what to do to fix it. Can you help me?'

It all comes out in a great rush of jumbled words and snotty sniffing, and can't possibly make any sense whatsoever, but the old lady seems to get it. She nods slowly, apparently considering my dilemma. Then she disappears behind some shelving and emerges a moment later with a bag of balloons, a selection of happy birthday banners in blues and pinks, and some party poppers.

She puts them on the counter.

'Thank you,' I say, more grateful for this meagre selection than she can possibly understand.

I pick up the balloons, two of the pink banners and a packet of party poppers and make a little pile of them.

The woman looks down at the pile, up at me and then her already wrinkly forehead crinkles still further as she raises her eyebrows.

'Not much of a birthday, is it?' she says with a lovely Miss Jean Brodie lilt.

I hang my head.

'No,' I admit, feeling like I'm being told off by a headmistress.

'I assume you have a card and a gift?' she asks.

Thank God I'm not that useless. There is a suitably amusing card in my case together with a lovely bracelet that Mel had admired on the wrist of a TV celebrity and which I managed to track down with the help of Google.

I nod by way of answer and wipe my nose on the heel of my hand like I'm some primary-school kid.

'Well, that's something at least,' says the woman, making me feel about two feet tall. 'Let's see. Does she eat sweets?'

Who doesn't eat sweets? I nod again.

'What about a nice bag of pick and mix?' the old lady suggests. She points to a string of pink and white stripy paper bags that hang from the shelf.

Then I have a great idea.

'Actually, could you do me ten bags?' I ask.

'Got a sweet tooth, has she?' asks the woman, as if this might be a cardinal sin.

'There are ten of us, on the coach. Eleven with the tour guide. Oh, and Dave the driver. Better make that twelve.'

'Do you mind what goes in them?'

She's climbing up on to a wooden stool so she can reach the higher jars. It can't possibly be safe, a woman of her age all the way up there.

'No,' I say, anxious not to make her do any unnecessary reaching. 'Whatever's easiest?' But then I add, 'But pear drops are her favourite so can you make sure there are some of those in every bag, please?'

'Right you are. And I'll put you light things in, so you get more for your money,' she says, as she reaches for a jar of white chocolate discs speckled in multicoloured sugar balls. 'Aren't you a wee bit young for a coach trip?'

'We've come with my grandma,' I say, hoping that explains everything.

'I'll not be putting any toffees in then,' she says, completely deadpan. 'Plays havoc with the dentures.'

I can see that this is going to take for ever.

'Would it be okay if I popped back for them?' I ask, hoping she isn't offended by the implied criticism. 'I need to catch the others up. They're following the Lowry Trail.'

'Aye,' she says. 'That'd be best. Have you got a cake?'

Shit! I hadn't even thought about a cake. My bottom lip wobbles and I shake my head dolefully.

'Call in at the bakery three doors down. My friend Pat is a marvel with a piping bag. She'll rustle you something up. Tell her Enid sent you. I'll add some candles to your order and you can collect them all when you come back round. Where are you staying?'

I give her name of the hotel.

'Tell you what. I'll send my wee grandson round with everything. And the cake. Easier than carrying it.'

I'm so grateful to her that it almost sets me off crying all over again.

'Off you go now,' she says. 'Don't forget. Tell Pat that you've come from Enid.'

'Thank you!!!' I say. 'Thank you so much.'

And then I skip out of the shop to find Pat.

42

CONSIDER IT DONE.

The bakery is three doors down, just as Enid described. It too has a gentle old-fashioned air about it. The window is filled with rustic-looking buns and cakes. None of your fancy French patisserie here.

I open the door and go in, feeling more hopeful after my encounter with Enid, but there's a man behind the counter. Could this be Pat? Have I just assumed Pat must be a woman because they bake? But then I remember that Enid called her 'she' most distinctly.

'Can I help you?' he asks. His accent is more Geordie than Scottish.

'Is Pat in?' I ask doubtfully.

'Pat!' he shouts at full volume without turning his head, so I get the full blast of it. 'Someone wants you.'

Then he stands and stares at me until I feel awkward and start fiddling with my bag.

Moments later a woman appears. She's younger and less fragile-looking than Enid, but still looks as if retirement age might have been and gone for her.

'Can I help you?' she asks in a similar accent to the man.

I'm suddenly aware that my eye make-up might now have dribbled down my cheeks and I rub at the skin below my eyes just in case.

'Enid from the paper shop sent me,' I begin, thinking that it all sounds a bit like a low-budget spy film. 'I find myself in need of a birthday cake. It's a bit of an emergency.'

Pat's eyes light up. Clearly emergencies are welcome around here.

'Tell me more, pet,' she says.

So I explain my dire situation. She nods along, showing that's she's following me, and she seems more sympathetic to my plight than Enid was.

'And when would you be wanting to eat this cake?' she asks.

'Tomorrow. But we're only here for the night and we'll leave early in the morning so I could really do with it today.'

'I have just the thing,' says Pat. 'I've cakes in the freezer. Bit hard to eat today but will have thawed out nicely by tomorrow. I can ice one, though, and the cake will keep it fresh as it defrosts. Victoria sponge or chocolate?'

'Chocolate,' I say, relief making my knees weak. 'Oh, thank you. You're a true lifesaver.'

Her smile suggests that saving lives is all part of the service.

'And what shall I write on the top?'

'Happy Birthday, Mel?' I suggest, wondering if that might be too many letters.

'Consider it done. Will you collect it later or will I have this great lummox drop it round?' She nods her head at the man who served me and who I imagine now must be her son.

'Actually, Enid said her grandson would bring it to the hotel,' I say, hoping that this doesn't offend anyone.

'Much better idea,' replies Pat. 'Far more chance of it getting there in one piece.'

I glance at the son out of the corner of my eye, but if her comments have offended him, he's not letting on.

'Thank you,' I say. 'You have no idea how grateful I am. What do I owe you?'

We settle up and I leave the shop feeling considerably lighter than when I entered it. Now I just need to catch up with the others. I have no idea where they might be. But I know a woman who might.

I pop my head back round Enid's door.

'All sorted with Pat?' she asks when she sees me.

'Yes. Thanks so much.'

'I'll get Archie to drop everything off at your hotel. You can pay him when he comes.'

My heart might burst at the kindness of these strangers, but instead I gush yet more thank-yous.

'I don't suppose you know which way the Lowry Trail goes next?' I ask her. 'I need to catch up with my party.'

'Old people, you said?'

I nod.

'They don't walk fast. Won't have got further than the pier. Left out of here, follow the road down to the river and then follow your nose. They're heading for the lighthouse. You can't miss it.'

Yet more thanks ensue. I'm just leaving when she calls after me, 'Good luck tomorrow.'

◆ ◆ ◆

I race down the street and soon find myself on the path by the river. Even though it feels like I've been with Enid and Pat for ages, I can make out Robin's red jacket followed by a little gaggle of people not that far ahead. I should be able to catch them before they reach the lighthouse. I don't want to miss the scattering of Grandad's ashes.

As I half-walk, half-run along the path, it occurs to me how unlikely I would have been to find either a Pat or an Enid if I'd been in Leeds. Yes, there would have been a wider range of celebratory birthday options available, but I doubt I would have got anywhere near the same level of service from some bored shop girl who didn't want to be there in the first place.

When I reach the group, Robin is explaining that ships have been trying to land in the harbour of the Tweed estuary for two thousand years.

'You'd have thought they'd have got the hang of it by now,' quips Frank, and then looks round the group for validation of his supposedly amusing comment. Vivienne lets out a shrill little laugh, but no one else reacts. Keith still looks as if his world has ended and Grandma has a distant air about her, as if she's not really there at all.

Mel throws me a questioning look. She must have wondered what I've been up to. I tap the side of my nose knowingly. She grins back at me, and my insides clench again, although not quite as tightly as they did earlier.

It's a fair way to the end of the pier, particularly at the pace we're managing, but the lighthouse calls to us, its red and white paint like a candy cane in the sea. Robin keeps up his cheery commentary, but today the group feels subdued and sombre. Even though I can't condone what Gloria did, she certainly livened things up a bit. Without her among us it's a bit like someone has turned the colour down.

I alter my pace until I'm walking next to Grandma.

'Okay?' I ask under my breath, and she smiles bravely.

I give her arm a little squeeze and gird myself.

I suspect this isn't going to be easy for any of us.

43

PETER KAY SHE IS NOT.

The seagulls are wheeling over our heads, calling out in that plaintive way they have. We finally reach the lighthouse, and Robin tells us that it's a Grade II listed building, but no one is really listening. We're all too aware of what is about to happen.

Angela looks very pale. She's gripping on to Ian's arm so tightly that it's making it hard for him to stand upright. I hadn't thought that scattering Grandad's ashes might be difficult for them too. Then again, isn't saying goodbye to a loved one difficult for everyone? We've all lost someone in our lives, or fear that we may soon. Having empathy for another person in that situation is part of what makes us human.

Grandma reaches into her bag and pulls out the pale green urn. My chest starts to tighten and I swallow hard. I can feel Mel linking her arm through mine as I try to keep myself in check. I don't want to fall apart, not when Grandma is being so strong, but it's not easy. Even though Grandad has been gone for months and I've had plenty of time to get used to the idea, there is something so final about this last moment of his physical time on earth. When

Grandma opens the urn and his ashes float away on the breeze, then he really will be gone for ever.

A hush falls across us. We seem to have arranged ourselves in a kind of semicircle around Grandma as she stands, her back to the lapping waves. I pinch my lips tightly together and stick my nails into my palm to stop myself from crying.

Grandma has been staring hard at the urn, but now she raises her eyes to look at us. She's smiling – not a tearful, brave kind of smile but the real McCoy, broad from ear to ear.

'I wish you'd known my Stan,' she begins. 'He was such a lovely fella. He could be a bit gruff. Well, show me the man that can't. But his bark was much worse than his bite. And he barely ever barked, not at me, anyhow.' Her smile softens into something fonder as she remembers. 'And he told terrible jokes. Didn't he, Emma?'

She looks over to me for confirmation and I nod my head, and then I smile too because the thought of Grandad's relentless joke-telling is funnier than most of his jokes ever were.

'He even gave me a joke for today. He told me I had to save it for this very moment. He was always doing silly stuff like that. But I remembered and so here we are.'

She removes a square of paper from her purse and opens it out with a flick of her wrist.

'You'll have to forgive my delivery. I've never had Stan's sense of timing.'

Then she begins to read, her forehead lined with concentration. Peter Kay she is not.

'I hear you can get glass urns these days,' she begins. Then she pauses, makes eye contact with me for a microsecond and then looks back at the paper.

'How will they go down? Remains to be seen!'

Keith laughs roundly and then immediately stifles it, but Grandma grins at him and shakes her head.

'No, no, Keith. You laugh away. Stan would have loved that. He adored playing to the crowd.'

Keith lets his face slide into a smile, even though he looks slightly uncomfortable about it.

'I miss his jokes,' Grandma continues. 'I've spent most of my life groaning at them, but now they don't come any more I realise how they kept things light between us. Even when I could cheerfully have strangled Stan for something he'd done, he'd tell one of his jokes and it took all the heat out of it. And it's taught me something, that has. We only get one life, and it's better to spend it smiling than frowning. Not that that's always easy. I know that as well as the next person. But I'd rather smile at what I've had and lost than be sad that it's gone. Youth, health, husbands. All of them slip away eventually. We can't stop that. I'm getting old, no matter what fancy face creams I use to try and delay it. And we can't stop those we love leaving us too soon. But what we can do it make sure that we make the most of what we still have.'

Grandma focuses her attention directly on Angela, as if it's her that she's talking to. I hardly dare look at Angela myself. It feels like such a private moment, but I can't help myself, and I think I see something pass between the pair of them, a kind of understanding, maybe.

'Stan would have loved seeing me on the back of Digger's bike yesterday,' Grandma continues. 'As me and Arthur raced through those waves, I could hear Stan in my ear. "Go on, my girl! You can do it!" And he was right. I could. And I did. And I can do this too.'

She turns her back on us and steps towards the edge of the pier, unscrewing the urn as she goes. I'd wondered before we got here if she'd want me to throw some too. I wasn't entirely comfortable with that, couldn't get my head round the idea of having Grandad in my hands. But then I'd got distracted, wondering about whether you did actually hold the ashes or just scatter them from a container, and I'd stopped thinking about Grandad and never reached a conclusion.

But while this is all running through my head, Grandma shakes the urn at the water without asking me to help.

A little cloud of dust hovers in the air for a moment, and then it gets caught by the breeze and is gone.

44

How wrong we all were.

Our mood should be subdued after we scatter Grandad's ashes, but somehow Grandma has managed to make it a joyful occasion, and as we walk back towards the city walls we are quite a jolly little group. Grandma is walking with Angela. They seem to be deep in conversation, which has allowed Ian, usually right by Angela's side in case she needs support, to drift back and walk with Keith and Frank. I can hear him explaining how modern online banking works to a disbelieving Keith.

Mel is walking with Cynthia. I can't catch what they are talking about, but it involves a lot of giggling and I hear Mel swear more than once, which makes Cynthia giggle all the more.

We've come a long way since Monday, not just geographically but also in our understanding of one another, and my insides squirm a bit when I think about how difficult Mel was at the start and how I let her be. We thought we had the measure of old people, and they of us, to be fair. How wrong we all were.

I'm aware of someone hurrying up behind me and then regulating their pace to mine, and when I look up it's Robin. My stomach flips and my hand automatically goes to try and straighten my wind-blown hair before I realise what I'm doing. I hope I'm not blushing too badly, but as we're walking side by side I don't suppose he'll notice.

'Hi, Emma,' he says. 'That was nice before, with your grandad's ashes.'

'Yes,' I reply. 'He would have approved. And have you heard anything more about Derek?'

'No, but I assume no news is good news. And can I just say . . .' He looks at me through his tangle of curls. 'I was so impressed by what you did.'

My heart does a little flutter but I'm not sure that's because someone has praised me or because Robin has praised me.

'Thanks,' I say. 'But it was nothing really. Anyone could have done it. I just happened to be in the right place at the right time.'

'But that's just it. I'm not sure anyone could have done it. I've done all the first-aid training. They make you when you get the job. But I've never had to use the CPR stuff. And, well, I'm not sure I could.'

'Of course you could,' I say modestly, but I know exactly what he's talking about. If you'd asked me if I could do CPR on Monday, I'd have said that I didn't know too.

'We all prepare for the bad stuff, but I wonder, when the chips are down, how many of us could actually do the necessary. You don't have other medical training, do you?'

'God no!' I say, with maybe a little bit too much emphasis. 'No, I dress shop windows for a living.'

'Oh yes, I remember you saying at the cream tea. Sounds interesting.'

I pull a face. 'It sounds more interesting than it actually is,' I say. 'And I just kind of fell into it after uni. It wasn't a career choice or anything. And what about you? Are you filling in time until the right job comes along too?'

Robin's face tells me that I'm wide of the mark before he can.

'No. Not at all. I love my job. I bounce out of bed each morning thinking about how I can make my tours better than they were the day before.'

Is he teasing me? I decide he probably is. I've always been a bit gullible. Mel is constantly telling me to look for the angle, but somehow it always passes me by.

'Ha. Yes, I hear you. But we have to work to pay the bills, eh?' I give a little resigned shrug and hope that he doesn't realise that I believed him to start with.

He turns his head and looks at me with a crinkled forehead, like I've just really confused him.

'No, Emma. I mean it. I really do love my job. I've wanted to be a tour guide since I was a little boy. I loved history at school. I always had my nose in some book or other, used to bore my mum to tears with my facts. So spending all day telling people interesting historical details is literally my dream job.'

How stupid do I feel? And a bit annoyed with myself because I read him right the first time. I should have had the courage of my convictions.

In an attempt to cover this up, I keep talking. 'You're very lucky then. But I've been wondering. It felt so right to me, stepping in to help Derek. I would never have said that I'd be so calm in an emergency, never in a million years. But I was. So, I'm wondering . . .' I hesitate. I haven't said this out loud yet, not even to Mel, and I don't want it to sound stupid or naive. 'I'm wondering if I could train as a paramedic. I know it's incredibly hard and the job is really demanding. But perhaps that's what I should be doing, like a calling.'

I cringe inside as I wait for him to laugh at me or tell me that the course is incredibly competitive or that it would probably be better suited to my brother, James, than to me, like Dad would do, but he doesn't say any of that.

'You should definitely look into it. And if you need a reference about the incident with Derek, then give them my number and I'll tell them how amazing you were.'

If my cheeks weren't blazing before then they certainly are now. It's good that we're walking along so he can't see.

'Actually, Emma,' he says. 'I was wondering, when we get back to Leeds I mean, whether you'd like to go out for a drink with me one night. No worries if not. I just thought it might be nice.'

Blimey!

'I'd love to,' I reply without even thinking about it, and that makes me realise how much I wanted him to ask.

'Great!' he says, sounding a little bit surprised, but in a good way, like he really wasn't expecting a yes. 'Let's do that. I'm looking forward to it already.'

'Me too,' I reply shyly.

'Robin!' I think it's Keith. 'Exactly when were these walls constructed?'

Robin rolls his eyes. 'Duty calls,' he says, and then drops back and starts telling Keith all about Berwick's Elizabethan defensive walls, leaving me to think about what just happened.

45

DOES IT COUNT IF HE ASKS YOU?

'Does it count if he asks you?' laughs Mel. 'I mean, the bet was the first one of us to ask him out. And you didn't. So I can't see how that means you win.'

'Well, I can't ask him now,' I object. 'I'd look like a right 'nana.'

Mel twists her mouth thoughtfully. 'Yeah. I can see that. But you definitely haven't won. Don't be thinking that. I guess we'll have to declare the bet null and void then.'

'I guess so,' I reply. She's totally wrong, but I'm so pleased that he asked me out that I can't be bothered arguing with her. It was a stupid idea anyway.

'And I don't have to do the washing-up.'

'Okay, but maybe, technically . . .'

'No,' she says with some force, and I throw a pillow at her.

She rolls over on the bed and props herself up on her elbows.

'You'll make a cute couple,' she says with a smirk.

'It's one drink!' I say.

'Still . . .'

I think she's right that we'll be cute together, but I'll keep that to myself for now.

◆ ◆ ◆

'This hotel has a spa,' she says a bit later as she flicks through the hotel services directory. 'Did you know that?'

I must have done because I've been carrying a rather optimistic bikini in my case all week. However, in all the drama of today, I'd forgotten.

'I think I did,' I reply vaguely. 'Did you bring your costume?'

Mel waves a low-cut one-piece at me.

'Sure did,' she says. 'Is there time to go down now before dinner?'

It's only four. There's plenty of time.

We grab some toiletries and our books and head down in the lift, a bit giddy with the excitement of it.

The spa is in the basement, but 'spa' might be overstating it a little. There's a rectangular pool with a hot tub at one end, a steam room and a tiny sauna that looks like someone just plonked a shed down inside. But there are robes and slippers and fluffy white towels, so that's enough for us.

We get changed and then head poolside, claiming a lounger each. I alter the back rest of mine so that I can sit up. I don't like to miss anything. Mel is content to lie flat on her back and stare at the ceiling.

'That was nice today,' she says when we're settled. 'With your grandma.'

'It was,' I agree. 'I think Grandad would have liked it.'

'That joke was bloody awful,' Mel adds. 'Just his kind of thing.'

We're quiet for a moment or two and I feel something shifting inside me, like I am finally able to say goodbye. It's a nice feeling, soothing somehow, and an involuntary smile makes it on to my lips at the thought. I send a silent kiss up to wherever he may be.

'Do you think they serve drinks down here? Alcohol, I mean,' Mel asks then, and just like that I'm back to the here and now.

There's no sign of a bar, but the loungers have little tables next to them. They can't all be intended for books.

'I imagine so,' I say. 'Shall I go and find out?'

Mel sits up and pulls her robe around her.

'No, it's okay. I'll go. Prosecco?'

'Need you ask?' I say.

'There is no escape from the pull of prosecco,' she laughs. 'It's like a magnet. I don't know why we think we're ever going to drink anything else!' Then she wanders off towards the entrance.

As she goes, I settle back into my lounger and open my book. I try to read a few words, but I can't get their meaning to stick in my head. The spectre of Mel's forthcoming birthday is still looming over me.

Enid, as good as her word, sent Archie round with all my purchases from this morning. Pat has done me proud with the cake. You'd never know that it had been in a freezer a few hours before, and she's decorated the top and sides in chocolate icing as if her life depended on it. I've never seen so many swirls on one item.

But, whilst the banners and sweets and cake are a great start, they don't alter the fact that I have nothing planned for the day itself.

I put my book down, pick up my phone and google 'What to do in Edinburgh'. The results all look very like what we've been doing all week – castles, walls, churches.

That won't do. I need to think outside the box here.

And then I have a brilliant idea. At last!

It was what Mel just said that put it into my head. She'd said, 'There's no escape . . .' and that made me think of an escape room!

Dizzyingly excited by the thought, I try to examine it objectively as my stomach fizzes. I decide that it would be fantastic – as long as we manage to get out without killing each other. We've never done one, but it's just the kind of thing that Mel loves. Pitching her brains against a problem.

I start searching and locate an escape room place right in the centre of the city. Within a minute or two it's booked, and Mel still isn't back with the fizz.

I'm on a roll now. I find a Thai restaurant that has great reviews. Mel adores Thai food and we've hardly had any since our favourite one closed down. Finally, I find a bar with a club attached. I book us a booth. Even though there are only two of us, I figure that we'll easily make some friends to share it with us. The Scottish are notoriously friendly, and who wouldn't want to spend their evening with two lovely single girls? Maybe 'girls' is no longer an age-appropriate description, but I don't care. I'm sticking with it.

The relief that washes over me as I pay the last deposit is immense. I've done it. A whole day booked. Thank God. Why the hell didn't I do this before we left? It was so easy once I got started. There was no need to make my life so stressful. When we get back home I shall try to . . .

The door opens and Mel is striding towards me with a bottle of prosecco in a metal cooler and two flutes.

'My birthday starts now!' she says as she sashays across the tiles. 'Who cares if we're a day early?'

We've just got it poured and have settled back for some serious relaxing when a pair of familiar twittering voices cuts through the sound of bubbling water. It's Frank and Vivienne. I try not to sigh. I really do, but somehow one still sneaks out.

'Here come the Chuckle Brothers,' says Mel under her breath, and I snigger into my glass.

There is something so irritating about these two. I can't quite put my finger on what it is, but I think it's that Vivienne is so wet and Frank is so eager to impress. Whenever he tells you something, he adds little gaps so that you can insert the appropriate positive reaction. It brings out the worst in me, and it definitely does in Mel. She's barely been civil to him all trip.

'Oh God,' she says now. 'They're coming over.'

'Hello, you two,' says Vivienne. 'We just thought we'd have a little swim before dinner, didn't we, Frank? It's nice here, isn't it? Is that one of those whirlpool things? I do like one of those.'

'And there's a steam room. That'll be good for your chest. She suffers terribly, you know. The doctors don't know why, but I think it stems from all that time she spent in cold water. We told you that she swam the Channel, didn't we?'

'I think you might have mentioned it,' says Mel with barely disguised sarcasm.

Frank doesn't appear to notice her tone.

'Mind if we join you?' he says, and before we can make some feeble excuse about having a highly contagious virus or a body odour problem he's pulled over two white plastic chairs and plonks them down next to us.

I sigh inwardly and resign myself to a few minutes of dull conversation before we can politely make our excuses and retreat back to our room.

'That was lovely today,' says Vivienne. 'On the pier. I thought your grandma did really well. It can't have been easy.'

I'm slightly taken aback. This is the most sensitive thing she's said all week. I didn't think she had it in her.

'Yes,' I agree. 'And Grandad would have loved it.'

Immediately, conversation dwindles to nothing. Maybe this isn't going to be so bad. After all, if neither of them says anything, it's hard to be irritated.

Then Frank pops up again.

'This reminds me of Spain,' he says.

This is a surprising comment. We are sitting on cheap plastic furniture beside a small pool with no natural sunlight in the basement of a hotel in Berwick-upon-Tweed. Even if we were drinking cava and not prosecco, it's hard to think of anywhere that reminds me less of Spain.

Vivienne nudges him and throws him a warning glance.

'Frank!' she hisses, as if he has spoken seriously out of turn. This isn't the first time this has happened, either. I'm wondering what the great Spanish mystery is all about. And so, it seems, is Mel.

'How come?' she says. 'I've been to Spain a few times myself, but I can't say this place is bringing it all back to me.'

Frank and Vivienne seem to be communicating by facial gesture, with all manner of twists and contortions.

'Tell them,' says Vivienne. 'What harm can it do now?'

'Yes!' agrees Mel. 'Tell us.'

46

I'LL REGRET THAT TO MY DYING DAY.

Frank and Vivienne shuffle in their seats and then there's that horrible scraping sound that sets your teeth on edge as Franks drags his chair across the tiles to get closer to us. Whatever this secret is, it appears to be for our ears only.

'We don't usually go on coach trips,' he says. 'We've always thought they were for poor people, or people with no imagination.'

My jaw is about to drop, but I manage to prop it up just in time.

'Well, we never had to, did we?' chips in Vivienne. 'We just always went to Spain. A gorgeous little place just outside Nerja. Have you ever been?'

We shake our heads.

'We went to Torremolinos once,' says Mel, but she's lying. 'That was delightful.'

I press my lips together to stop the giggle escaping and once again I have to make sure I don't catch her eye. If I give her an inch, I know she'll start talking about poor people and imaginations.

'Oh no!' says Vivienne, clearly missing Mel's naughtiness. 'Nerja is not a bit like that. It's much classier, isn't it, Frank?'

'Much,' says Frank, with absolutely no grasp of how they're coming across to us.

'Our son, Frank Junior, had a place there,' Vivienne continues. 'Spectacular villa, like you see in films, with views out across the sea, and a pool. One of those where you can't see the end of it and it looks like you're just going to swim off the edge. What are they called, Frank?'

'Infinity pools,' supplies Frank proudly.

'Yes. An infinity pool. And whenever we went to stay, Frank Junior would send a car to meet us at the airport. Not a taxi, but a proper executive limousine with black leather seats and a driver in a suit. It had air conditioning inside and everything, didn't it, Frank?'

'Well, you need it out there,' says Frank, as if we have never been anywhere warmer than Berwick in March. 'Especially in August. It's as hot as blazes, I can tell you.'

'Is it really?' asks Mel, all wide-eyed innocence. I'm going to kill her when we're on our own.

'Frank Junior would take us to the best restaurants too. He could always get a table. Everybody knew him. It was a bit like being royalty, entering a room with Frank Junior, everyone waving and saying hello. I was so proud of him.'

She gives a little sniff, and it crosses my mind that Frank Junior might have died as well. I hope not. I've had enough dead or nearly dead people for one week.

'We'd always tried to give him the best, hadn't we, Frank?' she goes on. 'We sent him to private school.' Her chest swells and she raises her chin defiantly as if we're about to suggest that they didn't. 'It wasn't always easy. We had to scrimp and save a bit, but everyone knows that a good education opens doors.'

'It wasn't Eton,' jokes Frank, rolling his eyes. 'Nothing like that.'

Vivienne seems irritated, her eyebrows pulling tightly together.

'It was a good school, Frank. And they got him into university. He did Business at Keele. Well, he started. He didn't finish in the end. Didn't need to because he set up his own business. "There's no point mouldering away just learning things, Mum," he said to me, "when I can be out there doing things instead."'

'The real world,' Frank adds. 'You can't beat it.'

Mel and I are enthralled. These two make such an entertaining double act. They should be on the stage.

'Well, it just took off, didn't it, Frank? One minute he was selling a few bits and pieces that he thought might go down well and the next he was running a whole import-export business. He got the stock from China, mainly. Not really to our taste, the things he sold, though, were they, Frank?'

'Tat, a lot of it,' says Frank. 'But people seemed to like it. Frank Junior bought it in at a song and then sold it on to bigger companies at a profit.'

'He always did have an eye for a deal,' says Vivienne. 'He used to buy Twix bars, split them and then sell them to his friends. He was only ten. Made quite a lot of extra pocket money.'

'Very enterprising,' I say quickly to stop Mel from saying what I know is on her mind. I'm with her on that one, though. What kind of ten-year-old boy rips his friends off for a few pence at break time?

'Things just seemed to keep getting better and better for him then,' Vivienne continues. 'He bought the villa in Spain and moved out there permanently. We used to go and stay when he was away on business, or on holiday. We went a lot, didn't we, Frank? Frank Junior was always off somewhere or other. Such a jet-set life. We could hardly keep up with all his comings and goings.'

Vivienne's doting smile slips into something darker. I am on the edge of my sun lounger. I can't wait to hear what happened to the villa, and Frank Junior. It's obviously not good, and as if to confirm this the two of them exchange looks and then shrug, like they're deciding that they might as well go the whole hog with the story.

'But something went wrong,' Vivienne says, dropping her voice so low that we have to lean in to hear her. 'We're still not quite sure what, are we, Frank? Something to do with customs. The rules are different in Spain, apparently. That's what Frank Junior told us. Anyway, somehow he got a bit behind with who he should be paying what to. He told us it was hard to keep up when they would keep speaking Spanish.'

'In Spain?' Mel says under her breath. 'Who knew?'

I give her a kick. I want to hear the end of this, and I don't need her sarcasm to seal their lips before we get there. I'm in too deep.

'Then he was arrested,' says Vivienne. 'It was awful. He didn't tell us at first. He wanted to save us from the worry, he said. It was just a little misunderstanding and it would get cleared up nice and quickly.'

'But it didn't,' says Frank, picking up the story baton as Vivienne blows her nose noisily on a tissue. 'They couldn't seem to get it sorted out. And the Spanish authorities wouldn't let him out on bail. Said he was a flight risk. They took his passport off him and everything.'

'That's when he told us what was going on,' Vivienne says, still dabbing at her nose. 'He needed some money to pay his lawyer. He told us that his was all tied up in the business and that he had a cash-flow problem which he couldn't sort out until they let him out. It was all very chicken and egg.'

I can see where this is going, and so, going by the expression on Mel's face, can she. But it's apparent that the whole thing had come as a terrible shock to poor old Frank and Vivienne.

'We didn't have much by way of savings,' says Frank. 'But we sent him what we had. That didn't seem to last very long and soon he needed more. So, we scraped together what we could and sent that over too.'

'He swore he'd pay it back when he got out,' sniffs Vivienne. 'And his business was so successful that we didn't doubt it, did we, Frank? We just never thought . . .'

'We lost our house,' says Frank, his mouth set in a grim line. 'We had to sell up and buy somewhere smaller to release the equity.'

'But we didn't begrudge him the money,' chips in Vivienne. 'I mean, he's our boy. You'd do anything for your children, wouldn't you?' She frowns at us. 'Well, you two don't have any children, do you? But when you do, you'll understand. If they need help, then you help. That's just how it is.'

I look at foolish, fluttery Vivienne in a new light. All week her silliness has been getting on our nerves. And she is a silly woman. There's no getting away from that. But part of me wants to get my hands around Frank Junior's neck and squeeze. How dare he, a grown adult, suck his mum and dad into his own sordid world and cause them so much heartache? No doubt they'll have spent their entire life working hard to build a nice home and a little nest egg, but they gave it all up to their seedy son without question. I bet he wasn't even grateful. It probably just got swallowed up into the black hole of his debt.

'And the villa in Spain?' asks Mel, although we both know the answer.

'The bank took it,' says Frank in a very matter-of-fact way. 'The bank took everything he had.'

'So, where's he living now then?' I ask. 'Is he back with you?'

They exchange glances that tell me exactly where Frank Junior is living before they answer the question.

'He had to go away,' says Vivienne, her eyes focusing on the tiled floor.

We wait a beat or two and then Frank adds, 'He's serving ten years in prison in Málaga.'

'Oh . . .' I say, not really sure what the polite response should be. 'I'm so sorry.'

Frank shrugs. 'They found him guilty on various counts of fraud, tax avoidance and customs and excise infringements,' he says. 'I know he's my son, and it's been hard on Vivienne and me, but I have to accept that he got what he deserved.'

'It wasn't just him and us that he hurt,' Vivienne says. 'There were all his employees as well. They all lost their jobs. His finance director is in prison too. They were in it together, you see. It was all such a terrible mess.'

'I'm so sorry,' I say again.

'You didn't deserve any of that crap,' says Mel.

Vivienne wipes at her eyes and then looks at Mel, gratitude in her eyes.

'Thank you,' she says.

'It's true,' Mel continues. 'I know he's your son and all that, but he's an adult. He's responsible for his own life and if he chose to live the way he did then he should have dealt with the consequences when it all turned to shit. Dragging you in and then making you dig him out is unforgivable.'

'Not many people see it like that,' says Frank. 'They think it's our fault that our son turned out a crook.'

'That's just bollocks,' says Mel sharply, and Vivienne flinches. 'Sorry,' she adds, 'but it is. It's judgemental bollocks. You did every-thing you could for him. He decided on a particular way of life and that was nothing to do with you. And no one should blame you for that. It's all on his shoulders.'

'Thank you,' says Frank. 'But it's more complicated than that. We couldn't just cut him loose and see him rot in jail. Not at the start, at least, when we truly thought the whole thing was a terrible mistake. But I do regret giving him the money from the house.'

Vivienne's eyes open wide and she opens her mouth to object.

'Well, I do, Vivienne. Giving him that money made no difference to him whatsoever. It just got swallowed up in legal costs and he still ended up in prison, which is what he deserved. We should have told him we'd given him everything we could spare, and then we'd still have our lovely house. I'll regret that to my dying day.'

I'm desperate to down some of the prosecco, but the bubbles hardly feel appropriate, given what we've just heard.

'Well, at least it's not all bad,' says Mel.

None of us have any idea what she's getting at. It all looks pretty much as bad as it can get from where I'm sitting. We eye her quizzically.

Mel raises her palms and shrugs her shoulders as if the answer is obvious. 'If your son hadn't selfishly screwed you out of everything you had, then you wouldn't have got to go on this fabulous coach trip and met me and Em!'

Worrying that this comment really could go either way, I give Vivienne a tentative little smile.

'So, cheers!' continues Mel, raising her glass in salute. 'Here's to new friends, no matter how they come into your life.'

Big smiles all round. Phew.

Mel stands up. 'I'm just going to get a couple more glasses and then you can help us finish this. It's my birthday – well, nearly – and that's as good an excuse as I need.'

She races off towards the door leaving me, feeling slightly shell-shocked, with Vivienne and Frank.

'She's quite a personality, your friend,' says Frank.

'God, yes,' I agree. 'Never a dull moment.'

'And is it really her birthday?' Vivienne asks in a slightly suspicious tone.

'Yes! Well, tomorrow, but we've started celebrating a bit early.'

'Oh, how lovely,' Vivienne replies, her face brightening into a smile now that we're back in the here and now. 'I do love a birthday. I imagine, as you're such great friends, that you have all kinds of exciting things lined up.'

And I am delighted to finally be able to say that I have.

47

Who are you and what have you done with the real Mel?

Mel and I lie in the dark in our room. It's almost midnight, but neither of us seems tired. I suppose it's because we're so chilled without any of the stresses and strains of our day-to-day lives. For all that this trip has had its unanticipated excitements, it is actually a proper break and the benefits of being away from the daily grind are just starting to kick in.

'I felt sorry for them,' Mel says, spinning the conversation on a ha'penny from what colour we could paint the sitting room in the new flat that we haven't yet found, let alone moved into. My brain has to do a couple of tumble turns to catch up with her.

'Who? Frank and Vivienne?'

'Yeah. Frank Junior sounds like a total shit. Who does that to their mum and dad? Although it probably serves them right for calling him Frank Junior. There's always something a bit suspect about a person who gives their child their own name.'

'You might even say it lacks imagination,' I quip, and I hear Mel's snorts coming from her side of the room.

'Could you believe that?' she adds. 'Coach trips are for poor people and people with no imagination! The cheek.'

I pause for a moment, considering what she's said.

'Isn't that pretty much what we thought too?' I ask.

Mel thinks for a beat and then replies, 'No. We thought coach trips were for old people. Not poor ones. And I still think that's right.'

'Fair point,' I say.

'But . . .' she continues, 'I'm slowly coming round to the view that old people aren't necessarily as annoying as I thought they were.'

This is interesting. It's rare that Mel admits that she might have made a mistake.

'I mean, don't get me wrong,' she muses. 'They are still annoying. All that fussing about stuff that doesn't matter, and not grasping things the first time they're told them. That's irritating, and there's no need for it. But I think I thought before that old people were just miserable. Not all of them,' she adds quickly. 'Your grandma isn't, for one. And that Gloria.'

'But she's a thief,' I add.

'Yes. Didn't see *that* coming. Cheerful with it, though.'

I laugh. Gloria had indeed been a cheerful thief.

'But when you look at the stuff that some of the others have had to deal with, Angela and Ian and their little boy, Arthur and his diagnosis, that stuff we heard this evening. Well, to be honest, it's a surprise any of them smile at all.'

I think about this for a moment.

'That's true about anyone, though,' I say. 'We none of us know what anyone else is going through.'

'Yes, but we make so many assumptions about old people. Or at least I do. I assume they don't return my smile in the street because they think young people don't deserve common courtesy, or push in front of me in a queue because they think their age entitles them to go first. It's never occurred to me that they might have been too lost in their own thoughts to smile, just like I am sometimes. And they maybe want to get to the front of the queue because they're not sure how much longer they can stand without their hips giving way. I mean, when you look at things like that they start to make more sense. Maybe old people get a bad press.'

'Who are you and what have you done with the real Mel?' I ask her, but I'm only partly joking. What she's saying does make sense, in light of all we've heard on this trip. She's on a roll now, though, so I just listen.

'I mean, take Keith as a case in point. We called him Mr Grumpy Aisle Man for the first two days. If there'd been a handy cliff, we'd have cheerfully pushed him off it.'

I nod into the darkness, because she's right about this too.

'It was only when we broke into his room and saw what he'd brought with him that we thought there might be a different side to him. And he was quite nice to you when you saved Derek's life. Plus, he was really honest with us when he told us about Gloria fleecing him. I hate to say it, and I really don't say this very often, but I think we might have been wrong about old Keith.'

'Are you coming over all Elizabeth Bennet on me?' I ask her.

'Do you know, I think I might be.'

We lie in the dark contemplating our various prejudices for a moment or two.

'We should probably go to sleep now,' I say, hating how sensible I sound. 'Big weekend ahead.'

'Is there now?' replies Mel. 'I wonder why that might be.'

'Can't think,' I say, and I close my eyes.

She's right. And it's not just that. We are going to find a decent place to live – invest in ourselves, as Mel said – and I . . . I pause for a moment and swallow hard . . . I am going to retrain as a paramedic.

As I drift off to sleep I'm conscious that I have some new feelings coursing through my body. Faith in myself and excitement about what is coming next. And I have a date! Life is feeling pretty good to me.

48

SATURDAY

THE PLEASURE IS ALL MINE.

Following careful consideration, I decide it would be better to decorate the coach rather than the bedroom. After all the effort that Enid put into getting the party items to me, it feels a little wasteful if they're only in situ for an hour or so. And something tells me that the old people will enjoy them . . . or is that me playing to stereotypes again?

So, when Mel wakes up, she does so to the simplest of birthday fanfares – just me and the gift-wrapped box containing the bracelet. It is beautifully gift-wrapped, though, even if I do say so myself. Mr Bean in *Love Actually* has nothing on my present-wrapping skills! (I do know that Rowan Atkinson and Mr Bean are not the same person, in case you were wondering.)

'Happy birthday,' I say, as soon as I hear her stir.

She sits up, pushing her hair out of her eyes and grinning like a loon.

'It's my birthday!!!' she says, giddy as a six-year-old.

Birthdays never grow old, though, do they? No matter how many of them you see.

'It is. Here. This is for you.'

I pass her the card and gift and then watch as she squeals her way through the ribbons and tissue until she reaches the treasure inside.

'Oh my God,' she says, looking up at me. 'It's not . . .'

'It is,' I reply, feeling smugly proud of myself. 'I tracked it down for you.'

She shoots forward and throws her arms around me.

'I love it! And I love you. You are absolutely the best best friend a girl could wish for.'

She puts the bracelet on, admiring it against her skin. 'It looks fabulous. Don't you think?'

'I do,' I say. 'Totally perfect.' Then I get to my feet. 'Right. You get dressed. I've got some things I just need to sort out . . .'

Mel gives me a comedy wink.

'Secret things?' she asks, but I just narrow my eyes enigmatically and let myself out of the room with my bag of tricks.

The weather has been kind to us on the trip up to this point, but it seems to have chosen today to pay us back for some grudge we knew nothing about. You know when people say that the rain is horizontal and you're never quite sure what they mean? Well, the rain is horizontal.

I stand at the front door, bag of decorations in hand, and wonder how I am going to make the twenty-metre dash to the coach without dissolving.

'Bit drizzly this morning,' says the man on reception without a hint of irony.

'It is,' I reply, and attempt a smile at this odd northern humour.

I peer through the sheets of water to see if Dave is already aboard and think I see a Dave-shaped figure in the driver's seat, although I can't be certain. I stuff the bag up my top and set off at a run, hoping against hope that he will see me sprinting across the car park and open the door before I get there. He doesn't, and I have to rap on the glass before he realises that I want to come on board. By the time the door finally hisses open I'm soaked through to the skin.

'You're a bit damp,' he says as I stumble up the coach steps. Everyone is a comedian this morning, apparently. 'Is there a problem?' he adds, apparently confused as to why I've arrived on his coach an hour earlier than expected.

'No, no,' I say as I try in vain to brush rainwater off myself. 'It's Mel's birthday today and I was hoping we could decorate the coach a bit.'

Dave's eyes light up and he rubs his hands together like this is the best thing to happen to him all week.

'I *love* a bit of decoration,' he says. 'I used to drive a school bus and it was the talk of the fleet. Christmas, Valentine's, Halloween. You name it, and my bus was decorated to the hilt to match. I even heard of kids walking out of their way just so they could ride to school with me. I used to have this brilliant Easter bunny that pooed out mini-eggs. It was great. Thinking about it, maybe it was the chocolate that pulled the extra kids in,' he muses, as much to himself as to me.

I smile in what I hope is an interested fashion, but I'm aware that seconds are passing. I check the time on my phone in a not very discreet fashion. This seems to bring him back to the here and now. He stands up and opens an overhead locker that is full to bursting with crinkly banners and streamers.

'Now, what did you have in mind?'

What with the things I'd got from Enid and Dave's not inconsiderable stash of goodies, we have more than enough, and forty minutes later the coach is almost unrecognisable. Happy birthday banners stretch along all the windows, balloons and streamers hang from the overhead luggage racks and Dave has rigged up some flashing fairy lights that he strings along the ceiling.

I step back to admire our handiwork. It might be raining cats and dogs outside, but in here it's like summer and Christmas and every party you ever went to all rolled into one.

'Oh, hang on!' I say, remembering the pick and mix, and I put a little striped paper bag on each seat and hand one to Dave. 'There! Perfect. Thanks so much, Dave.'

Dave is beaming at me as if he hasn't had so much fun for years.

'The pleasure is all mine,' he says, opening the little bag and peering inside. 'Ooh, liquorice torpedoes. My favourites.'

What a gent.

I race back through the rain just in time to meet Cynthia, Arthur and Grandma coming out of breakfast. They open their mouths to ask about my drowned-rat-like appearance, but there isn't time.

'It's Mel's birthday,' I say, as if this explains everything. 'Tell the others.'

And then I hurry back to our room. I'm still damp, but Mel knows enough about how secrets work not to ask. She's packed all my stuff as well as hers and is sitting on the bed replying to messages on Facebook.

'Aren't people lovely?' she says, looking up from her task. 'I know Facebook reminds them about birthdays, but they still have to take the time to post a message.'

It's true. Most people are lovely. Even old people, I think, as my mind returns to our conversation of the previous evening.

There isn't really time for a proper breakfast, so we make do with a rushed cup of coffee and a couple of croissants that we snatch from the buffet and eat on the hoof. Mel doesn't see what the weather gods have sent us until we're standing at the front door with our cases.

'Oh, for Christ's sake,' she says. 'What's that all about? Could it not have waited until next week, when we're back at work?'

'Maybe it's just passing through,' I say optimistically, the low, leaden sky belying my suggestion.

I pull my phone out and check the weather for Edinburgh. According to the Met Office, it's going to rain heavily and non-stop for the next thirty-six hours. I stuff my phone back into my pocket without reporting my findings to Mel.

'Better make a run for it,' she says.

Dave is standing at the luggage space gamely waiting to receive our cases, and is shrouded in one of those plastic ponchos you get at Disneyland. In fact, it looks like that's where it came from, as it's pink and has Minnie Mouse ears printed all over it. Despite looking a little incongruous, it is totally practical. Our ordinary coats will be soaked before we even reach the coach whereas Dave remains entirely dry beneath his enormous pink poncho. Go, Dave, I think. My mood is so buoyant that nothing can spoil it.

We charge across the car park, hurl our cases at Dave and then bound on to the coach, where we're the last to arrive. The rest of our motley crew are already sitting in their seats and staunchly ignoring the coach's new get-up. Mel gets halfway up the steps and then stops, stock-still, as she takes it all in. I have to budge her along a bit so that I can get in out of the rain.

'Oh, Em!' she says, with a tiny crack in her voice. 'Did you do all this?'

49

And so, just like that, it becomes a plan.

'It wasn't just me,' I say to Mel, feeling more than a little bit proud of our decorative prowess. 'I had an accomplice. Dave did most of it, in fact.'

'It's incredible. Thank you!' She turns and gives me a huge squeeze.

'You're so welcome,' I breathe into her hair.

Then she turns and hugs Dave too. His arms float in mid-air for a moment as he decides whether to commit or not, and then he hugs her back. I know they got off to a bit of a rocky start, but it appears that she is forgiven.

A tentative rendition of 'Happy Birthday' starts up, led by Cynthia. By the time we start the second line all the others have joined in and it becomes quite rousing. Keith has a lovely rounded tenor voice, and when we get to the last line someone adds in some harmony. I can't be sure, but I think it's Angela. The effect is lovely. We almost sound like a real choir.

For once in her life, Mel is speechless. She just stands there amongst the balloons and streamers with her hands covering her mouth, shaking her head slowly.

'This is amazing,' she says when she's recovered herself a bit. 'I wasn't expecting any of it.'

'Well, you obviously didn't factor in a friend like Emma,' says Vivienne, and my stomach clenches a bit as I think how far off all of this was when I woke up yesterday. Still, I tell myself, I got there in the end, and that's what counts.

'Happy birthday, Mel,' says Robin. He's smiling, but I'm not sure he entirely approves of my and Dave's handiwork.

'Do I get a birthday kiss?' Mel asks him, closing his eyes and puckering her lips.

I've rarely seen anyone look quite as uncomfortable as he does right then. He looks from Mel to me and back again.

'Er, I'm not sure that . . .' he begins.

Mel puts him out of his misery immediately.

'Only joking,' she says. 'And I wouldn't want to tread on anyone's toes,' she adds, and then pulls a conspiratorial face at me. I'm sure Grandma and Vivienne both notice, but luckily Robin is too busy having his narrow escape to realise. I could kill Mel sometimes, I really could.

We sit down in our seats and Mel finds the little striped bag of sweets on hers.

'Oh, Em. Pick and mix!' she says joyfully. 'My absolute favourite. And are there any . . .' She pushes the contents of the bag around with her finger. 'Pear drops! Yes! Thank you.'

'You're welcome,' I say as my mood soars. I did it!

Everyone agrees that the decoration and the sweets are all very thoughtful, and as the coach pulls out of the hotel car park, the windscreen wipers going like the clappers, I hear Vivienne whispering to Frank, 'I'm not sure it's entirely safe, driving with all these things dangling. Do you think he can see in the mirror?' and it doesn't even annoy me.

Robin launches into his spiel about the wonders of Edinburgh but, unlike on other days, I get the impression that he's not taking his crowd with him this morning. Maybe they have had their fill of castles, or perhaps it's the weather putting both a real and metaphorical dampener on everything, but as he runs through the itinerary for the day ahead there's no accompanying twitter of who is excited by what.

Mel turns her head and whispers to me, 'I assume we're not doing the tour thing today.'

'It's up to you,' I whisper back. 'It's your birthday and you can do precisely as you please. But I do have an alternative agenda to propose if you so wish. More details to follow!'

I give a tantalising twitch of my eyebrows and then fall silent so that we can listen to the rest of Robin's speech. I select a cola cube from my sweet bag and pop it in my mouth, running my tongue over its hard corners and sharp sugar crystals. Why don't I have these more often? I resolve to always have a bag of retro sweets handy from this point on.

The rain is relentless. The coach crawls up the A1, but visibility is appalling and I keep expecting us to aquaplane across the central reservation and tip over. We mustn't do that, though, because Pat's beautifully decorated birthday cake is carefully stowed in the luggage rack above my head and I want it to make it to our destination in one piece.

The journey should only take us a little over an hour, but the traffic is going so slowly that it's clear it'll take longer. Luckily, we're not booked into our first activity until 2 p.m., so I'm not anxious. I'm also very glad that I didn't choose the zoo.

Cynthia leans across the aisle to me.

'What have you two girls got planned for today?' she asks. 'Something more exciting than the Royal Mile in the rain, I hope?'

She says this quietly, but I think I see Robin stiffen in his seat. Poor Robin. His tours are far less charming if the weather is bad, and he's really up against it on that front today.

Mel looks at me expectantly.

'We have!' I say with gusto, hoping that what I'm about to reveal is as appealing to Mel as I've hoped. 'We're booked into an escape room this afternoon.'

'Fantastic!' says Mel, virtually piercing the air with her enthusiasm, and I am greatly relieved.

Cynthia's crinkly brow crinkles still further.

'I'm afraid that I don't know what that is,' she says apologetically, like lacking this knowledge is the worst kind of failing ever.

'It's as simple as it sounds,' I say. 'You get locked into a room and you have to escape.'

'Like Houdini?' she asks, eyes wide. 'With straitjackets and chains and such like?'

Whilst this is a wonderful mental image, I have to set her straight. 'No, not really. This is more about doing puzzles.'

'Ooh, I love a puzzle,' she says, waving her word search book at me. 'My niece says that a puzzle a day keeps dementia at bay. It's a little rhyme, you see. Like an apple a day keeps the doctor away.' She looks very pleased with herself and then she catches sight of Arthur, who is looking bemused, and she blushes. 'Sorry, Arthur, no offence intended.'

'And none taken,' replies Arthur good-humouredly.

'It's not really that kind of puzzle,' I say.

'So, what kind is it?' asks Ian.

By now everyone is listening.

'Well,' I begin. 'You start with a scenario. The one I've booked is set in a posh hotel. Some jewels have gone missing from a guest's room and she's accusing the maid of having taken them.'

'Ooh, how intriguing,' says Cynthia.

'But the hotel prides itself on offering the best service to its guests and they don't want to get a reputation for theft.'

'Well, no,' says Cynthia. 'That would really put their guests off.'

'Play havoc with their rating on Tripadvisor,' adds Keith.

It's the kind of comment that would have got my back up at the start of the week but which now actually seems quite funny. I grin at him and continue.

'So, they've called us, me and Mel, in to track down the jewels and solve the crime.'

'Like real detectives,' says Cynthia. 'Like Inspector Morse.'

I refrain from pointing out that TV detectives like Morse and his ilk aren't actually real.

'Yes,' I say. 'Kind of.'

'That sounds like good fun,' says Vivienne.

'But you've not heard the best part,' I say. 'They lock you in the room and you have to complete all the puzzles to solve the crime and get the code to open the door and let yourself out. And you have to do it all within an hour or you lose.'

Cynthia looks horrified. 'And if you don't solve it, do they keep you locked in there, like prisoners?'

'No,' I reply with a laugh. 'They let you out either way. It's just that if you haven't found the code, then you don't win.'

There's the general murmuring that we always get when new information has been introduced, each of them confirming their initial opinion to the person sitting next to them.

'So, it's a test of wits and intelligence?' says Keith.

'If you like,' I say. 'Although I prefer to think of it as fun.'

'How many can each room take?' asks Mel.

I assume that she's thinking Robin can book all the rest of them into another room. I pull the website up and check.

'Our room can hold ten,' I say. 'And the others seem to be between eight and twelve.'

'Well, why don't we all go and do ours?' says Mel.

I glance at her, my confusion no doubt clear on my face. Did I hear that right? Is she really suggesting that we share her birthday escape room with the rest of the coach trip?

'Really?' I ask, just as most of the rest of them say, 'Well, that would be great!' and 'And that's very kind,' and 'If you're sure.'

And so, just like that, it becomes a plan.

50

AND THAT'S NOT THE HALF OF IT.

Robin doesn't seem to mind that Mel and I have inadvertently staged a mutiny and agrees to let us all skip his afternoon tour without too much persuasion. Nor does he show any inclination to come with us to the escape room; which is handy, as there wouldn't be space, although I can't help but feel slightly disappointed. Still, today is about Mel and not me, so I try not to dwell on it.

Finally, the coach pulls up to our hotel in Edinburgh, and it's clear that we've been saving the best for last. This one has a canopy over the place where taxis drop off and a doorman in a top hat – the works. There are even those fancy luggage trollies I was looking for back in York. Hanging baskets and window boxes adorn the frontage and there are various national flags flapping about soggily in the blustery wind, welcoming international travellers.

The clouds are as grey as the stone of the buildings, so it's hard to see where the hotel stops and the sky begins. And still the rain falls. It's such a shame, but there's nothing I can do about it other than to go with the flow, so to speak.

We file through check-in for the final time. It runs like clockwork now. Vivienne barely even finds anything to complain about.

I can't decide if that's her lightening up a touch, or whether this hotel comes closer to matching her exacting standards. Either way, we make a jolly little bunch as we loiter in reception waiting for our rooms to be allocated.

'So, how old are we today?' Keith asks Mel, as if she's five.

I'm ready for the backlash, but it doesn't come.

'A lady never divulges her age,' Mel replies coyly.

Keith's mouth twitches but he manages not to make the obvious quip.

'But as I'm no lady,' Mel continues with a cheeky wink at Keith, 'I'm happy to tell you that I'm twenty-nine today. All day!'

'I was twenty-nine on 15 February 1971,' he says without missing a beat.

Either he's exceedingly good at maths or that day was significant for some reason. I have no idea why it might have been, but Grandma has.

'Decimal Day!' she says with a beaming smile.

'Exactly,' says Keith. 'Not a day to forget.'

I still have no clue.

'That was the day we changed from pounds, shillings and pence to the new decimal currency,' explains Grandma, but I still have no idea what she's talking about.

'New decimal currency?' I parrot back at her.

'It's the money we have now,' says Mel. 'A hundred pence in the pound, etc. But before that there were two hundred and forty pence in a pound.'

I stare at her as if she's just told me that the moon really is made of cheese.

'No,' I say. 'That's just stupid.'

'That's right, isn't it?' says Mel, looking to Keith and Grandma for confirmation. 'My grandad told me. He kept a few of the old coins and I used to play with them when I was little. Those old pennies were massive.'

'Yes,' Grandma agrees, nodding enthusiastically. 'They were. It really felt you had something worth having with one of those in your pocket. Not like those silly little pennies we have now. Then twelve pence made a shilling and there were twenty shillings in a pound.'

'What?!' I say. 'That makes no sense. Who on earth came up with a system like that?'

'The Normans,' replies Mel, and I look at her sceptically. Surely we weren't working on a system that old until the 1970s? But it seems we were. 'I kid you not,' she says. 'William the Conqueror and his mates.'

'No way!'

'And that's not the half of it. There were loads of other coins. Farthings and florins and . . .' She looks to Keith for help. 'What were those things you buy racehorses with?'

'Guineas?'

'Yes, those. Although they weren't actually coins. Just a price.'

'What?' I'm totally lost. A coin that isn't a coin?

'And crowns,' chips in Keith. 'Five shillings made a crown.'

I give up trying to make sense of the system and go back to where we started.

'And that's how it was?' I clarify. 'Until you were twenty-nine?'

'Yep. You should have seen the fuss there was about changing it,' he goes on, Grandma still nodding away at his side. 'It wasn't too bad for me. I was your age. Found it easy to pick up new things. But anyone over about forty was stumped, and the pensioners were convinced they were going to be robbed blind every time they went to the shops.'

'It's hard enough to get the hang of new coins when you go on holiday,' I say. 'I can't imagine our money all being different. It must have been really tricky.'

'My gran stopped going out altogether,' says Keith. 'She was totally overwhelmed by it. She used to talk other people into getting her shopping for her. Big changes like that can be a real challenge when you're older.'

I know what he's doing. He's having a gentle jab at me and Mel, and it's probably deserved. But I really think we've come a long way since Monday.

'I can see that,' I say. 'Change can be tricky for everyone, but especially if you're already a little bit anxious about where you fit in the world.'

I'm not going to say 'when you're old', although that's what I mean. But this is about more than just having had a lot of birthdays. It's caught up with being able to guess what's going to happen next through past experience, having worries about health and money, and loneliness too, as well as the fear of being left behind when the world is moving so quickly.

I get that. I've barely got the hang of my phone when they issue a new update and I have to start all over again, and I've never known a world without mobile phones. They are second nature to me, but Grandma has never mastered texting, no matter how many times I try to show her. She says she has no need for it, that if she wants to tell me something she can ring me up. And Grandma is on it with most stuff. What if you're Arthur?

'Well, we all worked the new money out in the end, though,' says Grandma. 'Even the old people,' she adds, raising an eyebrow in my direction. I give her a sheepish smile. But Mel and me are getting there too. Or, at least, we're trying.

51

Do you think these are important?

We spend a soggy morning at the Palace of Holyroodhouse wondering how you clean a crystal chandelier to sparkling glory (one part vinegar to three parts warm water, according to Vivienne) and giggling at what might have happened in the ornate four-poster beds. We conclude that we prefer the one Mary Queen of Scots slept in, with its drapes in calming blues and golds, than the showy red monstrosity that was the king's.

'Where do you think the Queen sleeps when she comes to stay?' asks Cynthia. One look at her earnest face tells me that she's asking in all seriousness.

'I think she probably has a comfy Slumberdown tucked away somewhere out of sight,' laughs Mel.

Cynthia looks horrified, as if the mere suggestion that the monarch sleeps in an ordinary bed is treasonous in itself.

We move on. Cynthia and I get a little behind the main group and so we need to make conversation.

'Do you have brothers and sisters?' she asks me.

'A brother. James.'

'Older or younger?'

'Older.'

'And is he very bossy?' she asks.

It's such a surprising question that it takes me a moment to reply.

'Not bossy,' I say. 'But he's always right.'

'Ah. One of those,' she says knowingly. 'A Keith then?'

It surprises me to hear her say this, but she's spot on.

'Precisely. When we were growing up he couldn't put a foot wrong. Whereas I could barely get anything right.'

Cynthia cocks her head to one side like a tiny bird. 'That must have been hard. We all need to be appreciated sometimes, don't we?'

'We do,' I agree. 'And do you have siblings?'

'I did. Dead now. It's just me and my cat.'

'No other family?' I ask.

'No. Oh, a couple of nephews and a niece, but I never hear from them. Young people are so busy these days, aren't they?'

She says this without any hint of an undercurrent and I imme-diately feel guilty, even though she isn't my aunt. Then I have an idea.

'Shall we keep in touch,' I ask her, 'after this trip?'

Cynthia's face lights up and her eyes shine. 'Ooh, yes, dear. That would be lovely.'

'You can give me your email address when we get back to the hotel,' I say.

Her face falls.

'Or your postal address, if that's easier.'

She beams at me.

Lunch is served in a low-ceilinged tearoom with plenty of wooden beams and tartan seat coverings. The unmistakable drone of bagpipes floats in the air, but I can't tell if it's a recording or if someone is actually playing them, albeit three streets away. I'd know if they were playing them in this building.

Then it's time for the escape room. As we race through the rain ('race' being a relative term, given the company) Cynthia gets quite excitable about the whole thing.

'I'm ever so nervous about getting locked in,' she confesses, and bites her lower lip. 'But it's very exciting too. Just imagine if we're able to solve the crime and return the jewels.'

Her eyes glitter at the thought and I worry that perhaps she hasn't quite understood that it's all pretend.

The escape rooms are in a repurposed 1930s building, squat brick with tall steel-framed windows. We push open huge wooden doors, and even that feels like stepping into the unknown. Inside, the waiting area is all mahogany panelling and monochrome floor tiles. It's beautiful, if not a little shabby.

We're greeted by a very smiley young man whose grin slips only slightly when he realises firstly how many there are of us and then our average age.

'Welcome, welcome,' he says gamely. 'Have you booked in?'

He runs a chewed finger down his list, clearly not finding a booking for quite so many people.

'It's booked under Emma Lewis,' I say. 'For two, but we brought a few friends.'

The host finds my name and ticks me off.

'The more the merrier,' he says. 'You're in Heartbreak Hotel, I see. Well, let's hope there are no broken hearts today.' He lets out a fake little laugh and I get the impression that this is a well-worn script. 'So, if you'd like to follow me, we can get started.'

We troop after him in a long line like a school outing. He pauses as we pass a locker room.

'Please feel free to leave any coats and bags in the lockers provided. They're free. You just turn the key and then it's locked,' he
says.

I brace myself for the flap that usually accompanies instructions like this, but there isn't one. Everyone selects a locker, places
their coats and bags inside and locks it with the minimum of fuss,
and I feel like a total heel for assuming that there would be more
drama. I put the bag I've been carrying as flat as I can inside my
locker and close the door.

We walk down a narrow corridor, still panelled in the same
dark wood, which gives it a slightly claustrophobic feel and adds to
the atmosphere of expectation. All the doors have signs on them.
Unlucky Lake. Banana-Skin Beach. Paradise Postponed. Vivienne
reads each one out and makes a little comment about what she
imagines is inside.

Then we reach Heartbreak Hotel and the host produces a
bunch of keys from his pocket and opens the door with a flourish.

Inside, the room is dressed, unsurprisingly, as a hotel room,
complete with a big double bed, a wardrobe and chest of drawers
and a suitcase sitting on the carpeted floor. Each has a rather omi-
nous-looking combination lock dangling from it.

'Here we are. Heartbreak Hotel. Now, here at Heartbreak
Hotel we pride ourselves on providing the very best service for our
guests,' begins the host, before trotting out the scenario that we
shared with the others on the bus. 'So, you need to solve the clues
to see if you can uncover either the jewels or the culprit. And you
have an hour from when I lock the door to do it. Any questions?'

Obviously, there are loads, not least, 'Where do we start?', but
no one asks anything. I think we're all stunned into silence as the
enormity of the task ahead dawns on us.

Hanging on one wall is a huge television screen with 60:00 on
it in big blue numbers. My stomach does a little somersault.

'Now, when I shut and lock this door, the clock on the screen will begin to count down to zero,' says our host. 'If you get stuck you may notice hints popping up there to help you along, but hopefully you won't need any pointers. Good luck!'

And with that he closes the door.

Keith tests it just to make sure it's locked.

It is.

'Right,' says Ian, sounding more in control than he has done all week. 'What shall we do first?'

Arthur sits down on the bed, smiling beneficently. I'm wondering if that's the most we can expect from him for now, but then again, he has surprised us before. I'm trying hard not to underestimate anyone any more.

I look over at Mel. Now we're all crammed into this tiny space I hope she's not regretting her decision to invite everyone along, but she gives me an excited little grin, eyebrows and shoulders shooting up in unison.

Frank is the first to do something. He prowls around the room poking and pushing at anything that might move. Keith follows his lead and it's not long before they discover that the kettle on the tea tray opens to reveal a clue inside.

Keith removes it and reads it out.

'The best place to start is always with a nice cup of tea.'

'Oh, yes. That does sound nice,' says Cynthia. Then she realises that this wasn't a suggestion and she giggles. 'Sorry!'

'Do you think these are important?' asks Mel, picking up some laminated pictures from the tray. She places them on the bed where we can all see them. One is of a tea bag, one a carton of milk and the last a sugar bowl.

Arthur picks one up to inspect it.

'There's a number on the back,' he says. 'There are numbers on all of them. Do you think they make up the code for one of those locks?'

Arthur is clearly still in the game.

'Yes,' I say. 'But how do we know which order they go in?'

'We can just try all possible combinations until we find the right one,' suggests Grandma.

I glance at the numbers ticking down on the screen.

'I'm not sure there's time for that,' I say doubtfully.

'Is it the order that you use those things?' asks Angela. 'When you make a cup of tea?'

'Yes!' shouts Keith, all enthusiasm.

'So that's the teabag first, in a pot I assume, then the milk, then the sugar,' she says, arranging the pictures in a line.

'No, that's not right,' chips in Vivienne. 'The milk always goes in first.'

Oh God. It's the first clue and we're already neck-deep in social etiquette. I have no idea about this, nor whether the cream or the jam goes first on a scone, not that that's relevant here. Grandma's suggestion of trying all combinations suddenly looks more appealing.

'No,' Angela says, her voice clear and calm. 'The milk goes in after the water.'

Vivienne looks as if she is about to object again so I jump in to avert disaster.

'Why don't we try it? Which of these locks only needs three numbers?'

Keith, Frank and Ian make a circuit of the room, examining all the locks, and land on the one on the bedside table.

'Read the code out,' I say to Arthur.

'It's always tea first,' says Arthur quietly as he arranges the images in that order and then flicks them over to reveal the code on the other side. '8 6 2,' he says.

Keith puts the numbers into the lock and it opens smoothly.

Vivienne gives a little sniff. 'Well, we put the milk in first in my house,' she hisses, tight-lipped.

'What's inside?' asks Mel as Keith opens the cabinet door.

'Another clue, and this.'

He holds aloft a bottle of bright blue nail varnish. He twists the lid, which won't open, shakes it and turns it upside down.

'No visible clue on it,' he says. 'We'll put it to one side for now.'

'What does the paper say?' asks Mel.

He hands it to her.

'You read it,' he says. 'As it's your birthday.'

Mel grins at him and reads it out. *'Don't ring me tonight.'*

It makes no sense whatsoever. She turns it over to see if there's anything written on the back. There isn't.

Silence falls as we think about it. Ian puffs out his cheeks and Keith resumes testing doors to see what opens.

The clock ticks down.

52

DON'T RING ME TONIGHT.

'Let's see if we can we find something else,' suggests Mel, 'and leave this clue until we have more of an idea about what it might mean.'

We could do that, but there doesn't seem to be anything else to find unless we can get into one of the locked spaces.

'*Don't ring me tonight*,' I repeat thoughtfully.

There's an old-fashioned telephone on the bedside table and I pick up the receiver, half-expecting room service to be there, but there's no dialling tone. I put it back down again.

'Let me look at that clue,' says Arthur.

Mel hands it to him. He thinks for a moment, his eyes narrowed as he examines the clue.

'Now, Emma, dear. Please could you look at the telephone and tell me what number corresponds with the letter D? I should know, but I can't remember.'

I pull a face at him, not sure what he's talking about.

'On the rotary dial,' he explains patiently. 'Where you put your finger in to pull the dial round. Are there some letters?'

I've never used a phone like this before and I peer at the dial. Then I see that above each number there are three letters.

'Oh!' I say, understanding dawning. 'Er, 2.'

'R?' asks Arthur.

'That's 7.'

'M?'

'Where are you getting these letters from, Arthur?' asks Angela.

'Basic Boy Scout coding,' he says. 'First letter of every word.'

'Brilliant,' says Keith. 'So M must be 6.'

I look down at the dial and then up at Keith.

'Yes, but how did you know that without looking?' I ask, mystified.

'When I was a boy, phone numbers were made up of both letters and numbers,' he says. 'The first three numbers were actually letters that matched the place where you were calling from.'

'We were STO 4816,' says Frank.

'Ooh, and there was WHITEHALL 1212?' says Cynthia, clapping her hands together in delight. 'That was the number for Scotland Yard, you know, girls. Which is highly appropriate, now we're chasing jewel thieves.'

'Yes, exactly like that,' says Frank.

'Fascinating,' I say, truly intrigued by the whole thing. 'So the last number must be' – I examine the dial on the phone – '8!'

'So that makes the whole code 2768,' says Angela.

I shake my head in awe. 'We would never have worked that out on our own, would we, Mel?'

'Not in a million years,' she says. 'I'm not sure I'd even have got the Boy Scout code part, let alone the numbers. Right. What does it open?'

The old people look all bashful, bless them.

We try the locks on the suitcase and the wardrobe, but neither budges and we're flummoxed for a moment.

'What about that?' asks Grandma, pointing at an innocuous door that I hadn't even noticed before. It does have a keypad on it, though, discreetly painted in the same cream as the doorframe.

'Ooh yes,' says Cynthia. 'How did we miss that?'

Cynthia almost skips to the door and taps the code into the pad. The joints of her fingers are swollen and red and it looks as if applying the pressure is uncomfortable, but she does it. Then she tries the handle and we all hold our breath as the door opens!

'What's in there?' asks Ian.

'The en suite bathroom,' Cynthia says with another little giggle. 'I didn't realise there was more than one room for us to escape from.'

We all charge in except for Arthur, who maintains his station on the bed.

As we enter the en suite I check the clock on the screen: 35.16. We have just over half an hour left.

53

STILL LIFE IN THE OLD DOGS YET.

The escape room fake en suite contains a vanity unit with a basin and a cupboard beneath, a shower and the loo. Vivienne dives on the vanity unit cupboard and emerges with some electric-blue eyeshadow, a lipstick, some red nail varnish and a yellow tube of mascara.

'I don't know what these are all about,' she says with a smirk, 'but Lady Whatever-Her-Name-Is has terrible taste in make-up.'

We find some more in the shower and then put all the make-up together on the bathroom shelf. Mel groups them by item, and then has a rethink and groups them by colour instead. We can't find anything else in there, though, and we're a bit stumped.

After a few minutes during which we make no progress at all a bell sounds from the bedroom. Grandma is the nearest, so she goes to see what it is and then calls back to us.

'The screen says "Check the toilet",' she says.

'Ew!' Mel, Vivienne and I all chorus in unison.

It hadn't occurred to us to look in there, but then of course it's not a working toilet so there's nothing to be squeamish about. Sure enough, there's another clue nestling in the bowl.

Using a combination of teamwork, general knowledge and guile, we work our way through the clues. The host doesn't have to intervene to help us again and there is only one sticky moment when we're required to use a digital camera to access some photos and Keith almost loses his temper because he can't work it out. Frank comes to his rescue and equilibrium is restored.

It turns out that the make-up gives us the code for a colour lock. Vivienne works that out by counting how many items there are of each colour, although Mel had probably started the process by grouping them like that.

The code that Vivienne finds unlocks the suitcase, and there we find the jewels.

'So, it wasn't the maid after all,' says Cynthia. 'Oh, I am relieved. I was worried she'd lose her job.'

I'm still not entirely convinced that Cynthia has totally got this.

The clock on the screen tells us that we've found the jewels with just less than two minutes to spare.

'Well, we did it!' says Ian, looking very pleased with himself. 'Still life in the old dogs yet.'

Angela elbows him in the ribs. 'We'll have less of the "old", thank you very much,' she says, but with a smile.

I'm not sure I've seen her smile more than twice all week.

'This was a great idea,' says Grandma. 'Thanks for inviting us all along, Mel.'

Mel grins. 'You're welcome.'

I was worried that having the entire coach party at her birthday treat would take the shine off for her, but it seems to have had the totally opposite effect.

'One thing . . .' Arthur says, still sitting on the bed. 'Aren't we supposed to escape?'

'Oh my God, yes!' I say, my eyes darting to the clock. There's only one minute left.

Keith rushes to the door, but it's firmly locked.

'Is there another clue in the bag?' Mel asks, desperately. 'Quick! Look!'

I drop to my knees and start going through all the pockets of the case. My heart is banging in my chest. We can't solve all the clues and in time and then fail to get out of the room. It would be like that athlete who started their winning celebrations too soon and got overtaken.

My fingers touch something in the last pocket and I pull it out. The others are crowded so close to me that I can barely get my hand up to read the words.

'*Last year diamonds were a girl's best friend,*' I read.

The room falls silent. The clock is electronic, but now there's an artificial ticking sound that I hadn't noticed before, and it's getting louder with each second that passes.

'Well, what does that mean?' asks Vivienne desperately, her voice at least an octave higher than normal.

I look over at Arthur, but this time he seems just as confused as the rest of us. The clock ticks on: 00.30. 00.29. 00.28. 00.27.

We are going to run out of time.

Then Cynthia goes over to the door.

'I wonder if . . .' she begins. 'I'm probably wrong . . . But I might just try . . . just in case.'

She pushes four numbers into the keypad with her swollen fingers and the door clicks open. The timer stops at 00.17.

We did it!

The room erupts. Everyone is cheering. Keith and Mel grab each other and do a little waltz. Ian hugs Angela and then hugs Vivienne too for good measure, and I squeeze Grandma.

'Well done, Cynthia,' calls out Arthur over all the hullabaloo. 'Excellent thinking.'

'But what was it?' Angela asks. 'What was the code?'

Cynthia looks as proud as punch.

'I just tried last year,' she says. 'Like it said in the clue. And it worked.'

There is a collective groan. It's so simple.

But only Cynthia thought of it.

As we make our way back out into the corridor, still chattering about our triumph and each individual clue, I hang back. I just want a quiet moment to take it all in, to bask in the success of my plan, if you like. I've just had the most fun I've had in ages, and with a bunch of septuagenarians who I had written off at the start of the week as miserable and unpleasant. Us all pulling together to solve the escape room puzzles feels like something I should make an effort to remember, click the shutter of the camera in my head and save a snapshot. I think it's going to be one of those things that stays with me for a long time to come.

54

A LADY CANNOT BE EXPECTED TO LIGHT
HER OWN BIRTHDAY CANDLE.

'What shall we do next?' asks Cynthia, eyes bright from her recent triumph in the escape room.

There isn't really any 'we' in the rest of the day's plan. Mel and I will go back to the hotel to get changed into our going-out stuff, and then it's cocktails, the Thai restaurant, a few bars maybe and, finally, the club. So this is all a tad awkward.

'Yes,' says Frank. 'We need to go and celebrate our timely escape from Heartbreak Hotel.'

'And the recovery of the jewels,' adds Vivienne.

She really should stop dyeing her hair that colour, I think again, even though I'm feeling more generous to her than I was when this first crossed my mind. The too-dark shade of brown is so unflattering against her skin. Maybe she hasn't noticed. Or perhaps she doesn't have a friend who's honest enough to tell her. I make a quick mental note to always try to look at myself objectively in the future, and thank God for Mel, who I know will never hold back with that kind of advice.

The old people are all staring at me, their faces full of hope and expectation, and I stop thinking about Vivienne's unfortunate choice of hair colour. My mind races with how I'm going to balance their request with my plans for Mel's birthday, but they really don't blend. It doesn't matter what I do – I'm going to disappoint someone.

But Mel is my priority here. This is her birthday celebration, and I can't inflict the coach trippers on her for a moment longer. If they want to go and celebrate our escape then that's fine, but Mel and I have other plans.

I'm about to open my mouth to say so, albeit in a slightly gentler way, when Mel beats me to it.

'Absolutely!' she says, punching above her head in a victory salute. 'Let's go and find a bar. Shouldn't be too hard. This is Scotland, after all. Someone ring Robin too. Let's see if he wants to join us.'

Cynthia claps her hands together and almost does a little dance on the spot, although I'm not sure her feet will move fast enough. The others all start talking amongst themselves, the buzz of excitement palpable as we retrieve our things from the locker.

'Are you sure about this?' I whisper to Mel. 'I can just as easily tell them we have plans and leave them to it.'

'It's early,' says Mel. 'Let's take them for a drink. Show them the high life. Then we can sneak off and get changed later.'

'Well, if you're sure?' I say doubtfully, but Mel just nods and grins at me.

'They're not that bad really,' she says. 'Not when you get to know them.'

◆ ◆ ◆

We end up in the pub that time forgot. Actually, what I mean is that it looks like the kind of pub you see in old TV programmes but that you rarely find in real life any more. The tables are heavy wood, the chairs no-nonsense and there is absolutely zero suggestion that they serve food, other than crisps, peanuts and pork scratchings.

Frank and Ian pull two tables together and Keith and I go to the bar. I fear an awkward moment, given that Gloria's made off with all his cash.

'My round,' he says as the bartender puts the last glass down on the sticky metal tray.

'But you've no money,' I begin.

He opens his wallet and waves a stack of bank cards at me.

'It's always good to have options,' he says.

I'm so tempted to remind him of his bank conspiracy theories of earlier in the trip, but then something about his expression tells me that there's no need.

Robin shows up just as we're paying and gets himself an orange juice.

'Really?' I ask him, eyeing his glass.

'I'm working,' he says. 'You lot might be letting your hair down . . .'

Right on cue, Vivienne lets out a whoop of laughter.

'But I have a responsible job to do, you know. It's not easy looking after a coachload of people. It requires constant vigilance.'

He grins at me, his fringe flopping in his eyes. It might be nice if this were our date, I think. But it isn't, and I'm reminded of that seconds later.

'Oi! Em! Where's my drink?!'

'Duty calls,' I say, lifting my tray to take the rest of the drinks over to the group.

'I'll see you in Leeds, though?' Robin says. There's an urgency to his tone that makes me tingle.

'Definitely,' I reply.

No one bats an eyelid at the unusual demographic of our group. Why would they? We're just a group of friends going out for a drink together. The only attention we draw is because of how loud we are, but no one seems bothered when we're clearly having such a good time.

Actually, I can't quite believe that I've just said that, but it is true. This unlikely bunch feel like our friends now.

When we're all three drinks in, I suddenly remember Mel's birthday cake. I've managed to keep it flat and safe from knocks and bashes for most of the day, but somehow as the afternoon progressed it's slipped my mind. And now it pops back in.

'Oh!' I say suddenly, cutting across the conversation. 'I forgot. I've got another surprise!'

Mel looks delighted.

'I love birthdays,' she says as I scrabble around under the table and pull out the bag. Even without opening it I can see that the box containing Pat's cake isn't quite the same shape as it was. I fear the worst as I put the squished box on the table in front of us.

'So, when we were in Berwick I found a lovely lady called Pat. Well, actually, first I found an equally lovely one called Enid . . .'

Mel pulls a face that tells me I'm rambling and makes a winding-up motion with her hand.

'Anyway. Pat made this for you, Mel. Happy birthday!!!'

I push the box towards her.

Mel looks at me and then at the box and then at everyone else and raises her eyebrows. Then she lifts the lid to reveal an enormous pile of crumbs and buttercream. The striped candle is just peeking out from the rubble.

'Well, isn't this delightful?' she says. 'My own birthday ruin!'

'Oh God, I'm sorry,' I say. 'It was so beautiful before. Honestly. Pat did such a good job.'

My shoulders sag as I survey the carnage that used to be Mel's birthday cake, but then I rally. At the start of the week I would have looked at this mess and convinced myself that it was how everything I try to do turns out – a bit of a mess.

But now I can just see the funny side. So the cake got squashed. It isn't the end of the world and it definitely doesn't make me a worse person. I doubt anyone could have kept that cake pristine, given everything it's been through. If anything, I've done well getting it to this point at all.

Mel looks at the cake and then at me. Then she plucks the candle from the crumbly wreckage and sticks it in the pile of crumbs. It's one of those that lights up like a mini firework and looks very grand standing there in the rubble of the cake.

'Match?' she asks.

I have matches. They're courtesy of Enid, who had added some to my order even though I'd totally forgotten I'd need any. I scrabble around in my bag, find the box and hand it over to Mel, only to have it snatched from my fingers by Keith.

'A lady cannot be expected to light her own birthday candle,' he says as he strikes a match and touches it to the wick.

It takes a few moments to catch and then the candle explodes into life. Sparks leap to the ceiling, lighting our corner of the pub up like bonfire night.

'Ooh!' says Cynthia, and I see Vivienne looking around to see if we're going to be in trouble, but the barman looks as if he has incendiary devices set off in his pub every day of the week. We break into another rendition of 'Happy Birthday' and a few of the old chaps who are sitting at the bar join in so that we end up with quite a rousing chorus. We watch as the candle burns its way to the bottom, eyes all shining in the sparking light.

When it's finished, Mel scoops up a handful of cake crumbs, tips her head back and drops them into her mouth.

'Delicious!' she says. 'Well done, Emma.'

'And Pat,' I add.

'Yes. And Pat. You can tell me about Pat later,' she adds with a grin. 'You really have been engaging your inner sneak, organising all these surprises for me. Thank you!'

'A photo for the Insta-thingamajig?' calls Vivienne, and I snap a selfie of us all.

Then Mel leans across and throws her arms around me and I feel her squeeze me tight and I know I am forgiven. It feels good to have finally got something right, but something tells me there's going to be more of this in my future.

'I'm so sorry for messing up your Valentine's Day,' I whisper.

'Well, you've more than made up for it now,' Mel replies, and plants a big kiss on my cheek.

Then she turns to face the others. 'Shall I tell you the story of how we ended up on this coach in the first place?'

They all nod enthusiastically.

'Oh yes!' says Vivienne. 'Please do.'

And so Mel begins her tale.

55

ABOUT ONE YEAR LATER

Please RSVP for catering purposes.

Our new flat is so lovely and, now that we're all settled in, I'm finding it hard to understand why we didn't move ages ago. The carpets aren't tacky and gross, and the kitchen cabinet doors can all bear their own weight and shut like they're supposed to. When visitors come, I don't spend the whole time apologising for the stains in the bathroom. 'Sorry about the brown marks in the loo. They were there when we moved in. I've tried everything to shift them, but nothing works. Just close your eyes and you won't see them!' None of that.

I'm proud of our home. It does finally feel like Mel and me are living like grown-ups and not perpetual students. Grandma has even been round, which never happened at the old place. I invited her and Digger for tea.

When she first told me that she'd seen Digger again after they bumped into each other on Holy Island, she was so apologetic about it. I think she thought I might see it as a betrayal of Grandad. Of course, I didn't. Life has to go on. Digger is great fun and he's given Grandma her joie de vivre back. He's even had her on the back of his bike, although only a couple of times. I'm not sure she's changed her mind on that score. Anyway, I decide that Grandad would have approved and I tell her so.

Mel's birthday isn't far away – the big Three-Oh – and this year she isn't taking any chances and is organising the celebrations herself. Not that she had a bad twenty-ninth in the end. I did manage to make it special for her, but it was a bit touch and go. Whenever I think of Mel's birthday now I'll remember Enid and Pat in Berwick, and how they saved the day for me. The thought always makes me smile: blue-rinsed Enid with her sharp tongue and her kind heart, and Pat with the cake that collapsed. This year we are going to Palma for a long weekend. I did suggest we try another coach trip, but on balance we decided against.

Anyway, it's Saturday morning. Mel is unpacking the groceries from our weekly shop and I'm finishing an assignment on arteries, veins and the circulatory system when an email pings in.

> From: ianandangela@truemail.com
> Good morning, fellow coach trippers . . .

'Blimey,' I call over to Mel. 'I've got an email from Angela and Ian. From the coach trip. Do you remember? With the little boy who died?'

'Of course I remember,' laughs Mel. 'That lot will be engrained in my heart till the day I keel over! What do they say?'

'Hang on.'

I read the message out loud.

We hope you're all well.

As it's been almost a year since our trip together, we thought it might be nice to have a little reunion. We would love to invite you for afternoon tea at our house (address below) on Saturday 14 March. 2.30 for 3.

Please RSVP for catering purposes.

Best wishes,
Angela and Ian (Robbins)

I look over to where Mel is just stuffing a bag of pasta into an already overfull cupboard. (We may have a swanky new pad, but we're not totally transformed.)

'What does 2.30 for 3 mean?' I ask, confused by the concept.

'It's old people talk for "arrive sometime between",' she says.

'Like a built-in time cushion?' I ask. 'Well, I can see the sense in that.'

I think back to our trip last year, and how we exchanged email addresses when we parted. Robin organised it. He seemed to think that we ought to, given how well the trip had turned out in the end. We haven't heard from any of them, though. I've written to Cynthia a couple of times and she's sent me lovely letters back full of news that wasn't news at all – her cat's comings and goings, some new biscuits they were stocking in her corner shop, that kind of thing. Come to think of it, I probably owe her a letter. It's been a while since her last one arrived, but what with moving flat and starting the paramedic training there hasn't been much spare time. I'll have to apologise when I see her.

'Do you think they'll all be there?' I ask. 'Except Gloria, of course.'

'They never caught her, did they?' muses Mel with a wry smile. 'I wonder how many more people she's fleeced since then. I suppose your grandma will be there. D'you think Robin will go?'

I look at the date again and shake my head. 'Pretty sure he's working that weekend. And he gets invited to loads of these reunions. I think he has a policy to avoid them.'

Mel nods. 'Very wise. And what about us? Shall we go or not bother?'

I stare at her, trying to gauge what she's thinking, and decide that she could be leaning either way. So I make the decision.

'Let's go!' I say.

56

IT LOOKS LIKE SOMEONE HAS RUN AMOK WITH SPRAY PAINT.

Angela and Ian's place is a neat semi in an upmarket, leafy suburb of Leeds. Even though it's barely spring, the garden is a riot of colour with bright yellow daffodils and purple and blue pansies in every bed. It looks like someone has run amok with spray paint and is in sharp contrast with next door, where the garden is still very much dormant. When I think of the sad, slightly shrunken couple we met a year earlier it's hard to reconcile them with this madly bright space.

'Wow,' I say. 'What a gorgeous garden. Did we know they were gardeners?'

Grandma and Mel shake their heads.

'Not sure they mentioned it,' said Mel. 'Puts our tubs to shame, Em.'

I grin back at her. We might have cracked living like grown-ups inside the flat, but outside is still another country.

Grandma leads the way to the front door and knocks confidently. I look at my watch. It's two forty-seven, which seems to fall squarely within the invitation window.

Seconds later the door bursts open and there is Ian, looking very much the same as I remember him, and Angela, who is looking very much not. Her hair has been coloured a gentle blonde and cut to show off her curls in a long bob that frames her face. She's wearing a gorgeous tunic in pale blue and tailored navy trousers. But it's her face where the real change is. With a little bit of foundation, a peachy blush and rosebud lipstick, she looks at least ten years younger than she did the last time we saw her.

'You've all arrived together,' says Ian. 'How very organised. Please. Do come in.'

He steps aside to let us pass, but none of us moves. We are all transfixed by the transformation in Angela.

It's Mel who gathers herself enough to speak first.

'You look amazing,' she says, and she sounds so astounded that I worry that Angela might take offence, but she just smiles back at her and nods, mumbling her thanks.

'No, seriously,' Mel continues, not quite able to let the transformation go. 'You look absolutely fabulous, Angela.'

A pretty pink bloom spreads up Angela's cheeks and she drops her head and then looks up through her hair, bashful but pleased.

'Doesn't she just,' says Ian, and the adoration in his eyes is enough to melt your heart. 'Now, come through. The others are already here.'

Of course they are, I think.

We follow Ian into a bright open-plan sitting and dining room that is full of people.

'Hi!' we say as we try to take them all in. 'Hi, everyone.'

Ian fusses about making sure that Grandma has a comfortable chair to sit in and Mel and I settle on the dining chairs, all the soft seats having already been taken.

Once I'm settled, I take a proper look at who's there.

I see Keith first. He's sitting on one of the sofas in very close proximity to a woman I don't recognise. She's around his age and looks like a thousand other old people, sort of grey and plumpish. Next to her is Arthur, very dapper in a three-piece suit and shoes polished to such a shine that I could do my make-up in them. Then it's Vivienne and Frank. Their skin glows with what might be fake tan but, given their age, is probably the remnants of some winter sun. Vivienne's hair is no longer the dark chestnut colour that was doing her no favours, and she has let it fade to her natural shade, which is still brown with almost no greys. It looks a million times better.

And then I spot Rita and Derek.

The last time I saw them, Derek was being wheeled away by paramedics, and the memory rushes to the front of my mind and makes my heart race. My hand flies to my mouth and my eyes start to prick, but I blink the tears away.

'Derek!' I say. 'How lovely to see you! How are you?'

I have to say that he doesn't look that well. He's holding a stick and his skin has that yellow waxy look, but he's alive. That's good enough for me.

'I'm well, thanks, Emma,' says Derek. 'Thanks to you and your amazing quick thinking.'

I wave his comment away, but I can feel my cheeks burning.

'It was nothing,' I say modestly.

'It was not nothing,' chips in Rita in that sharp tone that we heard so much of on the trip, and I have to remember that she's not having a go at me. 'It was everything, and we'll never be able to thank you enough.'

'I got the flowers,' I say, suddenly remembering the beautiful bouquet that had been waiting for me in Berwick. 'They were gorgeous. Thank you so much.'

Rita gives me a tight nod, and there are a thousand words contained in that small gesture. We don't need to say any more.

'Now, who would like a cup of tea?' asks Ian. 'Or I could do a glass of fizz . . .' he adds, looking at me and Mel with a wink.

'That would be lovely,' says Mel. 'We can consider it an early birthday drink.'

'Of course,' says Vivienne. 'It must be your birthday again soon.'

'Just over two weeks,' Mel replies. 'We're going to Palma, aren't we, Em? Because it's the Big One.'

Keith gives her one of those looks that we once thought were so supercilious but now seem light-hearted. 'You call thirty big? I'll be eighty in a couple of years. Now that's a big birthday!'

I can't even begin to imagine being as old as that, but when I am I hope I'm as spritely as Keith.

'And who's this?' asks Mel, as Ian scuttles off to join Angela in the kitchen.

'Do excuse me,' says Keith, trying to stand up but struggling against the cushions of the sofa. 'Allow me to introduce Muriel. Muriel, these are my good friends Emma and Carmel.'

Mel lifts a finger and points it at him in warning.

'But she likes to be called Mel,' he adds, and the smile he offers us is genuinely warm.

'Very pleased to meet you I'm sure,' says Muriel with a big, friendly smile. Her voice has a definite Scottish burr to it. 'I've heard so much about you two.' She casts her eyes around the room. 'Well, about all of you. It's so lovely to finally meet Keith's friends and put some faces to the names. And you must all come to the wedding.'

Wedding! Well, you're a quick mover, Keith, you sly old dog.

Keith is grinning from ear to ear and he lifts Muriel's left hand aloft to reveal a diamond engagement ring.

'Congratulations!' we all say at once, just as Ian and Angela reappear, each with a tray of sparkling champagne glasses. We've all taken a glass and we are about to raise them in a toast when I realise that someone is missing.

57

I can't find any words.

'Where's Cynthia?' I ask, looking round the room in case I just didn't spot her. She's likely to be sitting on a deck chair or behind the curtains so that she doesn't put anybody out at all.

But she's not here.

'Isn't she coming?' I continue. 'That's a shame. I was really looking forward to seeing her.'

The silence that drops over the room is absolute, like someone just unplugged the soundtrack. Rita reaches out a hand and takes Derek's. Keith lets his gaze fall to the floor and Arthur pulls a starched handkerchief from his breast pocket.

Even though I know what is coming next, I don't want to hear it. So I just wait, hoping that if enough time passes we will all realise that it's been a terrible mistake and she's just missed her bus.

But of course, she hasn't missed her bus.

I can't find any words. The shock is so profound that I just sit there. It's a good job my body can breathe on its own because I feel completely numb.

'Oh,' I say. 'She's not . . . She can't be. That's awful. Poor Cynthia. We had no idea, did we Mel? God. How awful.' I'm struggling to be coherent. The shock, I suppose. 'We'd been writing to each other, but then I was doing my new course and things got so busy. I can't think when I got her last letter . . .'

But I can think. It was in November. Then I'd sent her a Christmas card, but I hadn't written a letter to go inside, just a scribbled message saying that I'd be in touch soon. That was the last time. And now it's March.

'When did she die?' I ask, hardly daring to hear the answer, but I comfort myself with the thought that one of the rest of them would have been in touch with her at the end. It isn't as if she'd have been on her own.

I grasp on to this idea to protect me from the horror of the other thoughts that are starting to surface. Cynthia is dead, and we had no idea. I didn't bother to check in with her even though I liked her so much, and now it's too late.

Angela replies, her voice so gentle.

'It was at Christmas,' she says.

My throat starts to close. Christmas. When I had sent my hurried card and then forgotten all about her as I got on with my own busy life. A tear trickles down my cheek.

'But one of you was in touch with her, though,' I say. 'I mean, she wasn't on her own.'

All the heads hang. No one looks at anyone else.

Angela is the first to speak.

'We didn't know either, Emma,' she says. 'Someone replied to our letter about today, a lady from the hospice. Cynthia's post had been forwarded to them. It was cancer and very quick. The lady said that it was only a matter of weeks between them finding it and . . .'

In a hospice.

On her own.

'But she was so lovely,' I say, as if this fact alone should have saved her. 'We all loved her, didn't we? She was so funny and sweet.'

I stop talking. It doesn't matter how much we liked her. It doesn't make any difference at all. None of us bothered to keep in touch. No one was there when our friend Cynthia learned that she was going to die. No one held her hand or told her that it was going to be all right. Not one of us.

Tears pour down my face.

I can't control them.

I don't want to control them.

I don't even wipe them away.

58

It's all one giant experiment.

Despite the devasting news about Cynthia, we manage to rescue the afternoon. Once the shock at the news wears off, we all dig deep and bring the mood back up, maybe not to what it had been when we arrived but something better than it had sunk to. I can't help but think, though, that we really need Cynthia there to jolly us along over her death.

Ironic.

Grandma compliments Angela and Ian on their garden.

'Oh, it's all one giant experiment,' confesses Angela. 'We don't know the first thing about it really. But after Edinburgh we decided that we might have a go, so I bought lots of bulbs and we just stuck them in and hoped for the best. I have no idea what will happen when they die back, but that's all part of the adventure, isn't it, Ian?'

She looks over at Ian, grinning at her own hopelessness in the garden, and the look of pride and love that Ian gives her back is so warm that it could fill a million hot-air balloons.

'It is,' he says. 'Come back in the summer and see what we've managed to grow by then.'

'I can't wait to get to the garden centre when things warm up a bit,' adds Angela. 'It's a whole new world of colour. We're aiming to have the brightest garden on the road, aren't we?'

Ian rolls his eyes and grins. 'Apparently so,' he replies.

'Did you sell the bike?' Keith asks Grandma.

'I did,' she replies. 'Emma helped me. We put an advert on eBay and there was lots of interest, but I sold it to a young man whose dad was a mechanic. He said he wanted to learn about engines and what have you. I thought Stan would have approved.'

Arthur clears his throat and I realise that he hasn't really said much since we arrived.

'That bike ride was the most exciting experience I've had for decades,' he says. 'Really quite exhilarating. I mentioned it to the lady who helps at the memory clinic, but I'm sure she thought I was muddling my years up.' He smiles, clearly enjoying the idea.

'We have news too,' says Frank, and I immediately wonder how he's managed to keep it to himself all this time. I haven't noticed him trying to interrupt once.

We all turn in his direction.

Vivienne picks up the baton. 'We've found a lovely new town in Spain. Sitges. But this time instead of always going to the same apartment, we're working our way round them all, aren't we, Frank?'

'Well, maybe not quite *all* of them,' he says. 'But we're making a decent stab at it.'

I'm full of questions. Is Frank Junior still in prison? Have they managed to rebuild their savings to afford all these trips to Spain? But I don't know who knows what about their situation, so I just smile.

'How lovely. I've never been there. Have you, Mel?'

I know she hasn't.

'I have,' she says. 'Delightful little place. Have you found that fabulous beach with the dolphins yet?'

Vivienne's eyes open wide. 'No! Where is that?'

'Well, you follow that road that takes you out of town, you know the one?'

They both nod eagerly.

'And you just keep going down there until you get to that little white shrine thing, and then it's just along that path. Right off the tourist trail. Only the locals know about it really. But the dolphins are there every day.'

Vivienne and Frank look as if they want to set off right now this minute. I could kill Mel. She knows perfectly well that they will spend months trying to find the non-existent beach with its fictional dolphins.

We eat the tiny little sandwiches and the delicious cakes. I'm relieved that Angela has had the sensitivity not to include scones. The memory of Cynthia eating hers is so strong in my memory that I'm not sure I could have held it together.

And then it's all over. We all thank Angela and Ian for their hospitality and say our goodbyes. Other than another promise for wedding invitations to be forthcoming, there is no mention of meeting up becoming a regular event.

I'm glad. Words can be so empty.

This afternoon has shown us that.

We are quiet in the car as Mel drives Grandma home, each lost in our own thoughts.

Just as we're pulling on to Grandma's road, Mel says, 'I never thought I'd say this, but I'm so glad we went on that coach trip. Thank you for having us along, Phyllis.'

Grandma reaches over and touches Mel on the knee.

'I think that trip was just what we all needed,' she says.

I can't help but think that she's right.

ACKNOWLEDGEMENTS

Whilst the places in this book are real, my imagination is fertile, and so if something doesn't quite match the reality as you know it, then please consider it to be a matter of artistic licence and not a mistake.

There are a few people I need to thank for their help in creating this book. Firstly, thanks to my friend and walking companion Anna Hargraves, who showed me around many of the places that the coach visits on the Odyssey of the North trip. We spent a happy few days exploring the Northumberland coast together and had a night on Holy Island so I could experience what it was like when the tide rolls in over the causeway.

Thank you also to Justin Beevor for answering my questions about riding a motorbike through water, something I have never done.

As ever, the creation of a novel is a huge team effort, and I would like to thank everyone at Amazon Publishing for their hard work on my behalf. Particular mention must go to editors Victoria Pepe, Victoria Oundjian and Celine Kelly for their help, support and many, many words of wisdom.

Thank you to my family, who are always there for me through thick and thin.

And finally, thank you to you, my readers. I would still write books even if nobody read them, but it's a lot more fun knowing that you do.

If you've enjoyed this book, then please visit my website izzy-bromley.com, where you will find links to all my social media accounts. I also write book club fiction as Imogen Clark and you can find out all about that at imogenclark.com.

Best wishes,

Izzy.

ABOUT THE AUTHOR

Photo © 2022 Carolyn Mendelsohn

Izzy Bromley lives in Yorkshire with her family and when she's not writing books she is likely to be climbing hills. She also enjoys exploring new places both at home and abroad, singing soprano in her local choir and skating. If you can't find her in any of those places then try the cinema as that is her other big love.

Follow the Author on Amazon

If you enjoyed this book, follow Izzy Bromley on Amazon to be notified when the author releases a new book!

To do this, please follow these instructions:

Desktop:

1) Search for the author's name on Amazon or in the Amazon App.
2) Click on the author's name to arrive on their Amazon page.
3) Click the 'Follow' button.

Mobile and Tablet:

1) Search for the author's name on Amazon or in the Amazon App.
2) Click on one of the author's books.
3) Click on the author's name to arrive on their Amazon page.
4) Click the 'Follow' button.

Kindle eReader and Kindle App:

If you enjoyed this book on a Kindle eReader or in the Kindle App, you will find the author 'Follow' button after the last page.